STARLIGHT

JENNIFER M. EATON

For Scott,
If you crash landed
On an uncharted planet
I'd come get you.
I promise.

Chapter 1

MIA

Mia squinted in the bright light, clutching her communication pad as she rushed through the space station hallway. The orders to get to her first star cruiser had just appeared in her private inbox, and the sooner she got to her new baby, the better. If she fueled up and took off by the time command realized they'd just assigned a deep-space search and rescue mission to a five-day-old academy graduate, it would be too late for them to call her back.

The mission brief said they were heading out into the black sector, past the line where most of space had been charted—with the directive *to retrieve*. Retrieve what, she didn't know, but she wasn't about to ask questions when she had just thirty minutes to make the departure schedule. She hadn't even had time to pack a proper bag. She'd just grabbed her emergency essentials and run out the door.

She stopped to let a group of cadets running formations pass her in the hall. She'd been one of them not too long ago, and she'd been in front, outpacing the rest both physically and academically.

She straightened, adjusting her bag on her shoulder. This

assignment wasn't a mistake. She'd worked her ass off at the academy. She deserved to pilot her own ship.

She forced herself into a swift walk rather than a full-on sprint. She didn't want to draw attention to herself. One wrong move could set off a chain reaction, resulting in her being slapped back into basic training. Best to keep calm and in control, even if her entire body felt like it might take off on its own.

She'd been ready for this since she'd first seen a ship high in the sky over Calla Station. She'd looked to the stars all her life. Now she'd know what it felt like to sit behind the controls of a beautiful piece of engineering, capable of speeds beyond a normal person's comprehension.

She stopped at the edge of Bay Number 194 and took a deep breath. This was it.

The Alpha Cent was a Class Nine Reclaim and Rescue vessel, with long, high lines and sleek edging for added maneuverability in combat situations, and boy, was she a beauty.

Holding back her smile, she saluted the ground crew. A few narrowed their eyes at her, and she shifted her shoulder bag to reveal her pilot's stripes. Those simple marks brought them to their feet. Not that she needed anyone fawning over her. After all, most of these people were twice her age. It was kind of fun, though, to be recognized for a position she'd earned.

Mia ducked onto the boarding ramp and walked up the steep slope. Her heart rattled in her chest. It almost seemed surreal, experiencing the cool steel beneath her boots rumbling as the engineers tested the instruments.

The resonance seemed slightly off, but the next rattle proved smoother.

Good. The engineers were taking good care of her baby.

But... Where was the captain and the first officer? Protocol dictated that they should be here to greet her.

"Ground test complete," a man's voice sounded over the intercom. "I want to lift off within twenty. Has the pilot checked in yet?"

Twenty? She looked down at her communication pad. She was right on time, reporting as called. They should be here waiting for her.

"Start the sequences, Bernard," the voice said. "I am not missing this liftoff window."

"Yes, sir," another voice called.

Dang it! Mia dashed down the hall. Luckily, she'd done a short tour of duty on the same model ship and knew how to get to the pilot's station on her own.

But what in goodness' name was the rush? Not welcoming the pilot onboard... Well, it just wasn't done. She should be shown around, briefed on the ship, the mission, and the flight plan.

Two crew members turned into the hallway, huddled in conversation. They both wore light gray maintenance uniforms. Mia slowed so she wouldn't plow into them.

"Yeah, but her? What is she, like, twelve? She's barely out of flight school," one of them said.

The other shrugged. "She can't be that bad if they're letting her pilot."

"Yeah, but where we're going, I don't want to be anyone's guinea pig flight. I—" His gaze met Mia's before lowering to the stripes on her shoulder. His eyes widened before he saluted. "Welcome aboard, ma'am."

Mia gave him a curt nod, grinding her teeth. He didn't look all that much older than her. How dare he criticize her for just completing her training? Swallowing her frustration, Mia managed a smile. "Thank you. I'm happy to be here."

"We're happy to have you here too," the second crewman

said, saluting her. "I've heard so many great things. Top of the class."

At least someone knew of her accomplishments. "News travels fast. I won't keep you two from your work. We've got to get going."

"Yes, ma'am." They both gave her another salute.

She trudged past them, gripping her shoulder bag tighter. She'd worked hard for this position, and she'd earned it as much as anyone, despite her age. Everyone on board should have been honored to serve with her. Cream of the crop was becoming harder and harder to find these days. Sure, there were plenty of more experienced pilots out there—pilots who had more important missions to run than a search and rescue.

But to Mia, nothing could be more important than saving those who put their lives at risk every day to make the galaxy a safer place.

Mia continued down the hall and stopped at the wide, polished door of the cockpit. This was it, the moment of truth. She pressed her hand to the door. If she truly was meant to pilot this mission, it would open without a problem, responding to her DNA and her fingerprints.

The door slid aside, allowing her entry. Her heart fluttered, and she closed her eyes for a moment, reveling in the confirmation that she truly belonged here.

She stood in the archway, taking in her new office. Yes, she'd been in the cockpit of a similar ship before when she'd toured with Pilot Reynolds, one of the more senior pilots left in the fleet. It was different, though, knowing she would soon sit in that coveted chair.

"Beautiful," she whispered, taking in all the twinkling lights. Each blink represented a reading, a button, or a signal —all waiting on her.

"You barely made it," a rough voice said from up ahead.

The co-pilot chair spun revealing a young man close to her age with tightly cropped, wiry black curls. When his gaze caught sight of her he groaned loudly. "It *is* you. I thought they were messing with me."

Mia folded her arms in front of her chest. "Excuse me?"

The guy rose from his chair and stormed over. He had a good foot and a half of height on her, though that didn't take much. When he peered down at her, she made sure to hold her ground.

"I'm Bernard, and I don't expect you to remember me since I graduated from the academy a year before you did, but I've heard of you. Pretty much everyone in the academy has." He grabbed her helmet and connection tubes from off their storage rack. "It's important we stay on schedule or we'll miss the safest orbiting pattern."

She took the helmet and put it on before snapping all of the tubes into place. "You're only a year out of the academy and already a co-pilot?" Despite her early advancement, most people took years before getting anywhere near the controls of a ship this large.

"Not a co-pilot," he grumbled. "My official title has been junior assistant since I left the academy."

She glanced at him. "You're sitting in the wrong chair then," she stated. "Get my co-pilot here so we can go through the pre-flight checklist." She eased into her seat and butterflies took flight in her stomach.

Bernard sat in the co-pilot's chair and snapped on his own helmet. His voice popped into her earpiece nice and clear over the private communicator system. "You got this job because our previous pilot landed a snap promotion. When you were named his replacement, your co-pilot walked off. I got promoted an hour ago."

Mia cringed, but she guessed she couldn't blame the guy.

If she were a co-pilot and her pilot got a promotion, she would have expected to get the pilot job, too.

She shifted in her seat. It was probably better this way, though. The last thing she needed on her first mission was a co-pilot with a bad case of sour grapes.

Bernard pointed to the comm panel. "Captain Stevenson is ready on the bridge. He said to get started as soon as you got here."

Lights started flashing on the display panel.

This was it. She just had to hope Bernard had been paying attention while he'd sat at the assistant's station. If not, though, she'd done enough simulators with a dead co-pilot that she could probably fly this thing alone with her eyes closed.

"Let's go through the check-list so we can get going. I'd hate to miss the *safest orbiting pattern* the captain is shooting for."

Safest orbiting pattern... These were not always the easiest words to digest. The pilot was supposed to be briefed on the mission. She should have spent time running specific simulations if headed into a danger zone. Hopefully, once they were in route she'd be able to get some answers.

"Engines," Bernard said.

Mia observed the readings. "Good."

"Ionized propulsion."

"Two points above required parameters." She flipped a switch. "Pressurizing for separation from the station."

Bernard gazed at the meter. "Pressurized. Oxygen levels are good. Ready to request permission from the captain?"

Mia nodded. She hit the flashing button that read *Bridge*. "Sir, this is your pilot, Mia Walton. We're ready for deployment."

"Thank you for getting here so quickly," Captain Stevenson said. "I thought we were going to miss our window." The light flashed twice. "Sit tight. We're almost there." A few seconds later, his voice sounded over the intercom for the entire ship. "Crew of the Alpha Cent, we are ready for lift off. This is your last warning to strap in."

"Medical bay, ready."

"Engine room, ready."

One by one, each department of the ship sounded off. Mia tingled all over, her fingers at the helm, eager to guide the Alpha Cent out into the vast reaches of space.

"Pilot, we are go for launch," Captain Stevenson said.

Go for launch. Three words she'd dreamed of hearing since she'd been a little girl. A lot of pressure rested on her shoulders—pressure she relished, pressure that drove her to excellence. With the grace of a ballerina, she navigated the ship out of the docking bay.

Her eyes widened when they cleared the hangar, and stars stretched into infinity.

A simulation didn't do the experience justice. The metal framework of the docking bay disappeared from view within minutes. Other ships navigating their way to the space station became fewer the farther away the Alpha Cent moved, and then only a black blanket speckled in shining diamonds surrounded her.

Away from the station, the galaxies were so much more defined, each creating a distinct outline of shimmering reds and golds. It was all so much to take in, and it left her breathless. It seemed hard to imagine that only twenty years ago this immense, peaceful place had been a battleground.

The United Galaxy Alliance had started out as the galactic police when space piracy had been rampant enough to hinder the supply flow to the outer rim colonies. When the Hiverian Pirate settlement on Caspian Four had finally been discovered and taken out by the UGA, the Alpha Cent, like other C9R&Rs had returned to their roots as deep-space reclaim-and-rescue ships.

Now here Mia was, just one step closer to Heaven.

Bernard cleared his throat. "This really is your first time out, huh?"

Her cheeks burned. "Like you didn't do the same." He was right, though. She needed to focus and do her job.

She checked the vitals to make sure they were in fact still good before taking off her helmet. Chin-length blonde hair whipped around her face as she shook her head to combat some of the stiffness in her neck.

Bernard also took off his helmet. "It's an appreciation that won't last, sorry."

"Jaded much?"

He didn't laugh. "Captain Stevenson asked to see you on the command deck as soon as we'd cleared the station limits."

Mia nodded and tapped the bridge button. "This is the pilot. Transferring control to the navigators in five. Please confirm."

"Confirm," a woman's voice said.

Mia held her finger over the button. "Five, four, three, two, one." She pressed the button and the ship jolted as the bridge took control for the easier part of the flight.

Taking a deep breath, she stood. Under other circumstances, she'd have met the captain long before takeoff. The suddenness of their departure was a huge break in protocol. Now, maybe she'd find out why.

The Alpha Cent might not have been the largest star cruiser in the galaxy, but it was certainly big enough. From the cockpit, she had to climb a flight of stairs to reach the command deck.

Elevators were for the weak. Not to mention, she didn't want to be sidetracked by another member of the crew who wanted to thank her for her service or remind her that she'd just graduated.

Upon reaching the command deck, she found the door locked. That was strange. The passage between the deck and cockpit should only be sealed if under attack. That was protocol.

Again with the protocol infractions. What was going on with this ship?

Mia knocked on the door firmly and waited to be allowed in. A good minute passed before the door slid open.

"Is the door broken?" She stepped inside.

The command deck itself had ten times the floor space of the cockpit. Navigators inputted routes into the system while a tall man in captain's stripes spoke to a woman with hair pulled back into a tight bun wearing the first officer's insignia. Everyone ignored Mia.

Since when was a new pilot something to brush aside, as if unimportant?

She cleared her throat. "Officer Mia Walton reporting, sir."

Captain Stevenson gave her a glance, whispered something to the first officer, and then graced her with his full attention. "Officer Walton, thank you for joining me."

"Is the door broken?" she asked again.

"Excuse me?"

"The door." She pointed to where she'd entered from. "Is it broken? It didn't open for me."

Captain Stevenson pursed his lips. Tiny lines marred his face, drawing attention to the graying hair at his temples. "I'll have someone inquire about the matter."

The tone made the back of her neck itch, like he had no intention of inquiring about the matter. Still, she had to take the words at face value. It wasn't like she could call her new captain a liar. "Thank you, sir."

He pressed two buttons on a control panel. "Officer Walton, I'd also like to extend my thanks to you for taking on this mission on such short notice. As you know, our previous pilot was promoted, and all of the others at the station, frankly, had more important things to do with their time." He looked up. "You were the top recommendation from the academy."

Mia cringed. So she'd gotten the job because no one else had wanted it? Where could they possibly be going?

Captain Stevenson waved for her to follow him out of the command deck. "Now that we're cruising, would you like something to drink?"

Mia shook her head. "No, thank you." She took in the softer lighting on this part of the deck. The lower-level halls were mainly used for maintenance and quick access to the living quarters. These upper levels were frequented by the crew, and the softer light was supposed to simulate sunlight. Nothing was like the sun, but it was much better than the stark lighting downstairs.

She quickened her pace, realizing she'd fallen behind the captain. "Pardon me asking, sir, but what do you mean, the other pilots had better things to do?"

Captain Stevenson unlocked the door to his private office. He sat at his desk and pointed to a chair on the other side. She took a seat, though she'd have preferred to stand. Sitting implied they'd be speaking for a while, and she wanted to be back in the cockpit so she could keep familiarizing herself with her new station.

He leaned back. "Thirty-six hours ago, a relevant particle scan revealed a life signature in Sirius Alpha Nine."

The Kraken Nebula. Her stomach clenched.

"It was only there for about three seconds, but it was long enough to confirm a carbon-based life form, and three beats of what may have been a class seven sequential homing beacon."

She licked her lips. "Class seven would be a fighter plane."

His face remained placid. "That's what I'm hoping." He stood and walked to a star map posted on his wall. He ran his hands alongside five pins forming a circle. "What do you know about Sirius Alpha Nine?"

Mia shifted in her seat. "Well, it's a nebula, and we've lost a lot of ships there. One of my instructors called it space's Bermuda Triangle. I've also heard it referred to as *the Kraken*—"

"It's a death trap, that's what it is."

The weight in the room pressed in on all sides. "That's why you couldn't find another pilot? That's why you took off before telling me where you were going?"

He held up his hands. "You certainly could have asked questions first. No one dragged you onto this ship."

Fair enough. She had been well within her rights to make inquiries, but the window of opportunity had been slim. Now that she was here, though, she needed to be the officer she'd been trained to be.

She sat back. "A carbon signature is not much, though. It could be anything, and the last time we lost a fighter in that nebula was—"

"Thirty years ago."

Yes, thirty years ago. She remembered watching the news feeds. Of course, she hadn't been born yet, but her father had been obsessed with Jason Griggs, the fighter pilot who'd vanished into that colorful abyss. She'd sat with her dad day after day as he'd recounted all Griggs's accomplishments.

Her father had watched the footage of the mission where Griggs had disappeared over and over, hoping to find something that would tell them more about what had happened to the legendary pilot.

Even then, Mia's heart had been in the stars, and she'd watched, frozen, as one of the greatest heroes Earth had ever known disappeared over and over again.

The captain returned to the map. "What do you know about the Crengine disaster?"

Too much. She'd taken up her father's infatuation with Jason Griggs, the man known to the entire world by his call-sign, Captain Starlight. Many thought her fascination with the incident, and the pilot who had died that night, was unhealthy.

Instead, she played it smooth, cocking her head. "You mean the Crengine Rescue?"

He shrugged. "Rescue, disaster—I guess it's all relative."

She preferred the word *disaster* too, if she were being honest, but the history books used the word rescue, and facts were all that were required at the moment.

She took a deep breath and imparted what she knew. "The Crengine was a luxury liner. It had been hit by an uncharted piece of debris that left it disabled and adrift headed toward Sirius Alpha Nine."

She gripped the edges of her chair. The history books probably tamed down the horror, not wanting to discourage cadets, but she'd heard it called *The Crengine Disaster* before. Five fighter pilots had lost their lives trying to save that cruiser, the most notorious being Captain Starlight—the man whose photos had graced her bedroom walls since she'd been old enough to know what a hero was.

The captain turned to her. "I was a five-year veteran fighter pilot on a basic run on the outskirts of the nebula when that call came in." He rubbed his chin. "We were trained for combat, not rescue, but there was no one else close enough, so we went in."

Mia straightened. "You were in the 123rd? Did you know Jason Griggs?" The question slipped out before she could stop it. She gripped the arms of her chair, hoping to quell her excitement some.

Captain Stevenson shook his head. "Griggs...we all hated his guts."

Mia's jaw dropped. "Wh-What?"

"It was jealousy, really. That rat's ass got away with everything. He had no sense of rules or regulations. He just did whatever the hell he wanted to do, and he got away with it."

She stared at him for a minute. "B-But he was a hero—decorated twelve times before the age of twenty-five."

He waved his hands. "You don't have to tell me. He mentioned it. A lot. One thing that flyboy wasn't short on was ego."

A wave of nausea built in Mia's throat. Jason Griggs had saved hundreds of lives single handedly. He'd discovered new worlds, albeit somewhat unconventionally at times. How could his team not have loved him?

The captain looked back at the map. "Two of us had finished our cable runs, pulling the cruiser from the danger zone, when a piece of the ship broke off and careened into us. There wasn't a damn thing we could do. We were too close to the damaged ship to engage thrusters."

Mia shuddered. She remembered the cameras on those ships, and the frigid ice shooting into space as the air vented from the cabin cruiser.

"We were both disabled and careening straight for the nebula." He grimaced. "Starlight's ship came out of nowhere. He was singing some ridiculous song from the ancient radio era." He rubbed his face. "He bumped my wingman's jet twice, pushing him close enough to get grabbed by the cruiser's technicians."

Mia nodded. "I saw it on news reels. That was some amazing flying."

He nodded. "It was. I was there, watching it, and I still can't believe Griggs pulled it off." He stared at the floor. "Meanwhile, I got caught in the nebula's pull."

Mia's hands whitened on the armrests of her chair. No. It couldn't be... "He-He went back for you."

"I told him to back off, that I was lost." Stevenson grimaced, closing his eyes. "He laughed and said not to worry. After all, *Starlight was here*." He rubbed his face with his hands. "He spiraled around my ship at full throttle and bumped me so hard I landed in the infirmary with a concussion." He closed his eyes again. "He got me out of there."

Mia choked down the ball building in her throat. "And Starlight got sucked into the nebula."

The captain held on to the edge of his desk. "I hated that little piece of shit, and he had to go and die saving my life." His lower lip trembled. "I've been living with this for a long time." He pointed out his window. "That beacon is his. There is no other explanation."

Mia swallowed. "You can't possibly expect him to be alive in there. That was thirty years ago."

"If anyone can survive in an uninhabitable nebula, it would be that crazy son of a bitch." He looked at the map again. "But even if he's dead, we can find the ship and bring it back, give his family a chance to bury him."

It would be a hero's homecoming. Everyone loved him. Well, maybe everyone except the people on his team. Mia herself had a Starlight action figure and fashion doll. He was the stuff of legends and folklore.

Captain Stevenson chewed the inside of his cheek. This was more than a search and rescue to him, though. This was personal. He had a debt to repay, and he probably felt like a space worm for being jealous of the man who'd died saving his life.

Stevenson threw a folder on the desk. A few papers slipped out with her name on them. "You ran close to a thousand hours in simulators during your last two years of pilot training."

Mia looked up from the folders. "Yeah. And?"

"Ninety-eight percent of the simulations dealt with high convolution omni-gravity piloting and hostile environment landings."

She gripped the chair again. "Yeah. So?"

"There was a reason you were at the top of my list, Walton."

Her lips parted. "I thought no one else wanted to go."

"True. No one else the UGA approved wanted to go on this suicide mission. You were the next person on the list who was qualified to fly into that nebula."

Holy shit. He's serious.

She glanced at the map. The nebula was like space's boogeyman. People had nightmares about it without even stepping foot on a spaceship. No one in their right mind would go within miles of that place, but he'd picked her in case they needed to actually go in. "Do you really think he could still be alive in there?"

"Honestly, no. But I need closure as much as his family does."

Mia took a deep breath. Was this man seriously considering risking his ship and his crew on a mission to retrieve a body? Even the body of a decorated hero?

She shivered. The UGA's motto was to never leave a man in space, but not at the risk of more bodies needing to be recovered.

Now the lack of protocol and possible maintenance issues were clear. This guy might not be all that right in the head.

She straightened. "Permission to speak freely, sir?"

"Always."

Okay, here it goes. "You know how dangerous this is. It's fine for you to risk your own life, but what about the rest of the crew?"

He laughed. "Half of them are thrill-seekers, a quarter are anomaly freaks, and there are an easy twenty-five people who just want to be a part of history...and if we find that ship, we will be a part of history." He laughed again. "Go ahead and ask around. Everyone onboard is here because they want to be. The rest left in a rush when they found out I was serious."

Like the previous pilot? Maybe that sudden promotion had been a stroke of luck for him.

This was insane, but Stevenson was right. If they found that ship and brought Captain Starlight's body home for a proper burial, every one of their names would be immortalized in the historical databases.

This was the insane type of mission that Captain Starlight never shied away from. That was what made him a hero. He had always stepped up when others were too afraid to try.

The captain held out a palm to shake. "What do you say, pilot? Are you ready to make history?"

She stared at his hand for a moment before she stood and shook it. "I wouldn't miss it."

"Good. The first run will be over the outskirts of the active zone. When the singularity eases back, we zip in, we take another reading, and we get out. The less time we spend that close, the better."

She understood. "Take the reading, get out quick."

"Exactly."

"Not a problem." She saluted. "Thank you for your time, sir."

Captain Stevenson gave a slight nod, but his gaze was already on the map on his wall.

Mia took her leave and hurried to the cockpit. Everything about this was insane, but she picked up her pace. She was about to fly near the most dangerous nebula on record.

A smile burst across her face as she opened the door to the cockpit. She couldn't wait to navigate a real intergalactic storm.

Bernard had refitted his helmet and pushed a number of buttons on the dashboard. "I guess you just got the bad news?"

"You mean the *exciting* news? This is exactly what I signed up for."

His face paled. "You do realize that the pilot and the co-pilot, meaning you and me, are both a year or less out of the academy."

She settled into her station. "So?"

He pointed out the window. "We're headed for the star-blasted Kraken Nebula."

Mia looked out the window and nodded. She probably should be scared, but instead, a tingling sensation rushed through her veins. This was it, the real thing, and she'd never been one to skirt a challenge.

She gave him a level gaze. "Should I tell the captain the co-pilot wants to be let off at the nearest supply station?" Not that there was one near, but she needed to make sure where Bernard's balls hung. If he couldn't handle it, she'd rather know now.

His lips twitched before he strapped himself in. "No, ma'am. I just really hope you are as much of a hot shot as everyone says you are." He looked over at her. "Meant respectfully, of course."

She smiled and hit a few buttons on her control panel. She *was* a hot shot, and then some. Like the captain had pointed out, while others had been partying, she'd been in a simulator. There was a reason she'd been top of the class by such a high margin, and now she got to prove why.

Bernard called up the viewscreen. "This part of the outer fringe is filled with a lot of debris."

"I know. There used to be a large planet here that got blasted to pieces several thousand years ago." Mia put her helmet back on and checked her screens. "We're right over the point where the captain's initial readings were recorded." And only a few thousand miles from where Captain Starlight had disappeared with an entire world watching.

"Right, so we're supposed to go in and—"

"Check for any signs of UGA equipment, or carbon signatures." The tingling returned to her body. They were minutes from the spot where Griggs had given his final transmission. Even being here felt like absorbing history.

From a distance, the nebula swirled, a massive black-and-orange gas cloud with twisting fingers, earning it the name of the Kraken Nebula. UGA scientists believed the nebula had formed after a star explosion millions of years ago. Up close, the pockets of gas were full of planetary debris from a star system long dead. The Kraken Nebula didn't only look wicked, it also was home to the majority of space disasters in the galaxy. Only fools came close, and only imbeciles entered.

"Okay, crew. Let's get our reading and head to our next location," Captain Stevenson instructed. "Air pilot Walton, bring us in closer."

Mia complied.

"Call off when you can confirm there are no readings so we can get out of here," Bernard said. "This thing creeps me out."

Mia suppressed her smirk, wondering if he'd had the Kraken Nebula nightmares, too.

A red light started to flash on the dashboard. Mia drew

out her tablet and pulled up the data to inspect. "Captain, are you seeing this?"

"Yes, we're analyzing it now," Captain Stevenson said.

She frowned. The readings were hazy, but her analysis was solid. "There's life out there."

"There's also the possibility of a wormhole, or a black hole, or who knows what else," the captain said.

"But there's life out there," she repeated. "Our mission is the retrieval of life. That is our priority—always."

Captain Stevenson didn't respond for a long, agonizing moment. "You're right. Crew, prepare for exploration and possible retrieval."

"Preparing crew," came a woman's reply.

"Yes!" Mia settled in, resetting her grip on the controls. She glanced over at Bernard. His hands gripped the armrests of his chair tightly. "You okay?"

"I can't believe we found something," he managed. "You can fly, right?"

"Of course I can fly."

"I mean, *really* fly." His gaze remained glued to the floating rocks before them. "It's going to be hell in there."

Just like the asteroid simulators. Mia rolled her shoulders. "I promise you're in good hands."

She grabbed the controls and led them deeper into the gas cloud. The Alpha Cent sailed smoothly. Mia glided between the debris, maneuvering the ship closer to the point of life on her navigation system.

The nebula swirled around her. Pink, puffy clouds sparkled, emanating their own light. It was hard to believe anything so beautiful could have been the cause of so many deaths.

She eased up and over a charred piece of metal, maybe a piece of a ship.

She shivered. The beauty of this place was a mask for the

monster lying in wait. Too many had lost their lives here. The Kraken demanded respect, and it ate the unwary.

"You doing okay?" Bernard's voice sounded shaky.

She nodded. Actually, she was. She'd expected this to be a lot harder.

A large asteroid spiraled into view, rotated, then whisked toward them.

She banked right, but the controls froze, locked in place.

"What are you doing?" Bernard made a grab for the steering mechanism as a smaller asteroid scraped across the bottom of the ship. "Newsflash: We're not supposed to hit things."

"I can't move the controls," she said. "Well, I can, but the ship isn't reacting to my movements. The systems are just going—"

Dozens of lights flashed on her panel, and a red warning beep filled the cabin. A blue-green planet filled her viewscreen. "Where the snog did that come from?"

"We're caught in some kind of gravitational pull."

Yeah, great. Thanks for the info. Mia's hands shook on the controls. She grit her teeth, gripping harder, trying to pull up. "Come on!"

Captain Stevenson's voice came over the comm. "Pilots, see if you can get us out. We need to turn around."

Mia wanted to get them out, but she couldn't. The controls shook in her hands until deafening static filled her helmet. She grimaced, trying to tune it out, while Bernard yanked his helmet off.

"Get your gear back on," she said between grunts.

Bernard dropped his helmet and pressed his palms against his ears. "What?"

"Your helmet." She moved one hand off of the controls to point where it lay on the floor. "Get it back on."

He shook his head. "Hurts."

"Get your gear back on now." Even if he couldn't hear her, everyone could read the word *now* on someone's lips.

Logic won over in the end. He placed the helmet back on and essentially became worthless, cowering in his chair with his head in his hands.

Mia would be on her own.

She tightened her grip on the rattling controls. Not that it did any good at this point.

"Walton!" the captain screamed over the speaker.

Did she tell him the controls were locked?

Did she say the obvious, that they were caught in the planet's gravitational pull and there wasn't a star-blasted thing she could do about it?

The ship started to shake. The controls shifted in her hands...

Wait. They'd *shifted*.

Mia pulled up, but the ship started to spiral instead.

The planet raced toward them.

"Walton!"

A thousand hours of simulators had brought her right here, and all she could do was accept the inevitable. "Brace for impact!"

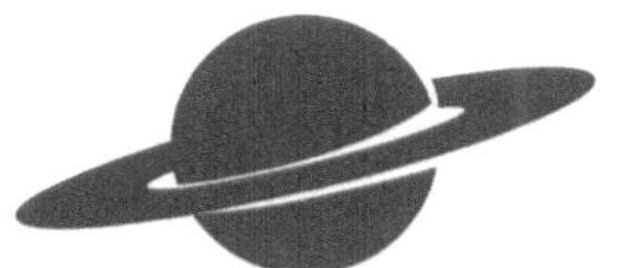

Chapter 2

Jason Griggs: pilot extraordinaire and hero of the galaxy —those were his titles before crashing onto planet *Bob*. Now he was simply master of his hut.

The sunlight poured through the window, stinging Jason's eyes. He'd placed his bed there strategically to catch the sunrise, forcing him to wake as soon as it was safe to go outside. Otherwise, he probably wouldn't get up in time and then he'd be screwed.

The other humans on the planet would stir soon, and the wildlife would scatter as soon as those imbeciles started tromping through the forest. Of course, Jason could join them, maybe even teach them to hunt properly, but then they'd try to suck him in to their colony again, and the least amount of contact as he could make with those guys, the better—both for his sanity, and for the good of planet Bob.

The planet wasn't really named *Bob*, he just liked to call it that because it was far easier to pronounce than the name the natives used. Bob was the name of a planet from an old animated movie his great-grandmother had had in her viewing files. Using the name gave him the warm and fuzzies

—and warm and fuzzies were good, when living on a planet that might eat you if you weren't careful.

If there was one thing Jason was good at, though, it was staying alive and making it look easy. Or maybe that was just the cocky attitude he still had yet to "grow out of" because that cockiness kept him alive when Bob was in a bad mood.

The hut itself didn't amount to much. Walls made from the wreckage of his ship and furniture he'd managed to construct from trees, leaves, and other Bob fauna kept him safe. Surprisingly, his sackcloth-stuffed-with-flower-petals bed made for the most comfortable sleeping he'd ever had in his life. What that said about academy cots, he wasn't quite sure. Either that, or he wasn't remembering his life pre-Bob the way he should be.

Life pre-Bob felt like a dream, anyway.

A high-pitched bark outside jolted the last of the sleep away. When he didn't answer, the scratching started at his door.

"Always punctual." Jason scratched his long, gnarled brown beard and hopped out of bed as he threw on his hand-made shirt—that had been a fun experiment in trial and error. Not only had he skinned the animal the cloth had come from, but he'd figured out that plant vines did not make for good sewing threads.

The barking turned into more of a whiny yip sound.

Jason groaned. "Dobby, come on. You know I'm not a morning person." The creature gave a firm yelp and he laughed. "Yes, even after all of this time."

He lifted the bolt across his front door and let Dobby in. A medium-sized animal, Dobby reminded him a lot of a huge, blue and yellow striped dog without fur and a tail twice the length of its body. Right now that tail was curled up nice and tight for convenience. As Dobby entered and jumped up to give Jason his usual morning greeting of a tongue bath, the tail loosened a bit to wag.

The locals had given Jason Dobby's real name a long time ago, but it wasn't a word he could pronounce. The little guy reminded him of a character from an old book about wizards his great-grandmother had read to him when he was a kid, so he'd gone with it, and Dobby didn't object to his new name. Over the last year or so, they'd learned how to communicate and understand one another. And thus a beautiful friendship had begun.

Jason eased away from the creature's lapping tongue. "Okay, Dobby, I'm glad you think I taste so delicious, but you need to get off of me. Please." Jason carefully pushed the creature away.

Dobby stood upright on his two hind legs and twitched his long ears. He looked an awful lot like a dog-headed person more than a canine-like being before he returned to all fours.

Jason scratched the animal's head. "Thanks. I want to get our visit over with so we can get straight to hunting. That okay with you?"

Dobby barked and lifted his head in a solid nod.

"Awesome." Jason waved for Dobby to head out. "After you."

Trotting out the door, Dobby raised his nose and sniffed. Jason checked to make sure the wood he'd stacked for a signal fire was still dry and then scanned the canopy, looking to the sky beyond. One of these days, a ship would fly overhead, and he'd finally have the opportunity to light those blasted logs.

Dobby shook his posterior and garbled, scratching the ground.

Jason threw his bag over his shoulder. "I'm not looking

forward to going to Perseverance, either, but there are a few things we need to pick up that only they have."

Dobby shot him a glare.

"It's true. Where else am I supposed to find ammo, or get freshly charged batteries? No one is sharing their solar panels with me." The gesture of poor faith still ground on Jason's nerves. Perseverance, the compound created by several ships of human crash survivors, just didn't like to play nice with outsiders. Not even Jason.

Ever since the first freighter had crashed here, Jason had been looking over his shoulder, waiting for them to pounce. At first he'd thought it would be great to finally have some human neighbors. The excitement was short-lived, though, when they'd opened fire on Dobby's clan, killing half of them before Jason could stop the madness.

Of course, that had labeled him an animal lover, as if that were a bad thing, and put a black mark on Jason as far as the newcomers were concerned.

That was fine with him, though. He was okay on his own.

His hut was a tiny efficiency built for one. He'd add to it if anyone ever wanted to leave that hellhole of a compound, but he doubted their self-appointed dictator, Vincent Chrona, would ever let them.

Dobby growled and barked four times.

While Jason couldn't understand the exact things Dobby said, he understood the general meaning, and he got Dobby's hesitation. If the supplies weren't so important, he wouldn't go near the humans, either.

Jason shook his head at his own stupidity. He'd still go, even if he didn't need supplies. Dobby was great and had probably kept him sane all these years, but seeing humans, hearing their voices—even the voices of assholes—filled a void he hadn't known had been there until the others had crashed. He *wanted* to keep away from them, he just couldn't.

Something squeezed around his ankle.

"Shit!" Jason grabbed for his knife as he was yanked off his feet. "Dobby?"

Jason clawed at his belt as he was hauled into the air, dangling upside down over the jaws of a deep violet mouth of acid-covered teeth. The giant purple petals shivered, flapping wildly as a thick stream of drool oozed down to the ground.

Not again. Not a-freaking-gain!

His knife slipped free, and he stabbed at the vine. "Let me go, Doug. You know you don't like the taste of Griggs." Not that this ever made a difference to the hissing flower.

The vine twitched, and he fell closer to the snapping teeth.

Dammit! He kicked its lower jaw, and the giant flower balked, dropping him.

Jason slammed onto the ground and rolled away in case Doug changed his mind. Luckily, the massive purple bloom closed its gaping maw and eased up into the trees.

A low moan sounded from a bush, and Dobby peeked his head out.

"A lot of help you were."

Dobby scanned the trees above, chattering in high tones.

"Well, you could've at least warned me he was hanging around."

Not that Dobby could always tell when the flowers were on the prowl. Most of the time the giant blooms were closed, digesting whatever they'd caught. It was only when they were open and pretty that you needed to avoid them.

Unfortunately for him, Jason had crash-landed near a really big one, and dealing with Doug was one more thing on his list of things to worry about each day.

Jason pushed up to his feet and rubbed his back. "Come on. We've wasted enough time."

Sighing, Jason ducked under a dangling branch full of

vibrant green, shiny leaves. He'd learned quickly to avoid those as well.

Dobby grabbed a few of the yellow leaves below to chew on as he poked the weapon in Jason's pack with his tail.

Dobby hated guns, and with good reason. He'd tried many times to get Jason to leave it behind, but not today.

"I need to protect myself, especially where we're going." It certainly was useless against the plant life. He just needed to keep a lookout for enormous flowers hiding in the verge.

Dobby lifted his head, an expression of sympathy in his big blue eyes. He nuzzled Jason in the leg before unleashing his tail and grabbing a tree branch with the long, curling appendage. Within seconds, he was gone from Jason's sight, running through the treetops above.

Those trees were Dobby's safe place after crossing the outer edges of Perseverance's territory. He and most other indigenous life had learned to steer clear of the humans.

Sometimes, Jason wished he could do the same. He spent most of his time on Bob by himself. Unlike the people of Perseverance, he'd bonded with the planet and found comfort in the trees, flowers, and animals who'd become his neighbors. One just needed to learn to navigate carefully and not get eaten.

Sometimes when Jason walked through the jungle alone, he could hear the trees whispering, or he thought he did. It was very possible he was losing his mind, though. Trees weren't supposed to have personalities.

Even Doug only acted on instinct, trying to eat whatever he caught in his creeping vines. Jason smiled to himself. The only reason Doug had a name was because he was the first creature Jason had run into after crashing on Bob. Even talking to a plant had been better than nothing at the time. Sometimes you needed to act insane to keep a shred of your sanity.

Voices carried on the wind, despite Perseverance still being nearly half a mile away. A few shouts, intoned like orders, made him cringe. Jason stopped walking and scanned the trees. The leaves didn't rustle with the wind, as if they were prepped to defend themselves from an unreasonable predator.

This close to Perseverance, they very well could be right. Dobby poked his head out of the leaves, looked at him, and then slipped into the full cover of the canopy.

Dobby might be onto something. Jason really needed to stop coming here. Jason was king at letting his pride guide him in whatever stupidity he'd chosen for a given day, and of course, today's stupidity was leading him right into the lion's den.

Hopefully, he wouldn't get shot again.

He fingered the dimple scar in his side, a byproduct of saving a native child from a Perseverance guard. He'd earned the natives' trust that day, as well as the recipe for healing ointment using the bark of the most dangerous tree on the planet. Now he'd use that miracle cure to get what he needed and hopefully get out in one piece.

Up ahead, Dobby yipped, pointing out one of Perseverance's lookouts. The guard got points for trying to hide behind the thick, teal leaves of the trees, even if he failed miserably. He wore black, but in this vibrant ecosystem, normal blending colors stood out. If Dobby hadn't alerted Jason, he would have seen the guy on his own about five seconds later.

Jason waved at the man. "It's Griggs."

"I already radioed the boss," the guard called down.

Jason raised his eyebrows, surprised. Someone who actually did their job correctly...a novelty out in the woods. He gave the guard one more wave before pressing onward toward the gates.

Much like his tree hut, Perseverance was composed of wood and old ship wreckage. Because the compound had more resources and people to build it, the walls and gate were actually quite impressive. They were around twenty feet tall and thick, protecting the squatters from the more powerful creatures living on Bob. Some of the larger, hungrier inhabitants of the planet still occasionally tried to attack when desperate enough, but they were learning that winning against the compound was becoming a lost cause.

Perseverance was indeed the perfect name for it. The people who lived there didn't quit, and Jason admired that about them. It was one of the only things he did admire about the people inside.

As he approached the gate, the doors slid open. A group of men with guns trained on him stood on the other side.

"Guys, come on." Jason gave them a weak smile in an attempt to hide his irritation. He held his hands up, gritting his teeth over their power games. "Is this any way to greet a friend?"

The group of guards glanced between one another before slowly lowering their weapons.

"We have a protocol, Griggs," a man said from farther away. The group of guards parted down the middle, revealing the one and only Vincent Chrona.

The hair on Jason's arms stood up, and he gripped his bag hard enough that his skin stung. He grimaced before he relaxed his features.

He could kick himself for his reaction. It wasn't like Vincent never popped up when Jason came for a visit.

Taking a deep breath, Jason offered up his politest of smiles. "It's me. Hasn't it been long enough that your protocol shouldn't apply anymore? I'm unarmed."

Except for the handgun hidden in his pack, but none of them needed to know that.

Jason spun in a circle with his hands up. "All I want to do is trade for—"

"More ammunition, batteries, and some fresh clothes, I'm assuming?" Vincent folded his arms across his well-muscled chest.

"Yes." Jason was very simple in his needs. He never asked for more. In truth, the planet could give him most of what he needed.

Vincent grinned in a way that would make children dive under their beds. As always, no creases could be seen in his outfit, nor were there any stains. His salt-and-pepper hair looked extra sharp today, completing the facade of a perfect commanding officer.

Vincent set his jaw. "That's ammunition that will be in the hands of someone who isn't a part of our family."

"All so I can kill those big nasty tiger piranhas and thick-hided rhino lions for you." Jason shrugged. "It's not a pretty job, but someone has to do it. The meat and the skins are well worth the cost, right?" He held out his hand. "There's no point in labeling me as an enemy. We've been over this." More than a few times.

"You're a human who won't live with his own kind. I'm not sure that makes you a solid ally, either," Vincent said.

"Then I won't give you my skins, or the herbs, seeds, and sap I gathered from the forest yesterday." With another shrug, Jason clutched his bag closer. "Too bad because I got fresh medical syrup. That stuff goes bad quick, and there's no way I'll need five bottles before they start to mold." Jason tilted his head. "Aren't some of your people sick?"

Vincent's jaw tightened. "A good man would let us have it."

"I'd be happy to let you have it, but you just said I'm not your ally, and half your men still have guns aimed at me."

He took a step toward Vincent. Several of the guns cocked, proving his point.

Jason raised his hands slightly. "Clearly, you think I'm some kind of threat just because I don't want to live with you. The only reason that I don't, I should add, is because I've become comfortable in the home I made before you all came along."

And because Vincent was an asshole who had no respect for this planet or the other inhabitants, but that was a conversation for a different day. Picking and choosing the right battles kept Jason alive, as well as comfortable. As long as he kept away from the stinking man-eating plants.

"You're resourceful if nothing else," Vincent said. "And your ability to command the wildlife is a great asset."

He nodded and all of the guns returned to their at-ease positioning. The guards returned to their posts, as if nothing had happened.

Jason needed to keep in mind how increasingly trigger-happy Vincent and his men had become. Something was up with them, which probably didn't bode well for Jason—or Planet Bob.

He shifted his bag. "I don't command the wildlife to do anything. They're happy to help me because we're neighbors."

"They're dogs and cats and trees, Griggs. Just because you trained a few doesn't mean they actually care."

Rather than argue, Jason followed Vincent deeper into the compound. He smiled at a few of the women sitting on the front stoops of the uniform homes built along the dirt road. None of the ladies acknowledged him. Their gazes remained firm on Vincent, and one of them shuddered.

Jason had never seen the women anywhere but in their doorways, or tending gardens attached to their modest homes.

It hadn't taken long for Jason to realize fear kept them close. It also didn't take a master's degree in population studies to figure out the greatly uneven ratio of men to women in the compound.

The colony only had a little over a hundred residents, from what he could tell. He tried to remember the women's faces he'd seen over the years, and he'd only counted eleven. That wasn't good odds if the men got unruly, and if the guy in command was an ass.

Vincent led him to the supply bunker, a place Jason had been a number of times. If he wanted to, he could easily break in and take what he needed, especially if Dobby was on board for a little snatch and grab. It would be weeks before anyone figured out anything was missing, but Jason valued his integrity.

Also, even though he hated this place, he didn't hate seeing people. Yeah, he was a badass, and he'd never admit it to any of these cronies, but he missed home, and this star-forsaken place was the closest thing he had to Earth at the moment.

Perseverance kept the hope alive that someday a ship would fly overhead rather than crashing, and he'd finally leave Bob far behind.

The door to the supply bunker opened and Vincent slipped in, leaving Jason outside to wait. A flash lit up the sky...probably another meteor pulled into the nebula. They usually burned up in the atmosphere and posed no threat, but the light show reminded him of thunderstorms back on Earth.

A few minutes later, Vincent returned with three large boxes of ammo, and two fully charged batteries.

"This should be more than fair," Vincent said.

Jason stared down at the boxes, unsure if he agreed. "I have skins too."

"I'll have the ladies sew them into something fresh for you. We don't have much of a need for them at the moment."

Jason considered the deal before pulling out his bottles of medicine and the animal skins. "All right."

The trade completed, Jason itched to take his wares and run. Vincent had never reneged on a deal before, but the mood in the compound seemed to darken with every visit, and Jason always had to wonder if each trade might be their last.

"As always, it's been a pleasure," Jason said. "I'll be back in a few days for the clothes, and I might have some more medicine or other goodies for you."

"We appreciate what you do. We might not show it well, but we know it isn't a simple task, and we're always grateful for your willingness to cooperate, unlike the other locals."

The other locals... The natives didn't want anything to do with Vincent, and for good reason, but this wasn't a fact worth pointing out to someone unable to see things from anyone else's perspective.

Jason gave the man a salute, knowing Vincent always appreciated a military touch. "We've got to look out for our own, sir," Jason said, meaning every word except the 'sir' part. That was just to butter up the imbecile in charge.

"That we do." Vincent returned the salute. "Until next time, Captain."

Jason flinched at the title. It felt wrong every time someone said it, but he'd gotten tired of correcting people.

He nodded. "Until next time."

Jason took his things and put as many of them into his bag as possible before walking out of the gates at as brisk of a pace as he could manage without running. He passed the same women on the porch, but this time they all jumped to their feet. He hesitated as they made eye contact. Their clothes were worn and dirty. The tallest of them had bruises on her arms that looked far too much like hand imprints.

One of them mouthed the words, *'Help us.'*

At least that was what he thought she'd said.

He stopped and looked to where he'd left Vincent. When he turned back to the women, the same girl mouthed, *'Please.'*

Jason gulped. The lack of women here always made him uneasy. After all, he was a guy. He knew how guys could get. He didn't even want to think about why they would ask for his help.

"Move along, Griggs," a guard called.

There really wasn't much he could do. Not now, at least.

He nodded to her. At least he could let her know that he understood, and he continued to the gates. As he passed through, he noted six men on one side of the gate, and five more on the other side. Yeah, Vincent was paranoid, but maybe it was founded. For the first time, Jason wondered if those guards were as much for keeping the people inside the gates as they were for keeping the wildlife out.

As soon as the gates were closed behind him, he slowed. The look on that girl's face tugged at his soul. The hero in him screamed to run back there, guns blazing. After all, that was what he'd have done a few years ago, before the crash, when he'd been young and stupid, his head filled with the ridiculous idea that nothing could stop him.

Then he got sucked into a nebula.

He moved deeper into the trees before Dobby chirped and dropped next to him, barking with excitement.

He scratched his friend between the ears. "Yeah, I got the stuff." He held up his bag. "Those medicines you gathered for me did the trick. I should be set for a while."

Dobby bowed his head and let out a happy whine.

"I'll have to return and get some clothes they're going to make me, though." He looked back toward the gate. "And I think there are some people in there who might need our help."

Dobby's ears perked up. He chirped twice.

Jason started walking again. "Yes, I know Big Ugly Man has guns." Goodness knew Dobby and his people had seen those overzealous soldiers use them. "I'll figure something out."

Dobby shook out his long ears, a movement that shifted through his body and ended in his tail. Jason had always equated that to Dobby's version of rolling his eyes.

His friend might have a point, though.

Jason didn't have a fighter jet to outmaneuver everyone else this time. He only had himself, Dobby, and whatever ammunition Vincent provided, which was always less than enough to mount any kind of offensive against Perseverance.

A boom sounded above, followed by a loud whistling sound that reminded him of an airplane. A fireball roared over the canopy, getting increasingly bigger by the second.

Stars of Mars!

Another ship was crashing, and it was headed straight for his hut.

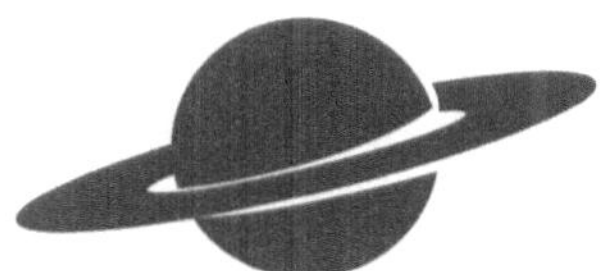

Chapter 3

MIA

Mia groaned as she came to. One moment she'd been doing everything in her power to make sure the Alpha Cent didn't get shredded to pieces by the atmosphere of a foreign planet, and the next, her head was smashed against an influx of bio-foam.

Her splitting headache proved that despite the safety protocols, they had crashed hard. She was still alive, though, as was Bernard, who cursed a number of times as he flipped switches and pushed buttons.

He fiddled with his earpiece. "Yes, Captain Stevenson, she's still alive. I just checked her vitals...uh-huh...good, the ship is intact, then, if there aren't any leaks in the hull. Yes, I'll..." Bernard stopped and gazed at her. "Walton just woke up. I'll have her come up to the command deck if she's able." He flipped off the comm. "Are you okay?"

"I'm fine." Mostly, at least.

She reached for her seat restraints and unclasped herself. Slowly and steadily, she got to her feet as the bio-foam retracted into her chair. The headache pulsed in a dull throb, but she didn't seem to have pain anywhere else. "Yeah, I'm fine."

"You don't sound sure," Bernard said.

He got out of his seat, offering her an arm. She gently pushed him away.

He held up his hands. "Just trying to be helpful. It seemed like the least I could do."

Mia shook her head and blinked. There were too many alarms going off, too many flashing lights. "Can we get rid of all this noise?"

"Captain Stevenson will take care of it after all of the departments check in. Until then, we're in a state of emergency."

"You think?" She plugged her ears. How could anyone think in a crisis with all this noise? "What's the status of the cockpit?"

"Banged up, but nothing major seems to have broken in the crash. At least, not here. The mechanics are in the process of doing a full evaluation now that it's been determined the hull hasn't been breached. That's all I got out of Captain Stevenson for now. No evacuation is necessary." Bernard gazed at her long and hard, then shook his head and headed for the door leading to the command deck. "Come on. He and Commander Cortenz want to talk to us. Now."

Yeah, she bet they did. Mia had just crash-landed their ship.

Hopefully, this would be a *'Thank you for saving our lives'* speech, and not a *'This is all your fault'* speech.

The lights flashed red in the hallway, the buzzing even louder, the tone more brash. No wonder so many people died after crashes. No one could hear or communicate over all this racket.

Bernard placed his hand alongside the entrance to the command deck. When it didn't open, he hit the pad twice with his fist, and the door slid open.

Inside, the various lieutenants gave out orders to their departments. Captain Stevenson spoke to his second-in-command. Several strands of the commander's dark hair had come loose from her tight bun, and there were scorch marks on her uniform. Their voices were hushed and their hands animated.

Mia stepped farther inside, and Commander Cortenz turned toward them.

"Glad you're okay, pilot," Cortenz said, her tone like ice. "Now maybe you can help us figure out a way off of this planet since you're the reason we got stuck on it in the first place."

Well, that answered that question.

Mia's lips curled. "Would you rather we'd all died in the crash?" Her eyes widened, wishing she could retract the words. This woman was a commanding officer and she could throw Mia into the brig until they were rescued—assuming there was another C9R&R captain crazy enough to enter the Kraken Nebula to save them.

Cortenz scoffed and pointed at Mia. "See this insubordination? She's too young for this responsibility. If she hadn't maneuvered us toward this cursed place, we wouldn't have been sucked in by the planet's gravitational pull, and—"

Captain Stevenson held up a hand, cutting her off. "While I understand your viewpoint, Commander, let me remind you that our mission is to retrieve life. A human life form appeared on our radar, and it is our duty to investigate it. Our pilots were responding to my orders just as much as their own instincts."

Mia's cheeks flushed.

Next to her, Bernard mumbled a "Thank you, sir." His hands trembled, though, along with his knees.

Captain Stevenson continued. "It isn't her fault that the

controls locked and the engines gave out in the outer fringes of the nebula, and you can't blame her for the gravitational pull, either." He held up his pointer finger. "What *is* her responsibility is keeping us all alive and the ship intact."

Wow. She hadn't expected this kind of support from the captain. They had, after all, crashed. If she was in the captain's seat, she'd probably be more like the Commander, looking for someone to blame.

The captain scanned the crew. "In case you hadn't noticed, we have zero fatalities, and our ship needs minor repairs in comparison to the disaster that could have occurred." He let those words sink in. "We should be thanking her, not accusing her."

A few of the people on the bridge glanced at each other, but it was hard to discern the expressions on their faces. Most looked at the floor.

"Blaming each other isn't going to get us anywhere. Period." The captain punched the palm of his hand. "We are in a less-than-optimal situation, and we're going to need a hundred percent from everyone to get out of this mess."

"Sir," a female officer with a long, dark ponytail said from across the room. "The atmospheric tests are complete. The air is compatible with our needs and should sustain us comfortably without life support aides."

Captain Stevenson breathed a sigh of what could only be relief. "Excellent. This should speed up our repairs. It also means that the human life on the radar may not have been a glitch."

"We're not sure of that," Commander Cortenz said. "There's no way of knowing for sure until we actually find what cast the humanoid carbon signatures."

"Correct. There is always the possibility that there is an indigenous humanoid population. Finding either would be exciting."

A few of the people at adjoining monitors glanced at each other, smiles bursting across their faces. At the academy, comms people frequently minored in extraterrestrial life, and most dreamed of first contact. Crash-landing on someone's planet, of course, wasn't the ideal way to say *hello*.

Captain Stevenson addressed the crew again. "Whatever the case, this is a small bump in our mission, but it's nothing we can't overcome." He turned to Mia. "Thank you, pilot, for keeping us alive. I know this is your first mission. I'm impressed by your skills. More importantly, that you held yourself together under pressure. That isn't common for a new pilot." He glared at Commander Cortenz as he said that last bit.

Mia saluted him. "No thanks are necessary, sir. I have no desire to die myself. I'm just glad all of my training paid off."

"Now I need you to put your survival skills to use and help the rest of the crew explore our surroundings," Captain Stevenson said. "You will accompany me on a team to secure our perimeters as well as find resources essential for staying alive. We need to find drinkable water and test the plant life for what is edible and what isn't."

Cortenz's eyes widened. "We have more than enough rations on board. Certainly that isn't necessary."

He gave her a level gaze. "Since we don't know how long we're going to be here, it's important we begin searching for native supplies right away." He looked her up and down. "Do I need to go over emergency protocols?"

Her cheeks reddened. She shook her head. "No, sir."

"Good." He turned to Mia. "Suit up, Walton."

"Yes, sir. Of course." Mia gave him another salute. "I'll be happy to accompany you after I've checked in with the medical bay to make sure I don't have a concussion." She tilted her head. "As per crash-landing protocols, sir."

He waved for her to return to ease. "Medical bay is full of

crewmen with more serious injuries at the moment. Now, if you feel your injuries need to be seen immediately, that's something else entirely."

Mia shook her head. "No, sir. I just wanted to follow protocol."

"Consider protocol overridden. Get your gun." His lips thinned. "Bernard, I want you to stay here and help the mechanical crew. Commander Cortenz, the deck is yours until I return."

Commander Cortenz gave a firm nod. "Yes, Captain."

"Walton, I'll meet you at the docking doors in five minutes."

"Yes, sir." Mia also nodded and turned on her heel to head back to the cockpit.

Bernard shared a goodbye with the captain before rushing to her side.

He ran a hand through his hair. His fingers trembled as he shook his head. "This is insane."

"It is." And a little exciting.

Mia had always dreamed of being part of a first contact team and getting to explore a new world. She never much enjoyed the massive cities on all of the planets she'd visited and trained on. Too much congestion, too much artificial life, and it all moved too quickly. Captain Griggs had explored many worlds and brought so many into the UGA. She dreamed of doing the same.

Poor Bernard seemed terrified, though, which might have been why he was ordered to stay behind despite the fact that he didn't seem injured.

She rubbed the incessant throb in her forehead and rolled her shoulders. A dull ache had started to set in. She probably did need that doctor. If she had a concussion, she should be resting, but the captain was right. They needed to worry about surviving first.

"I'll be on my communicator if you have any questions or need anything," Mia said.

Bernard shrugged. "While I appreciate the concern, I'm worried about *you*. You're the one walking out into who-knows-what." He raised both brows. "I'll be on *my* communicator in case *you* need anything." He grabbed a supply bag from a compartment in the wall. "Hopefully, I can help the mechanical crew fix the ship quick. I worked in that department for a while before I went to the academy."

"Yeah?" Mia grabbed the pilot's sidearm from the emergency weapon compartment and checked for bullets.

He nodded. "Be careful, though. It's habitable out there, but it's still dangerous. I swear I saw a plant that looked like it had teeth outside that window."

"A plant with teeth?" Mia laughed. "You're probably just imagining things."

He grabbed her shoulder. All mirth left his face. "I know what I saw."

Yeah, and he'd also probably hit his head even worse than she had.

Mia checked the charge on her communicator. She gazed at him and offered a smile. Belittling the man would help nothing. He seemed nice enough, even if he was hallucinating.

She adjusted her bag. "Thanks for the heads up."

Five minutes had definitely passed. She had to get going. With a wave, she left the cockpit and headed to the main docking doors. There, Captain Stevenson and three other crewmen waited.

"This is Leslie Karan, our head of alien biology," Captain Stevenson said, pointing to a woman a little older than Mia. He then motioned to the other, middle-aged blonde, woman next to Leslie. "And this is Ashley Johnson. I guess you could say she's a jack of all trades. Finally, there's Peter Schenectady."

The last crewman waved. He looked to be close to Captain Stevenson's age, minus the gray hair. "Peter is head of security. Everyone, this is our pilot, Mia Walton."

Leslie raised a brow, her dark eyes narrowing. "The pilot, huh? I wasn't aware those were good for exploring foreign territories. Shouldn't you be helping the mechanics repair the ship?"

Just as Mia was about to point out her amazing scores in self-defense and marksmanship, Captain Stevenson said, "Everyone on board is capable of exploring new lands. We need strength in numbers right now. This is as many as can be spared."

Leslie flipped her ponytail full of long, dark hair over her shoulder. The gesture seemed to only fulfill the purpose of showing her disapproval than anything practical. Her lips stayed glued shut, though.

Captain Stevenson frowned for a moment. "We're going to explore near our ship. We need to keep within one hundred feet of the hull at all times. Do not eat or touch anything with your bare hands. The air might be breathable, but that doesn't mean the rest of the planet is going to be friendly to us."

"Yes, sir," Peter said.

Mia nodded. "Let's go."

Captain Stevenson hit the docking bay release and the door opened. Warm, humid air surrounded them. It reminded Mia of a trip she'd taken to the tropical planet Tobaz. The heat mixed with the moisture wasn't an unpleasant feeling. Perhaps they'd stumbled upon another paradise-like world.

Captain Stevenson took the lead. While the others hesitated, Mia followed behind him eagerly.

A jungle walled them in on all sides. Mia's lips parted, transfixed by the beauty of massive green leaves in every shade imaginable, from bright and vibrant to dull and turquoise. Mixed throughout the verge rose flowers of red, orange, yellow, and purple—some the size of her fist but some spanning over six feet across.

A light breeze drifted through the trees, shifting one of the huge flowers so it faced them.

"Wow," she whispered.

Leslie stepped out of the ship next. She approached a nearby tree with long, thick, burgundy vines draped along its trunk. "I think I see berries on this one. I'll start gathering samples."

"Just a few," Captain Stevenson said. "And get your gloves on."

"Copy that." She pulled on her gloves.

Mia squinted at the tiny white berry shapes dotting the vines. She gazed up the length of the tree and noticed the vines weren't actually a part of the tree. They connected to a large, purple flower—a flower that had a large bed of rough petals and a great deal of slime surrounding what looked like...*teeth*. Her stomach sank. Bernard had been right!

Mia ran after Leslie. "Wait, don't touch that."

Leslie turned to Mia just as a vine twisted around the biologist's ankle. She screamed as it lifted her off the ground.

Her body spun around the tree trunk before the vine dragged her along the forest floor, her arms flailing. Leslie punched and tried to kick herself free from the plant's grasp as she was hoisted into the air toward the flower.

One of her legs came loose and she used it to push herself off of the jagged, tooth-like edges of the bright purple petals.

Mia and the others ran to the base of the plant. Captain Stevenson grabbed Leslie's hand, pulling with all his strength while Mia aimed her gun at the flower.

Leslie clenched her teeth and growled as the plant's mouth widened. A thick dollop of lavender goo trailed down the teeth, picking up particles of soil as it dragged the forest floor.

Mia tried to aim, but Leslie kept twisting.

"Stay still," Mia cried.

"Screw you!" Leslie spat.

Mia gulped. Yeah, she deserved that. She wasn't the one staring down the gullet of an alien life form. Taking a deep breath, Mia held up the gun and aimed at the center of the flower.

But something struck her in the back. She yelped with surprise and spun, but there were only leaves as far as she could see.

"I'm slipping." Leslie whimpered, tears streaming down her cheeks. One hard pull was all it took and she lost hold of Captain Stevenson.

"No!" he screamed, as her body lifted over the flower. The massive petals closed around her and she disappeared within.

Mia's eyes grew wide as the huge flower closed in on itself. The length of the throat contorted and twitched.

"Shoot it." Stevenson pulled out his gun.

Peter stood beside him, aiming.

"No." Mia held up her hands. "She's inside that thing. You'll shoot her, too." She looked down. "Shoot the roots, the vines."

Muffled cries came from within the plant. Mia held her breath and aimed low as the flower started to pump the length of its stem around Leslie. *Stars!* It was swallowing her whole.

Mia shot, but the vine whisked out of the way, reaching into the throat of the flower and yanking Leslie out. The acrid scent of rotten eggs and year-old decay filled the air as Leslie's body thumped at their feet.

Mia's gut churned, but she managed to keep what remained of her last meal in her stomach as she backed away.

Leslie coughed and gagged, spitting purple guck on the ground. The same sticky purple goo covered her body. She tried to wipe it off. "Oh, God...Oh my God..."

The flower retreated into the forest as if it could sense the danger of their guns. Weird.

"Breathe. You're okay," Mia said. "Don't go into shock. You're okay." She reached for her, then thought better of it.

"I'm itchy. It itches everywhere." Leslie started to roll across the ground. "Oh, God! It's so bad. It's stinging."

Captain Stevenson pulled off his jacket and used it to mop up some of the mess. "Everyone, be careful what you step on. It seems the plant life is carnivorous."

You think? Holding her gun steady, Mia gave the captain cover. Peter strolled circles around them, his gun pointed out into the jungle.

"Watch the ground for the vines," Mia called.

"Roger that." Peter continued his circular pattern.

Ashley drew off her own jacket and started wiping the goo from the sobbing woman.

With Peter watching the perimeter, Mia took the chance to grab her communicator. "Medical emergency. We need a team to..."

"No, we do not," the captain said. "I don't want anyone else out here."

Mia nodded. "Belay that. Prepare a medical team for possible burns and alien contamination. Leslie is down. We're bringing her..."

She heard a twig snap to her left. Both the captain and Ashley jumped to their feet.

"Did you hear that too?" Mia asked.

"Yes." Peter moved beside her.

"Are there more of them?" Leslie screamed.

Mia glanced back at the captain. "I'm going to go investigate. You get her to the ship."

Peter cocked his gun. "*We're* going to investigate. Groups of two or more in hostile territory, Walton."

She nodded. "Of course."

The captain narrowed his eyes. "Shouldn't I be giving you two the orders?"

The brush several meters from them shifted, and Mia tightened her grip on her gun.

"You're stronger than I am," she told the captain. "It seemed logical to me that you'd carry her, and Peter doesn't seem the nurturing type. I apologize for overstepping, sir."

Only she wasn't actually *that* sorry. Someone had to investigate, and the captain sure didn't seem all too interested in doing it.

She needed to be careful, though. This was a completely uncharted, unknown ecosystem. Something had thrown a rock at her when she'd tried to rescue Leslie.

Peter straightened his shoulders. "With your permission, sir, we'd like to investigate."

"Be careful," Captain Stevenson said. He gazed out into the forest. "As soon as you confirm what it is, come back. Do not engage. Understand?"

"Yes, sir," they responded in tandem.

"And keep away from the star-blasted plant life."

Mia didn't plan to engage anything unless whatever it was engaged with her first. She held her gun at the ready as she walked deeper into the forest, toward the source of the noise. A creature moved through the brush overhead, making a strange barking sound. To the left, Peter pointed his gun at a flutter of wings.

"Hold steady," she warned him.

"Roger that. I just wish I could see better."

That made two of them. But wildlife wasn't necessarily bad. This was obviously a thriving ecosystem. Whatever it was up there might just be curious. Shooting it would not give the inhabitants of this planet a kind how-do-you-do.

After taking a few more steps, she stopped. All around her, she could hear the soft, normal, ambient sounds that belonged in a jungle. Whatever creature had been barking before was now silent.

Just as she was about to return to the ship, she spotted someone in the trees. Or maybe he spotted her. He was human, or humanoid, wearing skins like the ancient cavemen in history books, and with a long, thick, brown beard covering his face. His steps were confident but not aggressive, keeping her desire to shoot on sight at bay.

The man's dirty hands raised in surrender. Mia lowered her weapon, but she wasn't dumb enough to let go of it completely.

"Who are you?" the man asked.

Her jaw dropped. "You speak English?"

"Who. Are. You?" His words were demanding now.

Peter raised his weapon again. "Don't come closer. We should be asking who *you* are."

"You're the one who landed on the planet, not the other way around," he snapped.

"So you're a native?" Mia asked.

"I am now." He glanced at the treetops. "Look, we need to continue this conversation elsewhere. It's not safe out here. There's a storm coming."

Mia scanned the sky through the leaves. It was crystal blue, not a single cloud. She reset her feet. "Why are you sneaking around?"

"Again, you landed on my planet. What should I have

done? Ignored you? And the way you're all swinging around the guns, you can't blame me for doing my best not to get shot." He dropped his hands.

Peter lowered his gun slightly. "Well, work on being a better ambassador for your people, then. You're failing badly."

He twitched, as if ready to run at any moment. "Can you at least tell me the year?" He looked at Peter, and enunciated, "Please."

"2347," Mia said.

His jaw dropped. He took a step back. His lips formed a word that didn't come out. "Wh-What did you just say?"

Mia repeated herself. Hadn't she spoken clearly?

He looked down, back to her, and then down again. "That long already? I could have sworn it's only been..." He rubbed his hands over his face. "I need to talk to the captain of your ship."

"How do you know I'm not she?" Mia asked.

"Because you're wearing three pilot's stripes, and your diplomacy skills are worse than mine." He dared to grin at her underneath his messy beard. He stopped a few feet from her and held out his hands to his sides. "Go ahead and scan me."

Mia cocked her head. "What?"

"Standard protocol. You need to check me for extraterrestrial pathogens, right?" He furrowed his brow. "Most protocols suck and are annoying, but that's one I tend to agree with. I think I'm fine, but I've been out here for a while, so who knows?"

Mia had actually forgotten about that protocol. Hopefully, Ashley had a scanner. Goodness knew, they needed it for Leslie, and all of them since they'd been attacked by the wildlife.

She tilted her head toward the ship. "Come on." She

waited for him to get in front of her before following. Her gun stayed down but was still at the ready. Peter followed behind, his weapon still cocked.

Mia appreciated his attention to security. This scruffy, bearded man had a bad attitude, but he was still human underneath all that grime. It was their job to save him if he'd crash-landed here. Besides, if he'd been here for as long as it seemed, he'd have valuable intel on the planet.

Captain Stevenson lifted his gaze from Leslie, who now lay in front of the ship. He stood slowly, his hand on the weapon at his hip. "Who's this?"

"Our mystery guest, and the owner of our carbon signature, I'd hazard to guess," Mia said.

The man looked up at the sky again. "Yeah, I wouldn't be the only carbon you'd be reading. I'll tell you everything inside the ship. We have to get in. There's a storm coming and it's not going to be pretty."

The captain stood. "Storm?"

The man nodded. "And once that passes, there are going to be other people. Humans—others who have crash-landed. They won't play nice. You need to get ready before they get here."

Mia and Captain Stevenson exchanged a glance. She gave a subtle shake of her head. She had no idea what to make of this person. Taking his word at face value probably wasn't the best course of action. Not to mention it was far outside the parameters of first contact protocol.

The captain called over his shoulder. "Ashley?"

She rounded the corner. Her eyes widened, seeing their bearded friend.

"Give me a full scan on our guest, please." The captain lifted Leslie off of the ground and took her into the docking bay.

Ashley collected herself and grabbed an instrument from

her pack. The man must have said something to her, because she blushed as she waved the wand over his lower extremities.

She nodded and turned from him. "You're clear. Welcome aboard the Alpha Cent, stranger."

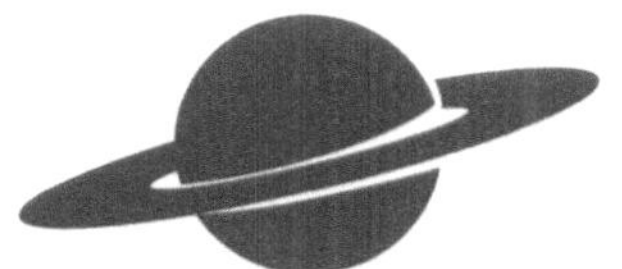

Chapter 4

JASON

It'd been a long time since Jason last stepped onto a star cruiser. The remains of his own ship had become the groundwork for his hut. What boggled his mind the most wasn't that he was on a star cruiser. No, it was the fact that he was on a star cruiser with thirty years' worth of technological advancements in it.

Thirty years. Had it really been thirty years since he'd crashed there? The updates in the UGA uniform were enough to convince him that perhaps time passed differently on Bob than it did on his home world.

Still, he'd almost accused the girl of lying, but why would she? She clearly didn't recognize him, either, which was a bonus, and not really unexpected if thirty years had passed. The world had probably already forgotten all about Jason Griggs.

Wind whistled outside of the ship. The storms hit hard and fast on Bob. He'd learned that the hard way a few days after he'd first crashed. The captain gazed at Jason with concern as the ship swayed.

"We'll be okay," Jason said. "Things will get rocky, so I'd

warn the crew, and get that ramp closed, unless you want it ripped off your ship."

"That bad?" the captain asked.

"I don't have the instruments to track the storms, but by my estimates, we're looking at a Category 2 or 3 hurricane.

The captain cursed under his breath, then made to mop his brow with his sleeve.

Jason stopped him, pointing to the green goo soaked into the fabric. "Trust me, you don't want that on your skin."

The captain gaped, lowering his arm. "The plant bile tested okay, but does it pose any harm to my crew?"

Jason shook his head. "Only if you touch it. Think of it as poison ivy on steroids. It itches and burns, but it's not deadly as far as I've seen."

"Good to know. Thank you."

Jason closed his eyes and took in a deep breath before looking at the captain again. "Yeah, no problem. There's a lot I need to fill you in on about this world, but would it be all right if I cleaned up first?" He held out his hands, showing off his soiled clothes. "It's been a while, as I'm sure you can imagine."

The captain's gaze moved over him as he nodded. "Yes, yes, I can." He nodded at the girl, the one who'd confronted Jason in the forest. "Pilot, help get him situated."

So, he'd read her stripes right. She really was a pilot. Cute —and a kindred soul. Imagine that?

"You've got to be kidding me," she said. "Protocol states that he needs to be questioned extensively."

Ah, one of those "rules" people. Jason hated those.

But he hated being this close to a shower while not actually showering even more. "I just saved your lives. Doesn't that earn me at least a change of clothes?"

The girl opened her mouth, but the captain held up a

hand, stopping whatever she'd been about to say. "Cut the guy a break, Walton. He just wants a shower."

Jason: one.

Cute girl: zero.

If she really was one of those *'ya gotta follow the rules'* people, she'd probably toss a fit now.

Instead, she shook her head and started down the hallway. His heart sank a little. For some reason, he'd hoped she'd argue.

At the end, she turned. Her eyes flashed. "Aren't you coming?"

There was that fire he'd been looking for.

He held back his grin as much as he could. He'd obviously gotten under her skin, and he hadn't even been trying. Maybe he needed to tone down his Jason-ness.

"Right." He joined her at the end of the hallway. It'd been so long since he'd met a girl with such spirit. Every woman he'd seen in Perseverance seemed empty.

Jason gave her a smile, hoping to charm her just a little. Hey, it always worked back home. At this point, he'd do anything to stop the death glares. She'd be gorgeous if she didn't look like she wanted to kick his ass, although it would be a hell of a lot of fun to watch her try.

"So," he said. "Pilot, huh? I used to be one of those. I could show you a few tricks some time."

Her gaze hardened. "See that door to the left with the sign that reads storage? Everything you need for a shower is in there, including some extra clothes."

"UGA uniforms?" he asked.

"Generic gray sweats. This is a training and conditioning area." She pointed to the right. "That sign says *bathroom*, and there are showers in there. Don't bother looking for weapons in the storage closet, by the way. Nothing in there can be used against us. Captain Stevenson will wait for you in the hallway."

"Abandoning me?" He pushed out his lip in a playful pout, determined to win this woman over.

Hey, he'd been dirtier than he was now after several missions, and there were still women waiting for him at the hangar bays when he'd returned.

The pilot crinkled her nose.

Okay, maybe there was a stink factor he needed to take care of. He hadn't considered that.

She took a step back. "Our ship is busted up from entry. I have more important things to do than stand here waiting for you to shower."

"I don't know. Women used to love watching me shower."

She groaned, turned, and left.

Okay, she definitely hated him. He must have been rustier with women than he'd thought. Then again, it had apparently been thirty years.

He sighed, staring at the bathroom door. Thirty years since he'd taken a hot shower...

Jason set his bag on the ground and walked to the storage closet to gather what he needed. Inside he found a pair of gray sweatpants and a white T-shirt still in its official UGA wrapping. The familiar logo was embroidered on the left breast. After thirty years, it hadn't been updated. Part of him still couldn't believe this was happening.

He grabbed soap, shampoo, scissors, and a razor. The latter might get him in trouble, but oh, how he missed a good shave. His knife could only handle so much. Every so often he got his hair cut by one of the women at Perseverance. Using them as a resource always sat wrong with him, though. It only encouraged Vincent's insanity and misogyny.

He froze, clutching the soap. He'd warned the captain to steer clear of the others, but not everyone in that camp was a threat. The face of the woman who'd asked for help haunted him. If this was his chance to leave, he needed to find a way to take her with him, and any others who wanted to escape Vincent's grip.

But first, a shower.

With everything he needed in hand, he went across the hall to the bathroom and slipped into a stream of warm, wet bliss.

Hot water... not even Perseverance had that. It definitely beat bathing in the river.

So much dirt washed out of his skin and hair, the floor started to cake in mud. He made sure to clean it as best he could before he got out.

Once finished, he went to the sink and began the grueling process of cutting off enough of his beard so he could shave. Getting his face completely clean at last took a few runs with the razor. When he looked into the mirror, he barely recognized himself. He brushed his hands over his new, smooth, chin. A strange sensation, and yet, for the first time in a long time, he felt like the real Jason Griggs.

He stepped out into the hallway.

Sure enough, the captain stood leaning against the wall, waiting. When his gaze landed on Jason, his jaw dropped. "G-Griggs?"

Jason took a step back and grimaced. He'd hoped he wouldn't be recognized so quickly. He used to eat up the limelight, but living on a planet that tried to eat you every day changed a man's perspective.

There was no use trying to deny who he was, though. He slipped his hands into the smooth brushed cotton sweats. "Yeah."

The captain laughed. "I-I..." He brushed his fingers through his hair. "I can't believe it. You're supposed to be dead."

"Sorry to disappoint you."

The captain shook his head. "No, sorry, that's not what I meant. Hell, I don't know what I mean, but you've been gone for..."

"Thirty years, according to your pilot."

The captain leaned closer, narrowing his eyes. "You haven't aged a day."

"Honestly, I didn't even realize so much time had passed. I never kept a calendar or anything, but I don't feel like I've been here for that long. Do you have time monitoring devices on this ship?"

"We have a science team."

Jason nodded. "They might want to look into that." Because it sure as hell didn't seem like thirty years. Jason took in the hall. Everything was so bright, so clean. "It doesn't look like you had that much damage."

"We have a topnotch pilot to thank for that. She might even give you a run for your money."

Jason snorted a laugh and then wished he hadn't.

The captain folded his arms. "What, because she's a girl?"

Jason held up his hands. "Didn't say that."

The captain's nose flared. "Thirty years hasn't changed you much."

"Excuse me?" Jason cocked his head. There was something faintly familiar about this guy. He obviously had a grudge against Jason, but Jason couldn't recall pissing off the captain of a C9R&R. A few hundred other captains, yes, but not this one.

The captain started walking. "Thankfully, the damage to our ship isn't critical. We're hoping to get her up and running soon."

Great, he'd managed to get under the captain's skin already, too. He'd definitely lost his charm. But maybe it was better to let the captain change the subject.

Jason ran his fingers along the edge of a computer panel. A ship that didn't lose its ability to fly after falling through Bob's atmosphere was a special ship, indeed. Either that, or someone special had been flying her. "She must be one hell of a pilot."

The captain nodded. "I'm sorry. I guess I should have introduced myself." The captain held out his hand for a shake. "Captain William Stevenson. This ship is the Alpha Cent. We're an official UGA vessel on a mission to retrieve life in the farthest reaches of space."

"Stevenson?" Jason tilted his head. "*Billy* Stevenson?"

His nose flared. "William."

Moons and skies, this was the snot-nosed kid in his squadron who always looked like he was going to pee himself.

Jason blinked twice. The last time he'd seen Billy had been through the windows of his cockpit when the kid's engines had gone dead. Now, he seemed so...*old*.

Jason looked away. "Wow. So I guess that means you got out of there that day."

Billy nodded. "We lost half our team, including you."

Jason balked. "Half?"

Billy nodded again.

"And the cruiser?"

Billy straightened. "No civilian casualties."

A smile burst across Jason's face. "Well, that's good news at least." But to lose half the team... Maybe he'd made a bad call, answering that distress beacon.

Billy placed a hand on his shoulder. "Hey, no one ever criticized your decision to help. There were a thousand people on that ship who owe you their lives."

Jason shook his head. "I didn't get them out of there. You guys did. Good work, Captain."

Billy blushed, and Jason couldn't remember if he'd ever complimented the kid when he'd been under his command.

Jason took the captain's hand and gave it a firm shake. "So, you landed yourself a rescue ship." Jason surveyed the hall again. "Pretty nice little bird you got here."

Billy touched the wall with a hint of reverence. "She's my baby."

Jason patted his arm. "You did good, man. I'm glad you got out." And he was. Knowing the cruiser had survived with no civilian casualties made getting sucked into the nebula worth it.

Well, almost.

Jason touched the ship, too, placing his forehead against the cool metal. The ship hummed, as if welcoming him. He'd almost forgotten the resonance of a living ship. He leaned back. "Can I see your cockpit?"

Stevenson pursed his lips. "Probably not the best idea. My pilot is a little wet behind the ears. She's almost as arrogant as you were."

"Does she have the chops to back that ego up?"

He snorted. "We're alive, aren't we? And this ship is getting in the air again. Since you're still on this planet, I'm going to guess your ship wasn't in this good of a condition."

Jason's cheeks heated. Billy's point was definitely taken.

"I actually need to do a standard debriefing with you," Billy said. "We need to know everything you can tell us about this planet."

"The cockpit." Jason turned to him. "The cockpit first."

Billy shook his head. "Starlight, my pilot is in the cockpit, and I'm afraid you've already made a classic Jason Griggs impression on her."

Jason quirked a brow.

"You talked down to her as if she were a child."

"I didn't..."

"You did."

Jason frowned. "That wasn't my intention, but maybe that's all the more reason to make things right." He held up his hands. "I haven't had a chance to flex my people skills out here. Besides, I'm sure you've got more important things to be dealing with." He lowered his hands. "How about you let her question me?" In the cockpit, so he could pretend to answer questions while soaking in the heart of the ship.

The Alpha Cent rocked a little as a gust of wind from the storm outside hit the hull. Jason lost his footing and stumbled.

When he righted himself, he gazed at the captain. "Do we have a deal?" He flashed his best smile. "I'm kind of dying to see the new technology."

"Fine," Captain Stevenson said. "But only because you're right, I have a lot to attend to. I'll take you down to the cockpit. Just don't treat her like a flyboy, or you're going to have to contend with me."

Jason ignored the last comment. If he'd been gone thirty years, she probably hadn't even been born yet during his glory years at the UGA. She'd treat him like a normal human being as he told his story, not like a starstruck kid. Between her and the captain, she was the better option. And she was also in the one place on the ship he wanted to see.

"The cockpit." Jason clapped his hands and rubbed them together. "Awesome." This was going to be just like going home again.

Chapter 5

MIA

Mia slipped into the pilot's seat and ran her fingers over a small burn in the control panel. With Bernard working in the mechanical department sifting through all of the problems on board, she'd probably have to sort out the issues here on her own.

Leaning back, she soaked in the silence around her. The throbbing headache started to pound fiercely in her skull as the last of the adrenaline faded. After fighting off carnivorous plants, she definitely needed a break before joining the repair team so they could get the heck off this jungle nightmare.

She rubbed at her forehead and closed her eyes. About three seconds passed before the door to the cockpit opened and Captain Stevenson entered. The door closed slowly behind him.

He shook his head. "I can't believe I'm about to say this, but our guest wants a tour of the cockpit."

She spun toward him. "You're kidding me, right?"

He smiled like a child hiding candy behind his back. "There's been some interesting developments with him."

"Since he took a shower? What, does he not smell like *katera* mash anymore?" She folded her arms.

He laughed outright. "This is definitely going to be good." He cleared his throat. "But seriously, try to get him to open up a bit. The ship is in great shape, but we're going to be here for a while. We need to know what we'll have to deal with out there other than giant man eating flowers."

Mia groaned. All she wanted was a nap and maybe a shower of her own.

"He said the plant goop reacts like poison ivy, and Leslie is in medical with burns over most of her body. I need to make sure it's not contagious since we were all exposed." He pointed at her. "Get him to talk."

"Okay, bring him in. I guess." She sat up in her pilot's chair, putting on her most professional of faces. "I'll play nice and everything."

"Actually, I think you're going to enjoy this."

She seriously doubted it, but she nodded anyway.

Captain Stevenson opened the door. "As you requested, the cockpit and our head pilot."

The strange man stepped through the doorway, and Mia let out a gasp as she met crystal blue eyes and a smile that could knock planets from the sky. The standard issue sweats clung to him, accentuating the lines of a man who'd worked his body for every moment of every day. She licked her lisps, reigning in her fluttering heart "S-Starlight?"

She'd never forget his face. It hung on the wall of her bedroom ever since she could remember. He didn't look a day older than his last known photograph.

"So you do recognize me. I wasn't sure. It's been...a long time."

"A long time? Try thirty years." Stars, he was still young. How was this possible? "Now I've got a million questions." Mia tugged at her hair, making sure it wasn't sticking up, before she caught herself and lowered her hands.

She gulped. She would have cried tears of joy if she hadn't been so exhausted.

"I'll leave you two to talk," Captain Stevenson said.

His stance suggested he'd rather stay and ask questions of his own, but she got it, the man had a ship to attend to, and apparently she had been promoted to interrogator...of Jason Starlight Griggs.

She took a deep breath and settled herself as her captain left the room.

Okay, don't make a fool out of yourself. "So, you look the same."

"So I hear," he said. "I wasn't sure since you didn't recognize me out in the jungle."

"In my defense you were wearing an animal on your face that seems to be gone now."

He ran a hand over his chin. "Time passes differently here, it seems. That, in combination with the composure of the atmosphere, must slow the aging process down. The air is rich with water and other nutrients."

Mia paused to consider his words. "There are studies about other planets with a similar phenomenon occurring. I'll give you the benefit of the doubt and assume you're not a clone or an imposter."

"I can take a DNA test if you want. But I think the captain is already sold."

"You knew each other."

He nodded. "He was on the last team I served with."

"You saved his life."

Griggs shrugged. "I've saved lots of lives."

"And so modest about it."

He smiled... the same smile that had graced her wall for so many years. Her heart fluttered. This was actually Jason Griggs...Captain Starlight. This had to be a dream.

She looked away. She needed to get a serious hold on

herself. "Since you've been here a while, I'm hoping you know a way to get us off of this rock."

He tapped a blinking light on the control panel, and the blinking stopped. "If you can get this ship fixed, then you'll be good to go as soon as this storm passes."

Outside, rain streamed down the window panels. Despite the thickness of the plexi, the wind still rumbled against the ship. "How long is that going to take?" she asked.

The Alpha Cent rocked hard as another powerful blast of wind hit.

Mia wiped back her bangs. "Do these storms happen often?"

She gripped the armrests of her chair as a wave of nausea added to the throb in her head. *Come on. Please, not now.*

"From what I've figured out, the storm is large—pretty much unending," Jason explained. "It passes over this area of Bob—" Her head tilted, a question forming on her lips. "I mean...the planet...over the course of a year. There are gaps in the system as it shifts and changes, but they're only slight," he explained.

"Like Jupiter."

"Yes, exactly, only I imagine the radar would show it looking more like Swiss cheese. Soon, the worst of it is going to have passed, and that's when you're going to be in the most danger."

Mia gazed at him for a long moment, waiting for him to say more. "Why would we be in more danger after the storm?"

"There's..." He wiped his face with his palm. "I think I mentioned before, there's another colony of humans who've crash-landed here." He sighed. "That happens every so often. Crashes, I mean. It seems to be about every year that's passed since I've landed." He leaned closer to the window and looked out, as if he could see past the torrent pelting the Plexiglas. "This colony is run in military order. They came from UGA, so at first I didn't think much of it."

Wow...an entire colony? "I'm sure it was a comfort to have other humans around."

"At first, yes," he said, his voice quiet. "But they have no respect for this planet. They're more interested in conquering the land than living within it."

Mia knew the type. She'd met a few during training...the ones who'd always argue with professors about the necessity of treaties that "hindered progress," as they'd put it.

He turned to her. "Their colony has grown in size, and there aren't a lot of women in the group, and I don't think the ones in there are treated well."

Mia leaned away. Certainly he didn't mean...

"Once they realize your ship is here, they're going to come and try to convince your captain to join them. When they see there are women onboard..." His gaze locked on hers. "They're going to *insist* that you join them."

Holy hell. What kind of insanity had they crashed into?

Jason looked away. "Their leader, Vincent Chrona, has staked a claim on this planet and plans to stay, but he's not dumb. He needs women to support a colony, and I don't really think he's above doing whatever it takes to add to his breed stock."

Mia gaped before a shiver went down her spine. That kind of treatment hadn't happened since...well, for hundreds of years. She wanted to believe he was just trying to scare her into talking the captain into leaving as early as possible, but something about his posture, the way his hands clenched and unclenched... He was telling the truth.

She gave a curt nod. "Gotcha, so we need to fix the ship and have it ready to go as soon as this storm hits a hole?"

"Yes, and it's going to hit that hole soon. How bad is the damage?"

"I'm not sure, but my co-pilot didn't seem concerned. He said it should be in order soon enough." She tucked two loose wires back into their places. "That being said, I don't know what kind of parts they're going to need, and if those are in storage."

"Whatever I can do to help, I will." He ran his fingers over two exposed wires by the door before pushing them back inside the panel.

Mia nodded, her lower lip running between her teeth. "Is this other colony really so bad? Or do you just have beef with Chrona?"

"A little of both," Jason mumbled. "I trade with them as needed, but I've made a point not to join them. I don't believe in Vincent's philosophy, or his goals."

Nodding, Mia processed his story. "Obviously, I need to share all of this with Captain Stevenson. The sooner the better."

"Right. Of course."

She stood. "We have some passenger lodging available. I'm sure you'd like to get some rest."

Mia glanced at him but had to look away. Seeing the face of her idol in the flesh felt far too surreal. She opened the door and waved for him to follow.

"Let me drop you off and then I'll return after I speak to the captain and the commander." She didn't turn back, just listened to the heavy gait of his boots behind her. "I know there's more to tell us about the planet, but the captain needs to know the crew might be in danger. I'm surprised you didn't tell him that first thing."

"I did—before I even got on the ship."

True, but he probably could have been more insistent.

He rubbed his face. "I'm kind of overwhelmed, if I'm being honest. And according to you, I'm out of practice by thirty years on protocols."

Fair enough, but still, he should have thought of protecting the innocent. Wasn't that always Starlight's motto? Heck, it was even printed on the packaging of his action figures.

"I'm going to check on the status of the repairs first. Especially if you think this Vincent guy might make a power move."

"He won't make a move. He'll attack. He's not going to stroll up and invite you to tea." He pointed at her. "Trust me, if he knows there are women here, he won't be diplomatic about what he wants. He's probably already preparing to mobilize. The colony isn't far from here. He would have seen your ship come down."

The threat was imminent, if he was telling the truth. "Good to know."

She pressed her hand on a panel beside a passenger door with a green light overhead, showing it was clear for a new occupant. The door slid open and she walked him inside.

Griggs dropped his bag on the floor and spun, whistling a long note. "Wow. Nice digs."

She wrinkled her brow. Most people complained about the close quarters of the three-room guest lodgings. It was better if he was happy, though. "The bathroom is over there, and there's a kitchenette, although most people eat in the galley dining area."

His eyes lingered on the bed before a lurid grin appeared on his face.

She found herself stepping back. "Something wrong?"

He shook his head. "It's just been a long time since I've seen a mattress. I gotta admit, that looks comfy."

She relaxed her shoulders and pointed at the control panel. "Most everything is voice activated. Just say 'System ready,' and the computer will respond."

"What can I help you with today?" The ship's voice filled the room.

"Thanks," Griggs said, slipping his hands in his pockets.

He appeared almost small, despite his six feet. He seemed...lost.

She needed to get back to the captain, but there were so many more questions that needed to be answered.

What had happened when he'd crashed?

Was he sucked into the planet's atmosphere like they were?

How had he survived on his own for all of this time?

Were there natives? Intelligent natives, at that?

What was with the plants eating people?

"Pilot," Jason said. "You still haven't told me your name."

Oh. "Mia," she said.

"Mia..."

"Yup." She had to turn at the sight of his grin. It was too much, too cute, too...everything that would only be a distraction and make her feel like some kind of groupie. She made her way to the door. "Nice to meet you, Captain Griggs."

His gaze swept over her. "And it's *certainly* been nice meeting *you.*"

What in the ever loving...? Is he flirting with me?

She opened the door. "Get lost." And she wished she could slam the sliding door to emphasize the point.

Yeah, he was *the* Jason Griggs, but she'd had enough of that garbage in the academy. She certainly wasn't going to put up with it out here.

Chapter 6

JASON

Did she just tell him to get lost? What had he said?

He'd said it was nice meeting her—was that a faux pas in this crazy new world?

Nah, it couldn't be. He needed to put her reaction out of his head. The ship had crashed, after all. Maybe she had a concussion and didn't know it?

He paced the room. The quarters were definitely nicer than his hut, but resting was too much to ask when he was standing in a living, breathing ship. There was too much to see and too much trouble to get into.

He smiled, feeling more like his old self than he had in years. She'd left him here to rest. Well, he felt plenty rested already. He placed his palm on the door and it opened.

Shame on them for not locking him in. They must have *wanted* him to take a little walk on his own.

He slipped out into the hall and made his way back to the cockpit. He snickered when the door stood before him, closed. Nothing stayed closed to Jason Griggs for long, especially when he'd been in that cockpit just long enough to rub his DNA all over the primary locking wires.

He pressed his palm against the pad beside the door. "Come on, baby. Come to Papa."

The door slid open. "Yes!"

He hadn't lost his touch. That little trick had gotten him into plenty of trouble through the years, and he just loved watching the commanding officers have to eat crow, glaring at him while they pinned yet another medal on Jason's chest for saving lives—after taking unsanctioned control of their ships.

Closing his eyes, he took a deep breath. A cockpit had a unique smell. This one had a hint of lavender mixed with the smell of copper and wiring, probably from the lovely Miss Mia.

Yeah, that had to be the prettiest darn pilot he'd ever seen.

He needed to keep it in his pants, though, even if it had been thirty years since he'd held a woman. He needed allies, and he seemed to piss her off, even when he was trying to be nice.

He settled into the pilot's seat and eased back in the chair. While the controls were higher tech, and there were more automated features inside, for the most part, the basic mechanics of the Alpha Cent were the same as many of the ships he'd flown.

He ran his fingers over the controls. *I could help guide this beauty back home.*

He glanced up at the rain pouring down the Plexiglas.

Home—a place he never thought he'd see again. Thirty years had passed on Earth. That would make his parents... He did the math... Skies, they'd be in their eighties, if they were even still alive. What about the rest of his family? Jillian and little Natty... Hell, Natty would be what, forty-six? He could have a family of his own.

His eyes burned. Jason hadn't gone home much after graduating the academy. He always figured he'd have time.

Now time had slipped away, without him even knowing it. All of his friends would be settled down, maybe even retired, and the world would be unrecognizable. Would it really even be like home anymore, or had Bob become that place for him?

He choked down the burning in his throat. For so long he'd thought all he'd wanted was to leave, and now he had the chance and he couldn't decide if he wanted to take it.

Chapter 7

MIA

Captain Stevenson rubbed his fingers through his hair. "And he's certain this colony is going to attack us?"

Mia nodded. "Regardless of his personal feelings about the guy, the way Griggs described the colony has me concerned about their motives. Being a breed mare isn't my idea of a good time, and I have a feeling they won't just let us go."

"I'm sure we could reach a diplomatic solution," the captain said.

Commander Cortenz tapped her fingers on the table. "One would think they'd want to leave this planet just as much as we do. Surely, they have homes and family elsewhere. We can use that as a bargaining point."

"With the way time passes here, it might change their desire to cooperate," Mia pointed out. "Depending on how long they've been here, they might not even have families back home anymore."

Cortenz pursed her lips. "The captain and I will discuss our tactics for dealing with this colony. You should remain focused on fixing the ship. It's where you'll be most useful."

Well, that was a dismissal if she'd ever heard one. It took everything within Mia to bite her tongue. "Yes, ma'am."

"Actually, I think she'll be most useful in dealing with this situation involving Captain Griggs," Captain Stevenson said. "He seemed to open up to you, and frankly, it was a little hard for me to remain impartial. I couldn't get over who he is." His gaze leveled on her. "Since you weren't even born yet, you hopefully won't have that problem."

Mia closed her gaping mouth. "But—"

"There's more information we can mine from him. Particularly, things about the planet that we'll need to know. For instance, this storm's weather pattern is going to make or break our attempt at leaving. Also, Leslie is still having a reaction to the acids from that plant." He got quiet, then nodded to himself. "Yes, start there. Let's see if he's aware of a cure, like a salve of some kind to help her." He looked up. "Let's also see what he can tell you about the planet's wildlife. This is going to save us time and we need to be prepared in case we can't make it out of here in our first window of opportunity."

Mia sighed. "Not that I'm unhappy we found him, but does it have to be *me*?"

"Yes, it does."

Commander Cortenz's expression softened. "This is a great chance for you to get to know one of the greatest UGA heroes in history."

"Yes, but..." *He hit on me.* She closed her eyes and took a deep breath. "I didn't think he'd be such a jerk."

"Most pilots are. Arrogance is a common trait in them." Cortenz raised a brow in Mia's direction.

Mia ground her teeth. "Maybe I'm not the arrogant one."

"Pilot, save the attitude for Griggs," Captain Stevenson advised. "I have a feeling you're going to need it."

She saluted her captain and then the commander. "Yes, sir, ma'am. I'll report whenever I find out anything more." And she'd try her best not to stuff it down his face sideways.

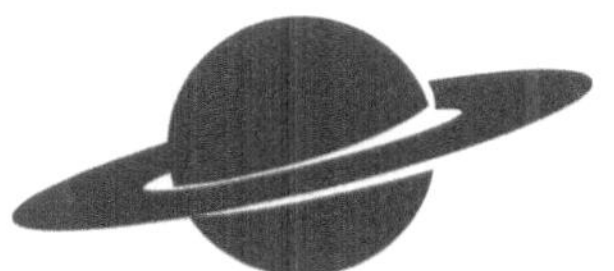

Chapter 8

JASON

Jason slipped out of the cockpit. Mia should be done debriefing the captain on the situation by now.

The pretty pilot wasn't like Billy, who maybe had some beef with him in the past. However, her gaze felt like a mixture of awe and annoyance every time she looked at him.

Funny, when she'd recognized him it had both excited and confused him. She shouldn't have known who he was, unless the history books were talking about him.

He'd pushed some envelopes, broken some records, pissed off a few admirals and saved lives in the process, but he didn't think his escapades would still be mentioned after —gulp—thirty years.

He turned down a side hallway, heading back to his room. He'd already made a pretty bad impression with her, from what he could see. The worst thing he could probably do is get caught hijacking the controls of her cockpit. Even though it would be fun getting her all riled up, he needed to play things cool with these people...at least until he decided whether or not he would be leaving with them.

He quickened his pace, taking in the clean lines and bright halls. The ship had held up nicely in the storm.

Outside of a few moments where it had rocked heavily, the vessel had absorbed most of the storm's tumult. Apparently, the UGA had learned a lot over the years in how to design for alien elements. It had certainly taken them long enough.

This storm had totaled three ships within days of them crashing. Jason may have been able to salvage some, if their hulls hadn't been torn to shreds from projectiles caught in the hurricane-strength winds.

He turned a corner just as the ship was slammed by another powerful blast of wind. Losing his footing, he stumbled into the next hallway—right into a pretty, short-haired blonde.

They tumbled to the floor and he managed to brace himself with his arms to keep from crushing her under his weight. Of course, she still lay underneath him, smelling like lavender and metallic machine parts. His hand trembled slightly, and when he dared to gaze at her face, he saw red cheeks and anger in her eyes.

He called up his best smile. "Nice to meet you again, pilot." Once the ship stopped shaking, he stood and offered her his hand.

Flaring her nose, she allowed him to pull her up. Her hand was soft and warm and... dammit!

He let go, wiping his palm on his sweats. "Sorry about that."

She settled her footing as another rumble rattled through the ship. She ran a hand through her adorable short curls. "It's not a big deal. I was looking for you anyway."

He widened his grin. "You were, huh? I knew you'd come around." He took a step toward her.

She used one finger to push him away. "I told you I'd come back, but you weren't in your quarters."

Oh, yeah. "I, umm, wanted to see the ship, and I started to get bored in there, all alone for so long."

She folded her arms. "Less than an hour has passed."

She was going to make it hard to win her over, wasn't she?

He exhaled sharply before trying again. "Did you talk to the captain?"

"I wouldn't be here if I hadn't."

Her chest rose and fell beneath her arms. She was round in all the right places, and he really wanted to... *Shoot! Down, boy*. He adjusted his sweats and looked up.

Her nose flared again.

He bit back his laugh. "I'm sorry. I've kind of been alone for a long time, and you're beautiful and—"

"And my eyes are right here." She pointed to her face.

Yeah, okay, guilty as charged. He'd definitely been looking at her chest. "Sorry. Again."

"And I would appreciate it if you didn't talk to me like I'm a child."

He tilted his head. "Maybe I'm just annoyed you haven't thanked me yet."

She glared at him. "Thank you for what, exactly?"

"Saving your life. Twice."

"You didn't save my life twice."

"The storm was one." He held up a pointer finger. "If I hadn't told you, you all would be splats on the trees."

She rolled her pretty blue eyes, and he didn't mind in the slightest despite her obvious intent to be disrespectful. "Fine, one time. When was the second?"

"The hungry flower."

She frowned. "That giant man-eating... I wasn't the one who almost got eaten."

"No, but—"

Mia gasped. "The plant... Leslie." She straightened. "She's not reacting well to whatever juice was in that thing. Do you know what might help? Our medics are stumped."

"So you do have a heart." He offered a soft smile. "Let me

grab my bag, and then take me to the infirmary. I think I've got something that will help."

She let out a sigh, her eyes closing for a second. "Thank you."

"There we go." He flashed a grin, so she'd know he wasn't trying to be mean.

The eye roll returned. "A simple '*You're welcome*' would have been fine, or you could just not say anything at all." She waved for him to follow her, and she waited for him to go into his room and grab his bag before they started walking again.

He flung the satchel over his shoulder. "You know, I'm not so bad if you give me a chance."

She glanced at him before pinning her attention to the hallway ahead of her. "Trust me when I say I'm trying to like you. I *want* to like you. Part of why I became a pilot is because..." She stared at him once more before shaking her head. "Never mind. I'm trying. Okay?"

"Noted," he said. *What did she almost say, though?* Part of why she'd become a pilot was... what?

Before he'd crashed, the academy had called him in once or twice a year to talk to the young recruits and get the kids excited. The kids had always fawned over him, telling him he was the reason they'd joined up. But again, this girl hadn't even been born yet. Which made him feel like a major dirt bag, because she had an amazing ass, but he was, what...

He did the math.

Stars, he had to be fifty years old, and she was barely in her twenties. His body screamed for him to forget numbers and go for it, though.

He adjusted his pants again. This should be easier... It had always been easy as far as women were concerned. Maybe he shouldn't try so hard.

Mia looked over her shoulder at him. Luckily enough, he

hadn't been staring at her ass at the time. "What's with the plants here, anyway? Are all of them so aggressive?"

He nodded. "The ones with the purple and red flowers, yes. They eat small animals and birds and large bugs. I've been snatched a few times myself, but they always spit people back out." He shook out his arms. Sometimes, he still felt the phantom burn, even years later. "The digestive juice wreaks havoc on the skin. Some people worse than others, of course."

Mia led him down a small flight of metal stairs. "It's not lethal, is it?"

"No, just painful, and it can leave scarring if the reaction is strong enough and not treated quickly." He reached into his bag and felt around for the healing sap. No matter what, he always kept a bottle of it on hand.

Mia opened the door to the infirmary. "Doctor Kelex, this is Captain Griggs."

Jason offered this hand. "Actually, it's 'Lieutenant Commander.' The *Captain* thing is a misnomer."

The doctor jumped up from her desk, smoothing back her dark, peppered-gray hair and straightening her lab coat. "Sir, it is an honor to meet you no matter the rank." She reached out to shake his hand. "I'm sure Mia has filled you in on our predicament."

Jason handed over the bottle of healing syrup. "This will do the trick. Apply a coat of it on the skin every three hours or so for the first twenty-four hours. After that, just once a day will be good until the infection clears up."

"Thank you," the doctor said, bringing it over to the poor woman who'd been grabbed by Doug's nameless cousin.

She groaned, but somehow managed to say, "Thank you" as well.

Jason raised a brow to Mia. "See, they know how to show appreciation to someone."

"Whatever." Mia headed out of the infirmary so fast, he barely caught the door to go after her.

He ran up beside her. "FYI, don't shoot those flowers. If they blow up, the toxins are released in a gas form. That's deadly."

She peered over at him. "So you're the one who threw the rock at me."

"Yes, I did. You're welcome, by the way."

"What?"

"Well, I figure by now you weren't going to say, 'Thank you,' and my mother always taught me to be polite to a lady."

He smiled, but she stopped and glared at him.

Dammit! What had he said this time?

She stared up into his eyes, her hands on her hips. "If you want me to like you, I suggest not being such a jerk."

His shoulders sagged. "I'm just trying to be funny. Lighten up."

"You're not funny, though, if you have to tear someone down for your punchline."

He held up his hands. "How in Neptune's moons did I tear you down? It was a joke."

She poked him in the ribs. "Jokes like that aren't funny. Especially with someone you don't know."

They gazed at one another for a long time, and his breath caught in his throat. He knew she was right. It'd been so long since he'd been with decent people. Vincent sure didn't have a sense of humor.

He held out his hand to her. "Fine, truce. At least until I earn the right to give you crap."

"I accept your apology." She shook his hand.

They resumed their walk. Passing a window, Jason saw a glimpse of the sun coming through the clouds. "Oh, no..."

"What?" she asked.

"The storm is breaking."

"That's a good thing, though, right?"

"Yes and no. Remember the colony? They're going to make a beeline for your ship as soon as they see it's clear." He grabbed her by the shoulders and forced her to look at him again. "Get the women together and hide. No matter what you hear happening outside, don't try to help. Don't make yourselves known."

Mia's gaze hardened. "Just because we're female doesn't mean we're weak. We can fight too."

"I'm sure you know how to, but these guys train day and night. They're strong. They'll overpower you. Please, trust me. Hide."

There had to be a way to explain to her just how dangerous Vincent and his men were without insulting her ego. Didn't she get this had nothing to do with Jason's perceptions of women, but the cold, hard facts?

A loud pounding against the hull of the ship echoed from the docking bay. Jason peeked out the window and saw several of Vincent's men stepping out of the foliage holding semi-automatic rifles.

He whispered a curse under his breath. "Too late. They're here."

Chapter 9

JASON

Jason made his way to the docking bay, completely ignoring every one of Mia's protests. He had to get to Billy...or Captain Stevenson—whatever in tarnation he was calling himself these days—before he went out to meet Vincent on his own. They arrived at the doors at exactly the same time, but instead of the small army Jason had hoped for, only Captain Stevenson stood by the doorway.

"You should call more of your men," Jason said.

Captain Stevenson tilted his head to the side. "Why? I know your interactions with this group haven't been pleasant, but that doesn't mean mine will be, too. I'm sure we'll be able to talk our situation over rationally."

"At least go out armed," Jason urged.

The captain pointed to a gun tucked in his uniform. "Just because I'm hopeful doesn't mean I'm stupid."

"Of course not." Jason returned his attention to the docking bay door. Someone pounded on the hull again. "Be ready."

"I am." Captain Stevenson released the latch and opened up the ship. He stepped forward, making sure to use his body size to block the way inside. Jason filled the gap.

At the foot of the ramp leading onto the ship stood Vincent Chrona. His gaze landed on Jason and narrowed. "Captain Griggs, I almost didn't recognize you all cleaned up like that. It seems you have no problem mingling with your own kind after all. There's hope."

Jason forced a smile. "I've never had issues with being around people. I just happen to be picky about the type of people I spend time with."

Vincent placed his hand on his chest and gave a mock pout. "You hurt my feelings."

"Good." Jason put a hand on his trusty gun, the one he'd had since he'd started in the UGA. It always got the job done in a pinch, and Jason happened to be an excellent shot.

Vincent must have caught the motion because he let out a heavy, dramatic sigh. He gazed at his men. "Guys, I guess we're in for a firefight after all. I was hoping we could take this vessel peacefully. Bloodshed is so unnecessary."

"I agree," Billy said. He gave Jason a stern look as he stepped out in front. "I'm the captain of this ship. We've come on a mission from the United—"

"To seek out life and return it to its homeland," Vincent finished. "Sounds a lot like our mission, too. We also went into this territory of space in search of all of the other lost ships of the ages. I hate to break it to you, but we're on our own and not going anywhere. It's better for you to surrender."

Billy pointed at the floor. "This is my ship and the people on board are under my command. I'm willing to work through a peaceful compromise, but I am not surrendering anything to you," he said. "As long as I breathe, you will not have control."

Vincent cocked his gun. All of his men followed suit. "Too bad it's going to have to come to that."

Jason put his fingers to his lips and whistled shrilly—

Dobby's call. The creature always stayed close, hidden in the trees. Dobby dropped down from the limbs above in between Jason and Vincent, standing on his hind legs, displaying his full height, which was almost equal to Jason's. His tail twitched behind him as he barked, and the forest grew eerily silent.

Jason recognized that call. Hopefully, Dobby's reinforcements weren't too far away.

Scoffing, Vincent pointed his gun. "Say goodbye to your pet."

A buzz filled the forest.

As Vincent pulled the trigger, a wall of beetle-like insects zoomed in and hovered between Dobby and the Perseverance men.

The bullet ricocheted off of the shells, and the men beside Vincent ducked.

Jason referred to these little workhorses as 'Tank Beetles' because their exoskeleton was practically indestructible. He'd tried smashing them with every object he owned, including a sledgehammer. All he'd done was dent the hammer. The only way he'd found to kill them was with the acid from the hungry flower that Mia's shipmate had fallen into.

Once he learned he couldn't kill them easily, he also learned he shouldn't. Jason embraced the bugs as part of his new life, much like all of the wildlife he'd encountered. They reacted in kind and were far more sentient than he'd given them credit for.

Vincent shot again and again, but the beetles simply buzzed louder as more and more came, thickening the wall. Yeah, this was one of his better friendships.

The beetles loved the nectar from the little yellow flowers in the low-growing bushes, but those flowers grew close to the spider warrens. Beetles were like a crunchy appetizer to the spiders, so the little bugs tended to steer clear. Harvesting the nectar once a week and leaving it out for the beetle colony had made him and Dobby fast friends to the giant bugs.

Billy's eyes went wide as the swarming cloud of beetles grew larger. "What in the world?"

"Dobby, help me disarm them," Jason said, ignoring the captain.

With a yip of agreement, Dobby swayed his tail back and forth. While Vincent kept shooting at the Tank Beetles, a group of Electric Squirrels ran down the tree trunks behind Vincent's cronies.

The small rodents charged the men, biting them in the ankles, not only sinking their teeth in, but also sending electric currents into the men's muscles. One guard dropped and convulsed, while the others all howled in pain or stood stunned from the reaction to the energy unloading on them.

Jason smiled. Electric squirrels loved the same sap that he'd given the doctor to heal the woman who'd been swallowed by the flower. He'd found that out one day by accident while leaving the sap out to warm in the sunshine between storms. These little guys were easier to make friends with than the beetles.

Another squirrel moved to bite Vincent too. He managed to dodge the creature before it could attack, all while unloading his last bullet on the Tank Beetle wall. His gaze fell on his twitching, flailing men and narrowed. "I thought I trained you all to be stronger than this. They're stupid animals, for crying out loud."

"They're more than that," Jason seethed. "Maybe if you worked with the planet instead of against it, you'd understand."

"And maybe someday you'll understand that I have more

men. No matter how many cute, fuzzy critters answer to your call, you won't be able to out match us." Vincent's face hardened as he pointed at the Alpha Cent. "This ship is mine, and I will be back for it."

Jason withheld an artfully crafted quip. Better to not egg him on.

He kept his hand on his gun as Vincent stormed off into the thick foliage. The egomaniac didn't even bother to help his men off of the ground. Why did they follow such a self-centered jerk so blindly? It didn't make sense.

One by one, the members of Perseverance retreated, leaving Jason and Billy alone. The captain still gazed wide-eyed at the Tank Beetles.

He reached out a hand to touch one. "These things are fascinating." Before his hand made contact with the black-and-iridescent bugs, they disbanded and disappeared into the bushes. "They're fast, too."

"I almost called them 'Speed Demons.'" Jason laughed. "But 'Tank Beetles' definitely fit better." His smile faded. "You need to up your security."

"Yes." Billy turned to enter the Alpha Cent again. With both of them inside, he shut the doors. "We've got a number of barriers and traps to arm ourselves with. All of our protective measures are still intact. This *Vincent* is going to realize quickly that we're not easy pickings."

Jason nodded, his mind drifting to Mia and the other women on board. For their sake, he sure hoped that was true. "Get all of your security team together. I'll meet you in a few minutes to cover what you'll need in order to protect yourself from Vincent's crew."

"All right. Come to the command deck when you're ready."

He gave the captain a salute. It felt strange performing the gesture to a kid who used to report to him. The gray hair made it a little easier at least.

Before meeting with anyone, though, he needed to check on the women. He'd probably get blasted for it, but fine. He needed to make sure they were okay, and that Vincent's men hadn't found another way inside.

He knew the chances of that were slim. As soon as those scum-suckers recovered from the squirrel bites, they'd run home with their tails between their legs. The same guys wouldn't return for quite a while.

Still, seeing Mia again would put his mind at ease and remind him exactly what he was fighting for.

Jason made his way toward the infirmary since that was the last place he'd left her. He didn't have to look so far. Standing in the middle of the hallway in a perfect squad formation was Mia and three of the other women on board— one of them being the victim of the hungry flower. All of them held guns at the ready.

For a long time, he just stared at them, impressed as well as confused. He had told them to hide, right? Mia knew what Vincent wanted. Standing out like this, even in foolproof formation, was...

"Shut your mouth before you catch flies," Mia said.

He did so, nodding slowly. "That's good advice since the ones who live here are bigger than your fist."

"Your jokes are the worst." Mia lowered her gun and put the safety back on.

"You didn't follow my orders," he said.

She laughed. "I rejected your advice. You're not my captain, so I don't have to obey you." She waved her hand at the rest of the women. "As you can see, we're more than capable of handling ourselves in a fight. We'll go down swinging and die before we let any man own us. Remember that, Griggs."

He held up his hands. "There's no way I'll forget that now." Wow, he'd seriously underestimated this crew.

Vincent had too, though, and he was a sore loser. He'd come back harder, with more men and more artillery. They needed to be ready for him.

Chapter 10

MIA

During the debriefing on the command deck, Mia listened to Captain Jason Griggs, her hero, direct the captain of the Alpha Cent as though Stevenson were the underling and not the other way around. She certainly respected Jason's knowledge. There was no denying he knew the most about the planet as well as the people who resided on it. What she couldn't get past was that awful ego.

An ego that greatly disappointed her.

"If we can have our technicians work on repairs all hours of the day, we should be ready for takeoff within the week," Commander Cortenz said.

Captain Stevenson nodded. "Although we do have a dilemma of resources. Particularly fuel. With heightened security, we're going to need to reallocate our energy from other basic comforts."

He started pacing, rubbing his chin. Reallocation was never easy. One department was about to be deemed non-essential, and that always led to bad feelings.

"We can cut down on air conditioning and unnecessary lights to start. The more things we can use the planet for, the better off we're going to be once it's time to go."

Interesting...most captains kept their creature comforts. It was going to get hot in this ship, though, and fast.

The captain turned to Jason. "Do you think it's safe enough to go outside and see about securing our perimeter? I can spare a few people to help."

"Of course, but I'll only need one." Jason's gaze landed right on Mia. "This is a good break in the storm. We should have plenty of time."

"This meeting is adjourned then. Griggs, feel free to select your counterpart and I'll give the rest of my crew their assignments." Captain Stevenson waved Cortenz to follow him. They walked straight to Bernard and started discussing how to reroute the power.

Mia had minored in shipboard functions, and if the captain had looked at her records as closely as she knew he had, he would know that. It stung that he hadn't come to her for help with onboard systems.

Then again, he probably assumed Jason would be enlisting her help, so why bother?

"Ready to go exploring, pilot?" Jason asked, putting an arm around her.

She gaped. "Sure am, but please keep your hands to yourself."

With a sigh, he lowered his arm. That smile from the posters returned. "By the end of the day, I'll have won you over."

"Don't count your cards until they are dealt, my friend." She turned away before he saw the heat rise in her cheeks. She'd spent so much time in the academy dodging advances just like this. Why couldn't she be treated like everyone else?

Then again, as much as she let her instincts kick in with him, like she would any other man, she really hadn't minded his touch.

Giving in to a guy's obvious advances, though, would

thwart everything she'd worked so hard to achieve. She was more than just a woman. More importantly, more than a beautiful blonde. Men had looked at her differently from the day she was old enough to notice. She needed to prove them all wrong, for herself as much as to shove her intelligence and grade point average up their pompous rear ends.

Still, his arms were strong, his body warm. Now that he was clean shaven, the beautiful smile that had graced her walls for years gave her all kinds of butterflies.

Then he'd open his mouth, and he became just like every other man she'd ever met—haughty, arrogant...and what was with the staring at her boobs?

She shook her head and made herself busy fixing the wiring in a compartment beside her on the wall.

Jason Griggs wasn't supposed to be like all the others. Captain Starlight was supposed to be better. He'd saved the galaxy. How could he be so...ordinary?

Mia shook it off and waved for him to follow her off of the command deck.

Jason's gaze stayed glued on her as they walked down the hall. "Why do I get the feeling that no matter what I say or do, I'm disappointing you?"

Wow. Good-looking and perceptive. Maybe the latter was what had kept him alive for so many years.

She kept walking. "You're... You're part of why I wanted to become a pilot." There. She'd said it. The truth. "So much of what you did during your time at UGA...it was the stuff of legends. You broke the mold, questioned authority, and saved lives." She held up her hands. "I wanted to be just like you."

His smile faded a tiny bit. "It's good to know all of the stuff I did was remembered so fondly. Frankly, I think I drove my superiors nuts."

"You saved three planets from being decimated and discovered five sentient species. Why would that make anyone mad?" She couldn't fathom it. Were his supervisors idiots?

"I did all of that because I went rogue," he said. "There were plenty of missions I obeyed my orders too, of course. When they retell all of my stories, they don't talk about me being the kid with attitude, though, do they?"

She shrugged. "It's been mentioned by some of your old training leaders at the academy. They always talk about it in a teasing sort of tone, so I didn't think much of it."

"So you decided to copy my attitude." His gaze bore through her before the smile returned. "I've noticed you've got some sass."

Her cheeks heated and she turned away. "I don't give my commanders sass."

"You sure do. Cortenz especially seems to creep under your skin. That look you gave her before spoke a million words you didn't have to say." He nudged her shoulder.

Inside, her stomach did a flip. She exhaled, desperate to regain her calm. "Did you notice how she talks down to me?"

"Like a good commander should." He pointed his thumb at his chest. "In my time here, with lots of reflection, I realized that my commanders did the same thing. It always annoyed me too, but you need to be careful." He grabbed her arm, stopping her gait. "I'm not the kind of guy you should be idolizing. I got lucky, that's all. Other people have done the same things and got themselves demoted, court-martialed, or killed in the line of duty."

She considered him for a moment before shaking her head. "That's hard for me to believe. I mean, you're a..."

"A guy. A regular, ordinary guy." His gaze was wide, pleading. "Can we drop the hero worshipping? It's uncomfortable."

Mia gave him a small smile. "Sure, I'll do my best. Keep talking to me like you have been, and the magic glow will fade in no time."

"I'm not *that* mean to you."

No? Then why did every word out of his mouth sting so bad?

She turned a corner and led him to the door for the ship's weapons storage. After typing in in her passcode, they entered. "I didn't say you were mean. Annoying, yes. You're definitely annoying."

He held up his pointer finger. "There's an old saying my great-grandmother used to use. She said, 'That's the pot calling the kettle black.'"

Mia laughed. "We must bring it out of each other." One thing she appreciated about him was that he seemed to get her sense of humor, finally. Or maybe she was starting to understand his.

Jason rubbed his hands together, taking in the weapons store. Guns, batons, flash grenades, and smoke bombs of all kinds hung from the walls in orderly rows. Then there were the weapons not on display. Knives, ropes— whatever they'd need to survive in the wilderness— most of it would be in that room, probably hidden in the cabinets. They just needed to find it.

He walked toward a drawer and slid it open. Large hunting knives glinted in the overhead lighting. His eyes lit up like a kid on Christmas.

"Good guess," Mia said.

"I've had a lot of practice at finding what I want." He glanced at her. "I can take anything?"

"Yes. I trust you're not going to turn on me," she said.

He snorted before spinning back to the case. "These knives are going to be the most useful. Guns are fine, but they're only good against certain animals. I honestly only use mine to hunt the Tiger Piranhas, and as a last defense against Vincent."

Mia packed a knife for herself and slipped a fresh battery in her gun. "Tiger Piranhas?"

"It's just something I call them. They look exactly like their name." He reached into the drawer and pulled out a sheathed blade before strapping it onto his body. "A lot of what we're going to do will involve setting traps using what the planet provides."

"Do you really think Chrona will fall for that?" She moved beside him, grabbing a small hunting knife.

"First of all, Vincent is too stupid to make the connection that the planet can be used against him. He'll be prepared for your tech, but not something primitive." He grabbed another blade. "Secondly, these traps are going to hold up better when the storm resurges."

He grabbed a magnifying glass. An odd choice, but she didn't question it.

"So...Tiger Piranhas?"

He walked over to the ropes. "The name might sound silly, but I'd already come up with my own names for things before I learned the local language, and the names I gave things just stuck in my mind."

"So there *is* a local language?" Which meant there were natives, something she'd already heard him imply, even if he still hadn't directly confirmed it as fact.

Once again, he dodged around the subject. "Let's head out. We're running out of time. The more daylight we can use, the better."

"I can grab a flashlight," she said.

"I'm sure you can, but that doesn't mean it's safe to be out in the dark. A lot of bigger, meaner things prowl during those hours."

Maybe, but he didn't know that she'd aced survival training on Dederon Four...the one training session the late, great Captain Starlight had failed miserably.

She grabbed a survival pack with a flashlight all the same. Extra food and water were inside as well. She tossed it at Griggs and then picked up another one. "Never hurts to be prepared."

Together, they left the storage room and made their way to the docking bay. Mia released the door and was once again greeted with the heat of the jungle. The air felt thicker this time, full of more water, like the storm still lingered. A musky, floral scent filled the air.

She wrinkled her nose. "Is it always like this after the storm passes?"

"Yes, the plants use the extra humidity to reproduce. They release spores into the enriched air before it becomes drier. It's the best time to gather medicines and herbs." He walked out into the jungle. "It's also a great time to get poisoned. Be careful not to touch anything."

Mia followed close behind. "That's going to be hard to do if we're supposed to make traps from the verge."

"Fine, don't touch anything unless I tell you to," he clarified. "We're going to get away from the ship to gather some supplies from plants that aren't here. Sticky webbing, thorns, and gas berries."

All of those sounded useful. "Are they not located nearby?"

"The plants are reproducing, so they're on the defense right now."

"You say that like they're sentient."

"They are." The look he gave her made it clear he was dead serious.

"So they understand what we're saying? They can think?"

"Kind of. I'm not sure they understand the language. I've had some close calls. Perhaps I should say that I'm not sure how much of what we say is understood. It might be more connected to emotions than any actual words." He waved a hand. "A lot of them shrink and hide when they feel threatened. A crash will definitely get that reaction out of them."

Mia gazed about her at the tall trees filled with thick leaves. A few vines dangled down the trunks, the same vines that had been used by the flower to capture Leslie. "I thought plants were stationary."

"Their bases are. I have one of those giant hungry flowers growing not far from where my ship crashed. He stays put, but he has these long vines that trail out, looking for food to drag back to him."

"Is that common here? For plants to have moving parts?"

He nodded. "Almost all of them have vines and roots that will expand and retract as needed. They use them like arms."

"Sounds like a horror movie."

"It was definitely a culture shock when I first got here."

And he'd been all alone.

With all the survival training she'd had, she still wasn't sure she could have lasted so many years out here with no back-up. She certainly would have given this planet a run for the money, though. But to be alone for so long, and being estranged from the others in the colony...no wonder he'd been so excited to talk to her.

They walked side by side through the jungle. Birds chirped above, and she thought she heard a smaller rodent-like animal running on the ground nearby. For the most part, though, it was only sound. The animals had a knack for not being seen.

After about a mile, Griggs held up a hand for them to stop. "Out this way is where the sticky webs are."

"Are they made by spiders?" she asked.

"Is this the part where you tell me you have arachnophobia?" He grinned at her.

She shook her head. "I just want to know what I'm getting into. Webs are usually made by spiders. If these are going to be big enough for us to use, then I'm imagining some pretty damn big spiders." A shiver ran down her spine at the thought.

Jason chuckled. "It's okay to say yes. I get it, they're creepy. Don't worry, though. They hunt at night here. They're all sleeping in their tunnels."

"Tunnels?"

"Yeah, they have a complete ecosystem under the entire jungle. It seems to be a symbiotic relationship with the Great Eater trees because they seem to work around each other."

"Great Eaters...you mean those big flowers?"

He snorted. "No. Hungry flowers spit you out. Great Eaters eat you."

Mia gulped, not sure what bothered her more: giant spiders or man-eating trees. Since they were looking for webs, the spiders were probably more of an immediate concern. "So there are spiders sleeping underneath us right now?"

"Probably." He waved his hand like giant spiders weren't a big deal.

Hadn't he ever heard of *The Lord of the Rings*? "But they're asleep and not going to come after us, right?" She stared at him, really needing that confirmation.

"Right. I promise no spider is going to eat you today."

Mia took in a deep breath. She could accept that answer. Out of sight, out of mind, right? "Okay, tell me how to get these sticky webs."

"You're going to want to pay close attention to where you're stepping. They look a lot like the ground," Jason explained. "They're placed over tunnel entrances for prey to land on. Then the spiders wake up and..."

She shivered. "Yeah, I get it. Game over."

He pointed at the ground. "Here."

Mia crouched beside a large, oval patch of dirt, dark gray like all the rest, but this area had a slight shine.

Wow. She never would have even noticed if she were out here for a casual hike.

She poked the edge with her finger. The web squished, but it didn't stick to her skin like she'd expected.

"Interesting," she murmured, pressing her hand more firmly against it.

Jason's gaze snapped to her. "What are you doing? I told you not to touch anything unless I said so."

"Relax, it isn't stick...ing." She frowned as she tried to pull her hand free from the web. "It didn't stick the other time I touched it."

He pressed a palm to his forehead. "It responds to different levels of pressure. Just hold still. I'll get you out in a second."

"I don't need you to rescue me." Why did he keep thinking she was helpless? It was just a stinking spider web.

Mia pulled her hand away from the web. The thick tendrils stretched with each tug, the microfibers getting thinner and thinner—but they didn't break.

Jason stared at her with his hands folded over his chest, waiting.

"See?" she said with a grin. "I got thi—"

The web gave a sharp yank on her arm as it snapped back to the ground. Her shoulder landed on the web, along with a large portion of her hair. She tried to sit up, but the elasticity drew her down.

Stars! What had she done?

Her breath hitched. Her heart rattled in her chest as she spun, trying to free herself, but the webbing only drew her in tighter.

Jason's laughter echoed between the trees.

She reached across to grab the ground and pull herself out, only to grab more of the web. Dang it!

His face appeared over her, partially skewed by a mixture of her hair and the web plastered over her right eye. He smirked, but his gaze swept over her, as if calculating his next move.

Mia growled. "Don't. Say. Anything."

"I wasn't planning on it." He knelt down and pulled out the magnifying glass. "I don't know if you ever did this as a kid, but back home, we used to use the sun to light insects on fire."

"That's cruel."

He laughed. "Maybe, but it's the same thing that's going to get you out of here before those spiders wake up. With all that struggling you're doing, they're going to be stirring any minute now."

"I thought you said they only came out at night." She started to wiggle. If the spiders were waking up, she needed to get loose. Now.

He put a hand on her ankle. "Every move you make sends a signal down into the tunnels. Those spiders are hungry. Calm down before you wrap yourself into a burrito." Jason angled the piece of glass somewhere beyond her head. When she saw the smoke drifting in from behind, she realized what he was doing.

"Don't burn me."

"All the more reason for you to hold still." His gaze stayed focused on his task, though. The look of determination on his face made her heart flutter just a tiny bit.

Mia closed her eyes and ignored the vision of spiders coming through the tunnels, eagerly waiting to suck her blood. Her heart tried to leap out of her chest. She hoped it was her imagination, but she thought she could hear the tattering of their legs as they crawled toward her.

She shuddered. Then she realized that sound wasn't coming from her imagination.

"J-Jason?"

He nodded curtly. "I hear it. Hang on."

"I can't do anything but hang on." The pull on her hair lessened, and she lifted her head.

He cradled the back of her neck. "Okay, go slow."

She did as he urged. Below her, something large, brown, and furry scuttled through the tunnel. "Can these things kill people?"

"It would take a lot. Their bites sting like a bitch, though."

Well, that was a relief, but only partially. A Doberman probably wouldn't kill her, either, but that didn't mean she wanted to be bitten by one.

The webbing around her arms softened.

Jason held her shoulder steady. "I want you to roll toward me, okay? If you go the other way, you're going to fall right into the tunnel and they'll be on you faster than warp speed."

She nodded and carefully shifted her weight toward Jason's voice. Her arm popped free just before a thick, furry leg prodded at her side.

In the hole beside her, several tightly knit, black and red eyes stared at her. A scream ripped from her throat as she backpedaled.

Jason grabbed hold of her, but she thrashed.

She needed to get away. The spiders! She punched, landing a solid hit to his chest.

He hissed out a curse and shoved her. His lips formed a word, but before he could speak his face paled. His jaw snapped shut and he reached for his knife.

She spun to check the hole just as Jason lunged over her. A creature with far more than eight legs and a dark, hairy body reared up, double his height. He stabbed at its belly, and it shrieked.

"Don't run," he cried. "You'll fall into another trap."

Another patch of glistening soil shifted beside her, then disappeared. She backed up, then remembered, sidestepping another web trap just as another smaller spider—but still more than half her height—emerged from the other hole.

Jason ducked and rolled beneath the other spider, jabbing it in the side.

He grimaced at the other huge, hissing creature. "Go for the eyes."

The eyes. Got it.

She set her footing, noting the placement of the traps, and pulled out her knife. The creature started to scurry toward her, and she lunged, stabbing at the patch of red and black. The creature shrieked and sidled back. Purple goo trailed out of a patch of fur just to the right of its eyes.

Mia gripped the blade tighter, balancing on the balls of her feet. She'd missed, but she wouldn't miss again. To her left, another patch of shiny dirt shook. "There's another one coming," she called out.

"Then I suggest we get out of here." He shoved his blade into the eyes of his beast.

The monster let out a high-pitched shriek that pierced her ears. Then he turned, knife in hand, and ran toward her.

She spun toward her spider. She did *not* need to be saved like a little girl. The spider lunged at her. She ducked, but the creature slammed into her, pinning her to the ground. Closing her eyes, she imagined she was on the practice mats and the academy, and this was nothing more than another two-hundred-pound asshole trying to pin her.

They never pinned her. Ever.

She kicked up into soft flesh and then grabbed and spun. The spider twirled with her, landing on its back below her. She stabbed three times, but a leg wrapped around her neck, pulling her away. The spider righted itself, holding her steady before its sparkling eyes.

The eyes!

She growled, plunging her knife into the center of the eye patch. The hold on her disappeared as the creature shrieked. She hit the dirt hard as the spider slumped beside her.

Jason stopped short, kicking up dirt at her side. He grabbed her arm, pulling her up. "Time to go."

They scurried up and over a fallen tree limb and he yanked her beneath a bush full of small yellow flowers. It barely shielded the two of them, and she might as well have been sitting on his lap.

One of the flowers reached out and sniffed her. She gasped, and he covered her mouth. "It's a baby yellow. It's only curious."

Her gaze darted to the flower as it tilted up and down like it was looking at her.

"Only the big red or purple ones will try to eat you. The others are just part of the wildlife," he whispered.

She nodded and he released her. She peeked through the leaves. Three more spiders had emerged from the ground. One poked at the body of the one she'd killed. "Will they come after us?"

"Definitely, but the smell of the flowers will mask our scent. Those things can keep a chase going for miles."

Her hair stuck to the bush, and she realized a piece of the web still clung to her. She tugged at it.

"Wait." Jason coaxed the yellow flower closer. The plant leaned toward the web and sucked her hair into its petals.

"Jason?"

"Hold on. Remember, it's not going to hurt you."

Her hair popped out of the flower—damp, but free of the web.

"Symbiotic relationships," Jason said. "The planet is filled with them. The spiders pull off their webs each night and toss them to the side to make new ones. The little yellows are always a good sign that there are traps around because they eat the discarded webs."

"Gross. Interesting, but gross." She wiped off another tendril of the web and held it up to the small flower, who snatched it off like a praying mantis grabs a bug.

Jason smirked at her. "Now are you going to start listening to me?"

Mia pursed her lips and peeked through the brush as one of the spiders wiggled underground. "You might know a thing or two."

"You're welcome, by the way."

"I was getting to the *thank you* part."

He laughed. "I'm sure you were."

Mia leaned against him. "How long do we have to wait?"

"Unless you want to get chased down, we wait until every last one gives up and goes underground."

His arms circled her, and she leaned on his chest. An odd reaction, she realized, when she'd normally bat a man away. He wasn't being a jerk, though, or he'd make a snide comment, or tell her how pretty she was again.

Stars! She hated it when men did that...like she was nothing more than the angles of her face and a highly toned body. When she found the right guy, he'd be more than all that. He'd appreciate her as an equal, and he wouldn't talk down to her. Ever.

That man obviously wasn't Jason Griggs, but still, his warmth seeped into her and somehow made everything okay...at least for now.

Chapter 11

JASON

Rather than risk another incident with the spiders, Jason decided to gather the sticky webs on his own. Solo, he couldn't free as many from their burrows, but a few would be enough. For the most part, Mia didn't act afraid as she waited for him near the little yellow bush they'd hidden in. She laughed as the flowers poked out their heads and she tickled their necks.

She probably thought they were playing. More likely, there were still remnants of the webs on her that they were helping clean off. Still, that laugh made him smile. There hadn't been much to laugh about out here on Bob in a very long time.

Every so often, she jumped at the sound of a twig breaking. Jason glanced around, watching for anything scampering through the verge. He didn't have it in his heart to tell her that there were more than spiders hiding beneath their feet to be worried about. She was smiling at the moment. There was no reason to change that.

As they made their way back toward the ship, he showed Mia how to place the webs so they blocked pathways.

"It'll force Vincent's men to go the way we want them to if

they want to reach the ship," Jason explained. "They're not the brightest stars in the galaxy, but I can guarantee they'll avoid the sticky webs because they hate those spiders as much as you do, and they still think they're deadly."

Mia nodded, her gaze intent on him. Good, he had her attention. Maybe the spider incident had finally woken her up. Now, if he could just make sure she didn't grab an acid berry, or set off an air-stealer, they might actually get through this in one piece.

Once the pathways were secured, Jason motioned her closer to the ship. "Remember the flower that ate your friend?"

"That's not the kind of thing a girl forgets."

He picked up a vine that connected to the hungry flower and gave it a sharp tug. The vine went taut. "This is going to sound insane, but watch carefully." He gave the vine a sharp karate chop and it went lax, drooping across his hand.

Mia's eyes widened. "Wow."

Her eyes were a deep, dark blue. They shone with an innocence and wonder that made him want to show her everything, if he only had time. She smiled, brushing back her blonde bangs. Those lips were so...

He blinked and looked away. It had been far too long since he'd thought about a woman like that. He needed to back off before he embarrassed himself again.

He held up the lax vines. "These creepers can stretch for miles on a full-grown plant. Not that we'll need miles' worth to guard the ship, but what you can do is tie them into slip knots and create triggers. If someone steps into the loop, the plant's instincts will kick in again."

"And eat whoever lands in the trap," she said.

"Exactly. But remember, it won't actually eat them. It'll try to and then spit them out. Whoever falls into your trap will just have a really bad day."

He walked her over to the base of a Great Eater, as the natives called them. He'd left these for last, until he was positive she'd listen to him and would respect the planet around her. Those trees were not the kind to be messed around with.

As they approached the base, he put a hand on her forearm, just in case.

She shaded her eyes, gazing up the long trunk until it disappeared into the canopy. "They're huge."

"They are, and their roots go deep and wide." He pointed to the divots in the ground. "Near the base, they make pits of something similar to quicksand, only a lot deadlier."

She stared at him. Good. That meant he had her attention.

"Smaller pocket pits are located along the root line, but you wouldn't notice them. They're used to trap small rodents in. The tree then absorbs the nutrients over long periods of time, essentially catching its own fertilizer." He pointed to larger divots. "Big pits are at the base, though, and they eat big animals. Including people."

"So stay far, far away from them," she said.

He nodded. "The sap on these trees has amazing healing properties. It's what I gave to Leslie. They can be climbed, but you need to be incredibly careful. The bark is edible and rich with protein, and it tastes like pure chocolate."

She rubbed her jaw, taking in both sides of the tree. "I'm sure that bark is tricky to get, though."

"It is. When I'm securing my boundaries, I always make sure to keep the paths to the trees open. Most of Vincent's men are smart enough to avoid them. Those who aren't can feed the plants."

She raised a brow. "Good to know. So if Vincent attacks, steer them to the pits?"

"They're the best defense." He pointed toward the hungry flower vines. "For now, I want you to make as many traps as you can. Remember, pull, then hit, and it'll relax. As long as it doesn't tangle around you, you're going to be fine."

She tilted her head. "You're making it sound way too easy."

"Because it *is* easy." He adjusted his bag on his shoulder. "Those things are only a pain in the butt if you're not paying attention or asking for trouble."

Mia gave him a weak grin. "Okay, I'll get on that," she said.

She'd stopped giving him sass whenever he gave her instructions, a small respect he appreciated. Something about her had softened, too. It made her look more fragile, and less like a person who could stand up to an elephant spider with nothing but her sass and a hunting knife.

He warmed a little, knowing she could be soft and also kick ass.

When she glanced at him, he waved, trying to be reassuring. Her chin lifted slightly before a dazzling smile lit up her face.

Well, crap, he didn't know what he'd done to warrant that, but he sure as heck hoped he'd keep doing it. That was galaxies better than her normal *screw-you* glare.

Part of him wanted to stalk through the bushes and keep an eye on her, but if that girl could take down a spider on her own, the hungry flowers shouldn't be a problem. Of course, he also trusted her to scream, and he would probably be able to cut her free before she got swallowed.

He hoped.

Jason picked up a vine of his own. The sooner they secured the area, the sooner he could start gathering more medical supplies like the healing sap. That Leslie woman would probably need more, and with a whole crew of newbies in the Alpha Cent, the chances were she would not be the only one caught unawares.

A chorus of jojo birds sang all around him. Through the

treetops, he could see the green undersides of their otherwise blue feathers. From above they blended in with the sky and from below they matched the trees.

He'd grown used to their songs over the years, and for some time, they were all he'd heard on the planet that resembled music. What made them more amazing was that they could copy any tune they heard, so over time, he'd taught them every song he'd ever known. These guys brought a small touch of home that brought him comfort in the mornings.

He whistled *Africa*, an old song from the ancient 1980s. After a few bars, the jojos caught on and continued the tune. Jason had no idea if Mia was an aficionado of ancient melodies, but he figured she'd enjoy a little music while she worked.

Mia had surprised him in a lot of ways. The longer they were alone together, and the more she accepted him for who he actually was rather than expecting him to be some sort of hero, the more they seemed to connect.

It felt strange, almost like they'd known each other for a lot longer than the day and change they'd spent in each other's company.

Maybe it had been longer, though. He'd only thought a few years had passed here on Bob, yet thirty years had passed on Earth. If that was the case, they could already have known each other for weeks by Earth's standards. He laughed, still baffled by the concept of time itself. General relativity hadn't been his best subject at the academy.

He looked through the verge until he saw her blonde curls bob over the brush.

Now, the laws of attraction, he'd been good at in class as well as in the real world. Attraction always made sense.

He smiled. When her frame had been pressed close against him in the little yellow bush, his body had come alive.

Parts of him had screamed to press it further, to take advantage of the close quarters. The smarter side of him had kept things at bay, though. The last thing he needed was a kick to the groin, and the spiders hearing them scuffle.

She hadn't pushed him away, though. In fact, she'd cuddled in when he'd expected her to slap him across the face. Maybe she wasn't as opposed to being close anymore, either. Then again, she'd almost gotten eaten by a spider. He probably shouldn't count his eggs before he stole them from the mommy Tiger Piranha.

A loud scream filled the air.

"Mia?" He jumped to his feet. "Mia, where are you?"

She screamed again. "Jason!"

He followed the sound of her voice, not too far away, thank goodness. Ten or so feet into the forest, on the backside of the ship, Mia stood with her hands up.

Shit!

He grabbed for his gun until he heard the firm sound of the native Bobonian tongue.

A wave of relief flooded him, but only a little. Vincent was an ass who wouldn't listen to reason. Hopefully, a Bobonian would give them a chance to talk things through.

He pushed his gun into his belt and eased forward with his hands raised.

Standing between him and Mia was a native warrior holding a weapon similar to a spear. She was naked except for the belts holding her weapons, and a small bag of supplies hanging at her waist.

The red flowers of the hunter adorned her long, brown hair tinted with the same green as the leaves. Similar to humans, the people of Bob walked on two legs and had two arms. Their hands had extra fingers, and their feet opposable thumbs to help with grabbing hold of tree branches.

For the most part, they walked above the forest floor, only

coming down to strike prey and pick flowers or berries. The huntress's skin was a deep green color painted in earthy hues of brown and gold to identify her to the others of her task, as well as provide her with camouflage.

He recognized her as one of the chieftess's daughters. Hopefully, she'd recognize him. They treated him as a friend for the most part, a title he'd earned.

Recently, though, with the arrival and colonization of Perseverance, they'd started to watch all humans a little more closely, even him.

"Adaranla, *Mopani areg sini caliodenesu aya.*" He didn't know what all that meant, but it was a standard greeting he'd heard enough between friends. Hopefully, he'd gotten the pronunciation right.

He bowed his head, but his gaze remained on hers the whole time. He kept his hands out and open so she knew he wasn't a threat.

"*Mopani,*" he repeated. He was reasonably certain the word meant *peace.* "She is friend of Griggs."

Adaranla tilted her head, and while her body remained tense, she returned her spear to her side. She still held the weapon at the ready, but at least the tip no longer pointed at Mia's head.

Mia exhaled and turned to him, her expression of a mixture of gratitude and disbelief. The huntress also gazed at him firmly. She snapped her right hand to her left shoulder before pointing at him.

The sign of the charge. He just became Mia's babysitter. If she screwed up in the natives' eyes, he'd end up paying for it.

Jason nodded in understanding. Adaranla ran toward a nearby Great Eater tree and climbed up its trunk in three bounds and faded out of sight.

Overhead, other hunters hid on the branches. They all made the same sign of the charge.

Perfect. His newfound ownership of Mia had been witnessed by the tribe. He'd labeled her *friend*, so she was his responsibility. She better not make him regret it.

Mia was trembling as he approached. Her eyes were pinned on the trees above.

He put both of his hands on her shoulders. "Hey, you're okay."

She took a deep breath. "So that's what the people of this planet look like." She rubbed her shoulders. "I didn't even realize she was here until she dropped out of the tree and charged."

Jason sighed. "They don't like humans much, mostly because of Vincent and his crew."

She scanned the top of the tree Adaranla had scaled. "They look so similar to us."

"Probably because our climates are comparable, and the carbon basing. I think the similarities stop there, though."

He looked up as the last hunter disappeared into the canopy. The way they moved was always a sight to behold.

"They're incredibly smart," he continued. "She wouldn't have killed you on the spot. That's not their way. They only kill when the guns are out and blazing."

He'd seen a few of Vincent's men be taken out as easily with a spear as with a gun, and it always hurt to see so much needless bloodshed.

Mia shifted her weight. "A sentient native population should have been first on your list of things to report to the captain."

"There's probably a lot of stuff I forgot to mention. It wasn't intentional. There's just...a lot." He held up his hands. "According to you, I have thirty years of knowledge to pass on."

Jason grinned, hoping to put her mind at ease, but her eyes were still pinned to the trees. He cupped her chin with his hand. "Hey, seriously, it's going to be okay. You trust me, right?"

Their gazes locked, and he felt his heart beat a tiny bit faster as he stared into those deep wells of blue. When he'd heard her scream, a little part of him had died inside. Yes, she would have survived the hungry flower he'd thought had attacked her, but the thought of her disappearing within, screaming as the acids rolled over her skin...he couldn't stand it.

He loved Bob, but if it came right down to it, he'd stand between his new planet and this bold, amazing woman if that was what it took to keep her safe, even if a protector was the furthest thing from what she wanted.

"I trust you," she said.

Three simple words that meant the world to him. Tilting her chin up, he brought his lips to hers. She was soft and warm beneath his weathered skin. Everything was right about her, but everything seemed so wrong about him.

He released the kiss and stepped away. His cheeks warmed.

Since when did he blush?

He rubbed at the back of his head. "Uh, sorry, I just... Look, it's been a while since I've been so close to a woman and you're...you're really beautiful, and smart, and damn good in a fight with an elephant spider. There's a lot to be attracted to and—"

"You don't need to explain." She closed the distance between them. "I get it."

She reached up to him, combed her fingers through his hair, and pressed her lips to his. She took charge, holding him firm and kissing him with so much confidence, it startled him. He took a step back to keep his balance before putting his arms around her waist. His lips parted ever so slightly, inviting her to do her worst. Or best. He really didn't care which.

Mia took advantage. She was sweet and warm, and everything he remembered loving about a woman, yet there was more there. She had a power about her, a strength like no woman he'd ever met. There was a challenge in that kiss, as well as tenderness. His mind spun, confused, but his hands roved across her back and up her spine, wanting more.

Something tugged at his leg, probably a vine poking for a meal. He stepped to the side, drawing Mia with him. The last thing he needed was this amazing moment interrupted by a hungry flower.

Another tug. He tried to ignore it, until a whine followed and then a bark.

Dobby. *For the love of fresh water and canna berries.*

He broke away from Mia. "What?"

Mia covered her hand with her mouth. "Oh my gosh!"

Jason held up a hand. "It's okay. He's a friend."

Dobby barked and jumped up onto his hind legs, using his upper ones to point to a place deeper in the forest.

Jason grimaced. "Trouble is coming."

Chapter 12

MIA

One second, she was kissing Jason Starlight Griggs, hero of the galaxy, and the next, he was pulling her behind a tree that she hoped wasn't one of those Great Eaters he talked about. With the way he pulled her close to his chest, both of them tight to the trunk, she assumed it didn't have pits lurking underneath.

Damn, he was warm. So was that kiss.

When she'd been trapped in that spider web, she'd thought she was done for. Then his face had appeared over hers, filled with focused concern. Yeah, he'd laughed at her, but she would have done the same, had their positions been reversed.

The way he'd slowly and carefully released her, and the panic in his eyes when the spiders began to emerge...she wasn't just a pretty thing to him. He cared.

Moreover, she'd impressed him when she'd taken out the giant spider. Back at the academy, men had scowled when she'd proven she could fight with the best of them. They'd seemed threatened by her strength for some reason.

She didn't get that from Jason. Not anymore at least.

He'd been alone for a long time. Maybe she just needed

to crack through the hardened exterior he'd adopted to stay alive all these years.

The alien creature, some sort of cross between a naked blue kangaroo and a giant yellow-striped rabbit, crouched next to them, peering through the vines. A long, black mane of spikes moved up and down with each of the animal's breaths, while its long tail twitched.

Not too far away, footsteps plodded through the jungle.

Commander Cortenz's distinct voice shouted, "I suggest you let go of me before my crewmates discover I'm missing. Once the captain finds out, you are going to wish you were never born."

Mia peeked around the tree. Her commander stood between them and the ship. She was probably about fifteen feet away. One man held the commander from behind while his three other companions cocked their weapons and approached the open landing platform.

Mia glanced at Jason, silently asking for direction. Instinct told her to go in swinging full force, but they'd seen how much of a bad idea that was on their very first day on the planet.

Jason held a finger to his lips before slipping around the side of the tree, his body low to the ground. He waved for her to follow. The alien creature took up the rear. Her instincts told her to not let the animal out of her sight, but Jason didn't seem concerned. Not that his lack of concern about anything should make her feel better.

Commander Cortenz's glare bored through her captors. Mia had seen the woman angry plenty of times so far on board, and all of them paled in comparison. Cortenz twisted her arms free of her captor, then landed a side kick in the guard's gut. The other two men went in to grab hold of her again. One ended up with a bloody nose from her elbow, and the other shouted out curses as he attempted to secure her other arm.

Mia's gaze landed on the vine trap she'd placed on the ground as the guy's foot moved dangerously close. Just a little farther... All he had to do was take one more step. Cortenz unknowingly assisted as she twisted around him and tried to shove him away. Unfortunately for her, he still had hold of her arm when he stepped into the loop.

Both of them flew back and slammed into one of the sticky webs they'd placed along the path. The vine's grasp on the man's leg tightened, and he cried out, reaching for his foot as the vine drew them both into the air. The web snared to the bark on the trunk, gluing them both to the side of the tree. Cortenz groaned, hanging upside down against the bark as the vine pulled over and over, just as stuck in the web as they were.

"Now?" Mia whispered.

Jason nodded. "Now."

Mia leapt from her hiding place. "You free her from the web. I'll take care of these guys."

Mia didn't wait for Jason to respond or protest. She moved to the man with the broken nose and swept his legs out from underneath him.

He landed backward, his arm catching in another vine trap. He too went flying through the air and disappeared from sight, hopefully landing inside of the hungry flower. That'd give him a reason to think twice before returning to the Alpha Cent.

Jason's jaw dropped. "Whoa. Remind me to never piss you off."

Mia smiled, standing a little straighter.

"Ugh, my head." Cortenz groaned.

That seemed to snap Jason out of his daze. He pulled out the magnifying glass and got to work melting the webs. Mia spun, readying her stance as one of Vincent's goons came charging at her.

Not today, sludge bag. Mia grabbed him under the arm and flipped him over her hip. He went down hard, tripping over a thick branch. No, not a branch, but the root of a Great Eater. Mia glanced over to the right and saw the massive tree looming overhead. The kangaroo-type creature barked and pointed.

Yes, she got it. She nodded, hoping the creature understood that she knew she was getting too close to certain death.

The guard made a grab for her feet. She jumped back and dodged his hands. He jumped to a standing position, glancing at the tree for a moment. A small smirk formed on his lips as he clenched and unclenched his hands. His uniform hung on him, as if two sizes too big.

"I don't want to hurt you, lady," he said. "In fact, my orders specifically said to bring you and any other ladies back alive. We need you."

She snorted. "I'm sure you do. It must be boring, getting friendly with yourself."

He narrowed his gaze at her. "You're not in a position to make jokes. Don't say anything you're gonna regret later."

She ducked as his arms swung around her, trying to make another grab. Plowing into him with her shoulder, she drove him back. He didn't budge quite as much as she'd hoped. Grunting, he reached for her again, but she drop-rolled out of his way. She had the energy to play this game of cat and mouse all day if she had to, though not the patience.

Mia circled around him from behind and kicked him hard in the back toward the Great Eater tree. The guy lost his footing and stumbled forward. While he managed to stay upright, his left food landed in the pit around the tree's roots.

The kangaroo-dog-thing barked.

Without solid ground to support his weight, the man fell. A splash of gray mud flew into the air as he disappeared into the pit. A hand shot out, grasping at air. It stopped twitching as it slowly sank to the ground.

Her stomach turned and Mia dropped to her knees and wretched. What a horrible way to die, and she'd done that to him. The animal nudged her with a slow, sorrowful moan.

Yes, that guy had come to take her and the others away. Yes, he was going to force them into their colony. But no one deserved to be eaten alive.

"Get over it," Jason called. "He wouldn't shed a tear for you, I guarantee it." He looked at them. "Dobby, give me a hand."

The creature—Dobby, apparently—ran to him as Commander Cortenz slipped farther to the ground. Mia ran over to help support the commander's body as she started to drop from the web.

"Hot water will melt the rest off," Jason said. "Unless you see a bush filled with little yellow flowers. They'd be more than happy to help you out."

Dobby barked twice and ran up the side of a tree and disappeared.

Jason called up to the creature. "Stay alert. There might be more of them."

A bark answered him in the distance.

Cortenz took in a few slow breaths. "Thank you."

"What were you doing out here by yourself?" Mia asked.

"Looking for you, Walton," Cortenz said.

For once, there wasn't any disdain in her voice. She shook slightly, and Mia realized it was from fear rather than rage.

"Captain Stevenson asked for me to get a status report on your progress. Your communications link wasn't working from inside the ship. I came out to see if I could find you." Cortenz leaned over with her hands on her knees. "I thought

I heard you talking not far from the ship, so I walked out. Turns out it was these idiots instead."

Jason scowled. "I didn't expect them to return so soon. Vincent's balls get bigger and bigger every day."

"I'm not sure if their intention was to come after the ship or simply spy on it. Regardless, they captured me and did a lot of talking as they tried to drag me to their camp." She shook her head. "We need to get inside and talk to Captain Stevenson. Now."

"You two go on ahead," Jason said. "I need to reset some of these traps."

"I'll help." Mia started toward a vine.

Commander Cortenz gazed between the two of them. "Okay, be quick."

"Yes, ma'am." Mia gave her a salute.

The commander returned the salute before making her way to the Alpha Cent.

Mia grinned. "I think that was the first time she and I have ever spoken without taking shots at each other."

"You saved her from a horrible fate." He lowered his eyes. "Watching you fight was amazing. You know a lot about how to take a man down."

She folded her arms in front of her chest. "That surprises you?"

"Well, not after seeing how you took that spider head on." He looked over his shoulder into the trees. "When I was at the academy, women weren't strong in combat training. It never came naturally to a lot of the female students in my class."

"Wow, see, that surprises me. In my class, all of us ladies kicked a whole lot of male ass on a regular basis." She chuckled. "I guess time does change a lot of things."

He nodded and took a step toward her. After a moment of

hesitation, he grabbed her hand with his own. "Every second, you impress me more and more."

Her cheeks flushed. If anyone inside the ship saw them...

She pulled her hand away. "I'll try not to let that get to my head."

Moving away from him was harder than keeping her hands off a Nova 360 sublight engine fighter.

She walked toward one of the vines as her heart swelled. *The* Jason Griggs was impressed by *her*. While she no longer viewed him as the hero she'd grown to love in her youth, she did see a man who'd conquered an ecosystem by learning to live in harmony with it, rather than muscling the world into submission.

She also saw a man who respected her strength, rather than being challenged by it.

She stopped and glanced back to him. All these things were far more worthy of her respect than childish expectations of what this accomplished man could never be.

She snapped the vine and it went lax in her hands. "You were right, though." She formed the vine into a loop and placed the thick, brown cord on the ground. "There's a lot we don't know about the planet and I wouldn't have been able to get through that fight without the things you taught me." She looked toward the massive tree trunks. "I'd have fallen right into that tree pit, for one. I appreciate how you've learned to use the planet's resources to survive."

"Thanks. That means a lot." He moved closer. "I also owe you an apology. Clearly, you can handle yourself and I should trust you to do more. At the same time..." He gave her a small smile. "This may make me sound like a Neanderthal, but it's important to me to make sure you're safe. You've kind of grown on me."

She laughed and took a step toward him. "You haven't quite reached the *growing on me* phase yet."

He gave her an exaggerated pout. "Not even a tiny bit?"

She held up her thumb and index finger a few inches apart. "Maybe a little, but I see a bright future ahead of us if you keep up the good work, soldier."

Jason closed the gap between them and gave her a kiss on the cheek.

She startled, glancing back to the ship.

Stars, she needed to be more careful. This was her first mission. The last thing she needed was to give the crew a reason to talk. That kind of reputation followed a female officer around for the rest of her life.

"Let's fix up the vine traps and head in," he said. "That was really smart, positioning your vine-trap to hit that web by the way. I'd never thought of that."

The trunk of the tree rose high into the sky. She'd actually had no idea the vine would yank its victim into the trap, let alone hit and stick to the tree. She'd just gotten lucky.

She wasn't going to admit to that, though. "I'm a natural, what can I say?"

They got to work, finding more vines and tightening up the security around the ship.

He entwined his fingers with hers as they returned to the Alpha Cent. She glanced down at them. The last time someone had held her hand, she'd been six.

"Is this okay?" he asked.

She looked at their hands again. *Was it?*

His fingers were rough but warm. There was something oddly soothing about being held like this, which should have sent up warning bells all over the place. She didn't pull away, though. Jason wasn't trying to prove anything. He wasn't being egged on by friends at the academy, seeing who'd be the one to break the *cold-hearted bitch*. He was simply here, helping to protect her ship and enjoying her company.

She tightened her grip on his hand. "Yeah, it's okay."

When they neared the ship, though, she let go.

He frowned at her, but he needed to understand her position. Falling for a guy she'd just met would make her appear weak in the eyes of the crew.

She opened her mouth, but she wasn't sure what to say. "I-I..."

Jason glanced at the ship and his lips thinned. "I get it." He looked down before turning completely away.

Stars, they'd only known each other for a few days. Getting involved would be frowned upon, at least for now. This was her first mission, and she needed to prove that she could do the job without letting childish emotions take over.

She walked faster, not even looking at him. She wasn't sure she could take the look of disappointment that she knew would be on his face.

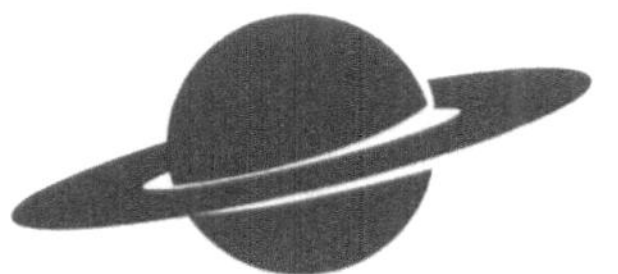

Chapter 13

MIA

Once inside the Alpha Cent, Jason and Mia headed straight to Captain Stevenson's office. Jason glanced at her a few times, but she kept her face forward.

He was a career pilot. An officer. He needed to understand how important appearances were. Of course, according to people who'd known him, Captain Starlight tended to hold up an inappropriate finger to anyone else's conventions, including what anyone else thought about him.

Mia knocked on the captain's door, and Commander Cortenz answered. She nodded at Mia before her gaze latched onto Jason's "As appreciative as I am for all of the hard work you've done to protect us, we need to speak to the captain alone."

"Of course," Jason said, though Mia detected an agitation in his voice all the same. She couldn't blame him. He wasn't just any old civilian they'd found on the surface. This was Jason Starlight Griggs. It was wrong to shut him out, especially since he was the one with all the information they needed to protect themselves.

Cortenz was one of Mia's commanding officers, though,

and Mia might have pushed the limit on giving her attitude one too many times. If there was a reason she didn't want Jason to sit in on their next discussion, it had better be a good one. Or maybe Cortenz wanted to speak to the captain without Mia as well?

She moved off to the side, preparing for dismissal. Then she and Jason could go down to the cockpit and she could show him more of how the ship worked. He used to be the greatest pilot who'd ever lived. He'd probably love to sit in the control seat and take a look around.

Her cheeks heated. Maybe being alone with him wouldn't be the best thing—for her career, that was.

"Walton," Cortenz said, snapping her out of her thoughts. The captain's door was opened and both she and Stevenson were staring at Mia. "Are you going to be joining us or not?"

Mia stood straighter. "Yes, ma'am, if you wish."

"I do," she said sternly. She gazed over at Jason and Mia saw a hint of apprehension in his eyes. "We shouldn't be long."

"All right," Jason said.

Commander Cortenz ushered Mia inside and closed the door. "Forgive me for not including him, but after my experiences today, I'm not sure I fully trust him."

Mia worked at not reacting, at keeping her face calm. How could she say that? The man had saved her life...cut her free from the webs.

The captain sat down at his desk and motioned for the women to take a seat as well. "It sounds like you had quite the ordeal."

"Yes," Cortenz said. "And it seems my radioing for help didn't connect with the ship or the crew."

Mia frowned. "Something in the atmosphere must be messing with all of our devices. I don't know if you noticed it,

Commander, but the air felt a lot thicker than when we first landed."

"I'd wondered that," Cortenz said. "I also wasn't sure if perhaps there was sabotage on board."

"If you're implying that Captain Griggs did something to our devices, then—"

"I'm not implying anything." Cortenz held up her hands in front of her. "The colony on this planet is more than capable of such a feat as well. Those guards told me they've been preparing the area for a conquest, beginning with our ship."

Both of Captain Stevenson's brows raised. "A conquest?"

"Of the planet." Cortenz laughed sourly. "I'm not sure if they're that lonely or that arrogant, because they spilled a great deal of their plans. There were mentions of preparing drills for mining."

"Mining?" Mia frowned.

Cortenz nodded. "Deeper underground, there's an element that can be used as a fuel source. It sounds like something similar to oil. They seem to think it will keep their colony fully functional for a long time." She leaned forward. "That compound Griggs warned us about isn't temporary. They plan on staying. Colonizing."

"Colonizing?" Mia found herself gaping. It took a lot to surprise her. She'd have thought Vincent and his men would prioritize going home again, not settling on a planet that had almost killed them. "Is he crazy?"

"I think so." Cortenz folded her hands. "They were very excited to find me." She shuddered. "Their intentions for us are clear. If they're to create a successful colony, they need women to..."

Make more colonizers with. She didn't have to actually finish the thought. Jason had said the same thing, but he hadn't said anything about Vincent's crew wanting to settle on the planet forever.

Captain Stevenson sat back. "Why would they think it a good idea to take over this planet and start a new civilization? It's dangerous. The planet alone is a force to be reckoned with, and if that storm is constant, with only breaks in the maelstrom here and there..." He shook his head. "It doesn't make sense to me."

"Ashley brought some samples back, and Leslie has been analyzing them in between treatments for the plant acid," the commander said. "The land is rich. Growing food would be easy. The idiots who grabbed me were going on and on about how the crops in the base camp are flourishing beyond expectations." She laughed. "I think they were bragging, hoping I'd come along peacefully."

"They are right, though. If you look at the trees and those dangerous plants, you'll see how strong they are," Mia said. "Growing food and other resources isn't that far of a stretch. I'm sure it wouldn't be difficult to bring in more crops from Earth to start producing. If they can grow potatoes on Mars, it'll be no problem here."

The captain chuckled a little. "Good point. So it seems Vincent and his crew have no interest in actually leaving the planet after all."

He tapped his fingers on the desk, and Mia narrowed her eyes, not sure why he'd laughed. She had been trying to make a point that there was a valid threat that Chrona and his people might want to stay, but he seemed so matter-of-fact about it. Didn't he understand the problems that would cause?

The captain looked up. "At first, I thought they wanted our ship so they could escape. Originally, I had been willing to invite them on board once we were up and running again. That is, until they showed their true colors."

The captain pushed a replica of the *USS Enterprise* sitting on the edge of his desk. He seemed to be working something out in his head. What, Mia wasn't sure. Chrona's plan was against all the UGA stood for. This should be an open-and-shut case.

"It's not a bad idea," he finally said. "The UGA is always looking to expand its reach. Having a settlement out this far would make sense. Especially if we could find a way to safely navigate the nebula."

Mia's jaw dropped. Was he serious?

The captain waved a hand before continuing. "Don't get me wrong. I'm not a fan of Vincent or his methods, but I'm saying we could find a way to work with him. If we promised to go to the UGA and return with aid, or perhaps lend a few of our officers as resources to help assist with his project..."

"A few female officers, you mean?" Mia said stiffly.

"I don't see why gender has anything to do with this," Captain Stevenson said.

She ground her teeth. It had everything to do with it, and Stevenson knew it.

He stared at her for a moment. "Okay, yes, I suppose they'd have to be male officers, things being what they are. I didn't mean to imply that we'd support him with women. But maybe we could—"

Mia took a deep breath, trying to prevent herself from going off on him. "So we go to Vincent and tell him we're cool with his plan to take over the planet as long as he claims it for the UGA. That's what you're saying?"

The captain shrugged.

She ground her teeth until her jaw started to ache. "We're here on a rescue mission, not one to settle foreign lands. Also, I'm sure the native people of this planet will have lots to say about us coming in and taking over."

"There are natives?" Captain Stevenson blinked. His lips parted.

"Yes, sir. There are natives. I met up with one outside the ship. They're intelligent and seem to have a culture and their own language. It might be a good idea to touch base with them before returning to the UGA and starting a petition to claim their planet."

He looked to the side. "True, but if Vincent is already on a quest to set up a human civilization—"

"With all due respect, sir, Vincent and his crew crash-landed here. Just like we did. Just like Captain Griggs did." Mia glared at Commander Cortenz for good measure. "None of us have been sent to this planet to explore it. It's all been by accident. I understand and respect that Vincent and his crew are attempting to make the most of a horrible situation. They're trying to survive, I get that." She exhaled before continuing. "But, sir... His methods are hostile and frightening. While certain aspects of it might seem logical to you, they set a precedent for a tyrannical future. It's not a future I want to take part in."

Captain Stevenson folded his hands in front of him as he thought over her words. Every so often, he tapped his chin with his index fingers. "You make a sound argument. What do you think of Lieutenant Commander Griggs?"

Lieutenant Commander... not Captain. She needed to remember that. Still, she flinched. "W-What do you mean what do I think of him?" Her cheeks heated. Had someone seen them kiss in the woods?

Chuckling, the captain relaxed his posture. "Still starstruck, I see. It's okay, Walton, I understand. I was a little flustered, too. I've been living with the guilt of his loss for a long time." He held up his hands "And here I am, the one who gets the honor of saving him."

Mia managed a weak laugh.

"You're doing a great job with him," Commander Cortenz said. "Keep up the good work and see what more information you can get out of him."

In other words, keep him out of the captain's hair, but Mia needed to do that without losing herself in those eyes, in that smile—which could be pretty damn easy to do when he opened his mouth to talk.

She'd seen a softer side of him out there, and she hoped he'd stay that way.

Then again. Maybe she didn't.

She took a deep breath. Griggs could be infuriating, she got that, and apparently Stevenson wanted the glory of saving Captain Starlight without actually having to deal with the man he admitted to hating when he was younger.

At this point, whether she liked it or not, she was the logical choice. "I'll do my best, ma'am," Mia said.

She doubted Jason had much more he was willing to share. The fact that he didn't want to talk about the indigenous people of the planet still bothered her. It almost seemed like he was protecting them. Then again, if he'd been protecting them from Vincent from all these years, maybe it was force of habit.

She needed to know more about the indigenous people, though. Maybe she needed to ask the questions directly, which was what they all should have been doing all along, had they time to follow protocol. Service in space was one part training, one part rules, one part instinct, one part luck. Landing on a hostile planet, though, added another part to the equation. They needed to do whatever they had to do to survive and worry about protocol later.

Of course, spending time talking to Jason, rather than interrogating him wouldn't be all too hard a chore.

Her cheeks warmed again, and she held back her smile.

Keeping a level head around him would be easier if he hadn't been such a good kisser.

"Is everything okay, Walton?" Commander Cortenz asked.

Mia nodded quickly. "There's a lot to process."

"Yes," Captain Stevenson agreed. "Set up a meeting with the natives. See what information you can get about them."

Mia balked. "Shouldn't Leslie go? She's an alien biologist, right?" Not that this made her a good communicator, but Mia hadn't expected them to send their pilot out there.

He shook his head. "Doc says it'll be a few more days before she can return to full duty. We'll also need Griggs to give us all a lesson in the plant life before anyone else leaves the ship." He pointed at her. "You have the most time outside the ship at this point, and I believe you have a secondary degree in indigenous studies."

"Yes, sir." Wow. He really had done his homework.

"Excellent. I'd like to hear their perspective on things before we make any decisions on how to move forward."

"Sir." Mia gave him a salute.

Stevenson was a good guy. He wouldn't side with Vincent, there was no way. Just the fact that he'd considered it for a moment gave her a reason to pause, though.

As if he could sense her uneasiness, he gave a genuine smile. "Our primary objective is to leave this planet. I do not have any interest in settling here permanently. The UGA will take an interest in this world, though, and we must make sure that we tell them everything. Meeting with the people who originate here is greatly important so we don't do anything to disturb their way of life. We don't want to make the mistakes of our ancestors."

"Yes," Mia said, sighing with relief. "Making an alliance with them will be better than forcing them into submission."

"Correct."

She nodded. "I'll talk to Captain Griggs... Umm, Lieutenant Commander Griggs. I'm sure he'll be happy to assist."

"Thank you, pilot."

Commander Cortenz bit her lip before adding, "Be careful with him."

"I will, ma'am." Mia gave her a quick salute, but she knew it was far too easy to promise to be careful when she wasn't looking into Jason's blue eyes and fending off that beautiful smile.

Chapter 14

JASON

Jason clenched and unclenched his hands as he held the thin wire of the centralized air evacuation panel up to his ear. It was an old trick, similar to how kids connected string to cups and pretended to have old-fashioned wired telephones.

Like those makeshift phones, though, he only got part of the conversation when the people on the other side shouted. Still, he'd heard enough.

This crew was actually considering helping Vincent. He couldn't believe it. He rubbed his temples as the words he'd heard played over and over again in his mind.

"Growing food and other resources isn't that far of a stretch. I'm sure it wouldn't be difficult to bring in more crops from Earth to start producing." That was what Mia had said.

And then Billy, saying he'd send the UGA to assist in the process... Was this what the UGA had devolved to over the last thirty years—allowing humanity to become an invasive species?

He agreed that colonization was an important goal. After all, humanity couldn't live under the false reality that a meteor strike like the one that took out the dinosaurs wouldn't happen again. But that colonization needed to happen on uninhabited worlds. Bob had an indigenous population, a population that had rights, according to the UGA charters. Well, according to the UGA charters he'd been taught and still upheld.

He stared at the flickering overhead lights. He couldn't be a part of an invading force. He refused. The Bobonians had lived peacefully for too long. They deserved to remain untouched, if that was what they wanted.

He paced through the hallway, unable to hold still, but he needed to hear as much as he could. He needed to know if the crew of the Alpha Cent could still be trusted, or if Vincent had just earned a beautiful, nearly functional ship, and more women to add to his harem.

No, he couldn't imagine the women who'd gathered in perfect defensive formation—let alone a woman who could take down an elephant spider on her own, subjecting themselves to such a thing.

Commander Cortenz seemed pretty hot to get off this rock, and there was no way she would support helping the guys who'd just tried to kidnap her.

Jason took in a slow breath. He was probably overreacting. Mia was strong-willed and ready to do the right thing no matter the cost—much like he'd been when he'd first left the academy. She'd fight any attempt to support maniacs like Vincent, let alone join them.

"I understand and respect that Vincent and his crew are attempting to make the most of a horrible situation. They're trying to survive." Mia's muffled voice drifted through the door. She continued on, and he only caught bits and pieces...the word "hostile" being one of them, and "tyrannical" another.

What did Jason even make of that? He shook his head. Waiting and eavesdropping was agony. He hated being excluded from the conversation.

Had he done something wrong? Cortenz had seemed bent on him staying out of the room, and he would have expected Mia to fight for him to stay. After all, who better to advise them on the planet than the guy who'd been here for years?

It almost sounded like Mia was rolling over now, though. How could she even stand in that room, contemplating helping Vincent after everything he'd told her?

The door opened, and Mia came out. He wanted to stare her down, make her tell him that they'd decided to support Vincent, but he couldn't help the grimace that formed on his face. He looked away.

"Sorry about that," she mumbled. "Cortenz is on edge after her run-in with Vincent's men and has lost faith in anyone who's not a part of this crew." She motioned for him to follow her down to the cockpit. "It should be obvious by now that you're nothing like them."

"It should be," he echoed, his tone a bit stiff.

Mia glanced over at him. "Once she calms down, she'll come around."

"I'm not worried."

It was only partially a lie. Cortenz was just a single star agitating a supernova waiting to explode. She was not the problem. Billy—sweet little Billy, who'd peed himself the first time his controls had locked on an interstellar mission—was setting himself up to betray the very oaths they'd both taken to protect indigenous species of other worlds.

Then again, maybe Jason should have expected this. Billy had never had any balls. Maybe it was just easier for brave, wise Captain Stevenson to give Vincent what he wanted, rather than standing up for what was right.

He'd seen too much of the same during his career—people too worried about rules and not pissing off someone, even when that someone might accidentally kill people in their idiocy. That's when he'd started saying *screw it*.

That attitude had him up for court martial three times—all of them thrown out, and had earned him twelve medals by the time he'd turned twenty-four. Mia acted like Jason was a hero. If that was true, too bad the academy didn't grab on to that and teach the principles Jason had lived by. If they had, the galaxy would be a better place.

Now, he found himself alone again, maybe with more enemies than he'd had before. He had to find a way to protect the Bobonians, and get those women trapped in Chrona's camp out—and it looked like he was going to have to do it all solo.

Mia's short hair bobbed as she walked. A grim determination coated her features. Too bad it was for the wrong reasons. He'd hoped she'd stand beside him. She could be damn good in a fight. They'd still be outnumbered, but at least they'd have had a fighting chance.

That dream, of course, was gone like so many others.

"There's something we need to discuss in private," she said, placing her hand on the cockpit door.

Yeah, Jason bet she did. Probably a good call for her to get Jason alone before he bit her star-blasted head off.

She stopped short before stepping in. Her hand whitened on the doorframe. There was a guy sitting in the co-pilot's seat, twisting a screwdriver into the stabilization panel.

"Bernard, get out, please," she said.

He spun toward her. "What? I'm working." His gaze landed on Jason and his head tilted before his eyes seemed to sparkle, an expression Jason knew all too well. "Wow, so it *is* true. Starlight's alive." He popped to his feet. "Welcome aboard, Captain Griggs. It's an honor, sir."

Jason forced a smile through gritted teeth as he shook the kid's hand. "Yeah, I'm alive. Doing great and happy to help you get home again." He was beyond caring or wanting to get into a conversation with this kid. He was about to explode, and he wanted to get it over with.

Bernard kept shaking far longer than customary. "I have a million questions about how you learned to maneuver the model 7T Star Cruiser through the—"

"Lots of practice and a lot of luck. The whole thing was instinct. I'll tell you the story sometime over a drink." Jason led Bernard to the door. "And I hate to interrupt you. I'm sure you're working hard on getting this girl back into the air, but your pilot and I need to talk about something alone and this seems to be the only unoccupied space available. I'm sure you understand, right?"

Before Bernard could say anything, Jason gave him a shove out the door. Right before it closed, a big goofy grin appeared on Bernard's face, so he couldn't have been too upset over getting tossed out of his workspace.

Of course, now Jason owed the kid a drink and long, boring stories about things Jason had done years ago.

Whatever. He'd live.

Mia folded her arms across her chest. "Okay, what's your problem?"

"Me?" She had to be kidding, right?

She cocked her head. "Stars, you are on a short fuse for someone who always seemed to put others before yourself."

He snorted. "I like to think of it as being mature and thinking before speaking."

"I don't believe in mincing words." Mia lowered her arms. "Or hiding what I'm feeling."

"You did a good job of it in the captain's office just now," he grumbled.

"Excuse me?"

He glared at her. "You heard me."

"Yeah, I heard you, but what is that supposed to mean?"

"You didn't try to defend me when Cortenz suggested I sabotaged the communications, and I think I heard you say you *respected* Vincent Chrona?"

Her nose flared, and her lips thinned.

Good. He refused to stand down. What they were considering couldn't be allowed. Someone needed to stand up for what was right, and if it had to once again be Jason Griggs, then screw it, he'd put himself in the line of fire.

Something changed in her eyes. Was it...hurt?

What did she expect? He wasn't about to back away from everything that was right in the galaxy just because he cared about her.

But those eyes...dammit! She was almost enough to make him forget the right thing. *Almost.*

Mia's lips skewed before she puffed out a laugh. "You think I respect Chrona?"

Jason pointed at her. "Your words, not mine."

She swatted his finger away. "Context is everything. It's one of the first things we're taught in the academy when dealing with foreign cultures. A rule you must have forgotten." She lifted her chin. "I said I respect his wanting to survive. That doesn't mean I respect *him.*"

Now it was his turn to laugh. "I did hear that part. It still doesn't change that you didn't bother to try and talk your captain out of helping Chrona."

"Excuse me? If you're going to listen in on a conversation, you should at least make sure you hear the whole thing."

"I did." Jason seethed. "It's like you didn't even try to tell him otherwise. You have to understand how infuriating this is. You fought and fought and fought before, so I have to wonder why you're not fighting *now* when you know he's wrong. Why all the diplomacy all of a sudden? Also, I can't believe you want to sell this place out to the UGA."

She held out her hands. "We can't hide this place from

the UGA. That's not how it works. We go out and explore and then we report what we find to our superiors so they can maintain peace and order in the galaxy."

"And set up an encampment here, one that will probably support Chrona's ideas about colonization." He held up his hands as her glare intensified into one of pure rage. "That's how they function, Mia. I might have crash-landed on here because of a UGA mission, but during my time here, I've grown fond of the place. The last thing I want to do is see it ruined by a bunch of...humans."

"UGA isn't going to ruin the planet. There are laws about that now. We can't just take over and forget about the people who are here already."

"It's not like you're reaching out to make peace with them first," he pointed out.

Mia pointed a finger at him. "If you'd have told us about them from the beginning, we'd have known there were people to make peace with."

He winced. She could have that one. He had no arguments to respond with.

Maybe, deep down, he was hoping to get them off the planet without finding out about the Bobonians, and part of him hoped that incident with the hungry flower would be enough for them to wash their hands of this place and never return.

"Also, you must have missed when I told Captain Stevenson I wanted to meet with the natives of the planet so that we could make an alliance of some kind." She stepped toward him and poked him in the chest. "If we can talk to them, align with them, and start the pathway to peace with the UGA, then we can work on protecting these people and their culture from Chrona and his crew of degenerates." She stepped closer, running a hand down his arm. "We want to help you. *I* want to help you."

Bile built in his throat. He pushed her away.

This wasn't his first rodeo, and it definitely wasn't the first time a commanding officer had sent a beautiful woman to push Jason off-track. "Who wouldn't want to help me? I'm Jason-freaking-Griggs. Captain Starlight."

Her eyes widened and her cheeks turned pink.

That was all the confirmation he needed.

Had this been going on from the start? Had that been why they'd sent her out into the jungle alone with him? Had he totally fallen for it, kissing her?

Dammit!

Why did he have to kiss her in the first place?

More importantly, why did he have to like it so much?

"Ugh." He groaned. "I can't believe..."

"Can't believe what?" she asked, her voice quiet.

That tone was sincere, though. Either she was a darn good actress, or maybe she'd enjoyed that kiss in the woods as much as he had.

Either way, he still needed her as an ally, albeit one he would watch more closely than before. Pissing her off by calling her out might just be the sand that blasted her into Chrona's camp. Although he still couldn't understand why she'd even consider it.

What he needed was to take what relationship they had and use it to his advantage. Maybe if she was any bit the woman he'd hoped she was, she'd see the Bobonians for the great race that they were, and she would fight tooth and nail alongside him, keeping this planet free of human hostility.

He straightened. "You're right. I should have told you about Ka'Raziel sooner."

"Who?" Mia blinked.

"Ka'Raziel," he said. "She's the leader of the Bobonians near here."

"The what?"

He waved a hand. "Just a name I made up for them." If he told her he'd nicknamed the planet *Bob*, he'd never hear the end of it. "Their language is complicated. I know enough to get by, and they've been kind enough to simplify their names to a form that I can pronounce easily."

"Wow. Well, that would be great. We definitely need to arrange a meeting as soon as possible," Mia said.

"Good." He moved to the door. "Let's go."

She gaped. "What? Now?"

Damn, she was cute when she was surprised. That, in and of itself, was the best reason for dropping that on her so quickly. That and the shock gave her less of a chance to argue.

Mia's gaze stayed glued to him, and he could see the sadness in them still. "I know that's not what you were going to say originally. You were going to say something else. I don't know what, but I want to know." She reached for him. "You're important to me."

But *why* was he important to her? That was the part he didn't like.

Did she care about him the way he'd hoped, in the way she'd promised with that kiss?

Or was it because he was some kind of hero back home?

Or was it because keeping the infamous Captain Griggs in line was part of her assignment?

He cringed, knowing that two of the three options were ten times more likely than the one he wanted.

There was way too much uncertainty surrounding this girl, and as much as he wanted to, he couldn't put his trust in her completely. Maybe he shouldn't have trusted her at all to begin with, but that was his fault. He should have known, dealing with Vincent all this time, how bad humans could be when they were out for number one and nothing else.

"Hey." She traced his temple with her fingers.

Shit, why did her touch still send shivers through him?

"I meant that," she continued. "You mean a lot to me."

He stepped back. "Of course I do. I'm Captain Starlight. I'm everybody's favorite flyboy." He grimaced. "I'm sure you'll get a nice medal for bringing me home. And it'll be well-deserved. You've worked hard, and you've fought with honor. I'm proud of you. Everyone else will be too."

Her gape and sorrowful eyes burned into his soul. He wanted to grab her, hold her to him, and tell her how sorry he was for hurting her. The hero inside wanted to make this right. The realist in him stood his ground. The people of this planet deserved that much.

"You're more to me than a medal or a trophy." She pushed past him toward the door. "At least you were." She kept walking. "Let's go see this Kazrail."

"Ka'Raziel," Jason corrected.

"Whatever."

He followed her out the door, hurrying to keep her pace.

Yeah, it looked like he'd done a pretty good job of pissing her off. Probably because she realized she'd been caught. What did she expect, that he'd just roll over and be okay with this?

He heard a sniff, and his veins iced. This pilot was a hard-ened warrior, one who could give most of the guys he'd trained with a run for their money...and she was *crying*?

Stars over Mars...what if he'd been wrong?

They turned a corner and made their way to the docking bay. Mia slammed on the button to open the doors.

"Aren't you going to tell your captain you're leaving?" he asked.

Mia snorted. "Someone said I needed to stand up for myself and go against my commanding officers to do the right thing. If I go up to the command deck, Captain Stevenson will demand I go through all kinds of official protocols first."

She paused and typed into a communication panel on the wall. "There, I told them we were leaving. Let's go before they try to stop us."

A smile burst free. "Careful. People are going to say I'm rubbing off on you."

She stepped out, muttering. It sounded like she said, *"They could say worse things."* He wasn't sure, though.

She walked ahead. No, she *stomped* ahead, even though she had no idea where they were going. "Are there any unexpected dangers that you conveniently forgot to mention that I should know about before we go?"

"Just the acid-spitting snakes. Watch out. You're about to step on one."

She stumbled, landing in his arms. Her breath hitched, and a knife twisted in his chest.

"I...was actually kidding. Sorry."

She slapped him and pushed away.

He really needed to work on his sense of humor with this woman. "Don't you want to know if you're going the right way?"

She spun, her eyes on fire. "Am I going the wrong way?"

"No. Actually, you're good." Damn, she was beautiful when she was ticked off.

"Fine." She spun and continued walking.

She expertly circumvented a Great Eater and slowly passed through a patch of sticky webs. She was a quick study. Hopefully, she'd listen once they got to the native city, too. This little attitude sparking with her, while totally adorable, wouldn't fly with the Bobonians. She needed to show respect in every way or this was going to go south really fast.

After the spitting snake joke, though, it would probably be best to let her calm down a bit before going over the rules. She stomped ahead, rattling a few bushes. A patch of little yellows poked their heads out to look at her as she passed.

Although her posterior wasn't an unpleasant sight, he missed the easy conversation of their last trek into the jungle. He missed her warmth, and not just the kiss.

He'd hoped that there had been a connection there. There were so many things he wanted to tell her, so many incredible things about this planet that he wanted to share... but only with someone who could appreciate them and not look for a way to exploit this amazing ecosystem.

He'd been chastised back home, called "one of a kind" by his superiors, who hadn't meant that as a compliment. Maybe he was the only human being left who thought this way. Maybe the academy had spit out troops whose only goal was exploiting the universe for humanity's gain.

If that was true, then his decision was made. He'd help her and the Alpha Cent get off the planet, and then he'd figure out how to deal with Vincent Chrona and anyone else who dared try to take advantage of his planet—and he'd do it on his own. Maybe, for the first time in his life, he'd be able to really live up to the legend of Captain Starlight.

Chapter 15

MIA

Mia slowed so Jason could catch up with her. She wasn't scared, but it would be foolish to stay too far ahead in an unknown ecosystem. Especially one where the plants might eat her.

Every so often, he'd look her way, but only for a moment. She wished she knew what his problem was. Last she'd checked, she hadn't committed any great sin—only voiced an opinion. Would he get all up in arms every time she did? If that was the case, then they were over before they'd even started. That made him just as bad as Chrona.

Well, almost.

He put out his arm to stop her from walking. He was all strength and muscle, and he still protected her, even though she'd obviously ticked him off. His hand warmed her right through her uniform. She should have pushed him away. She didn't need his protection or his touch, yet at the same time, she wanted both.

Closing her eyes, she took a deep breath. She needed to get over this guy. They were here to meet with the natives, not to have another romantic moment in the woods.

"Are we here?" Mia asked.

Jason nodded. "Stay put. I'm going to let them know we're friends."

She knew better than to disobey, though she did want to know just how he planned on alerting the hidden civilization of their arrival. After all, no one was around.

The verge of thick, massive leaves pressed in on all sides, the jungle twice as thick as around the crash site. Almost unnaturally thick, come to think of it.

Carefully, Jason approached a thin tree. It was as tall as one of the Great Eaters, but smaller in width than Jason's body, the color of its trunk an ashen gray. The branches themselves didn't start splaying until far up in the canopy, and its leaves billowed out in brilliant shades of red and orange.

Jason tapped a pattern into the bark, then spoke into one of the knots in the trunk. His voice was too quiet for her to make out the words. What she did hear sounded like gibberish, most likely the local language.

After a few long seconds had passed, seconds that felt a lot more like minutes, something in the foliage shifted before the verge split into a narrow alley. A handful of native warriors stepped into the pathway.

They all had skin painted tan, though beneath seemed more green than any skin tone she'd seen on Earth. It helped them blend seamlessly into their surroundings, and she wondered if any of them had followed her and Jason from the ship.

Their dark hair was pulled into tight braids or dreadlocks, and all of them wore flowers or leaves interwoven in their locks. The decorations seemed to be part practical and part art, as they all flowed in a pattern that was masterfully beautiful.

Their clothes were tight and a dull brownish gray that matched both the tree trunks and the ground. The outfits the natives wore seemed to blend with their skin as well, and the fabric covered most of their bodies despite the hot, sticky temperature.

One of the warriors stepped forward and gave Jason a salute. Jason in turn, pressed a hand to his chest and bowed. He spoke a few words to the warrior, a male, from what Mia could tell. The warrior shifted his attention to Mia and frowned. More words were exchanged between the two before they were waved to walk onto the path.

Mia swallowed. "Everything okay?"

"They're nervous about outsiders," Jason said quietly. "For a moment, they weren't interested in letting you into the city. When I pointed out that I was once an outsider too, and that I wouldn't allow anyone to come here who was unworthy, they relented."

He took her arm, guiding her between a circle of guards forming around them.

"That being said, you're going to be watched—closely. They don't trust you. Please, don't make it worse by going rogue on me."

"I don't plan on it." Mia considered the numerous spears. "I have no desire to become a shish-kabob."

He laughed. "I didn't mean to imply that you'd do anything dumb, but there was that incident with the web..."

"Fall into one spider web, and you're branded for life?"

They both laughed. It was nice, like it had been when they were laying traps in the woods. She warmed in all the right places. His smile seemed sincere, but then he frowned, staring at her as if he had just remembered she had the plague or something. What was up with him?

Mia kept her hands in front of her, not wanting to give the natives any reason to feel threatened as they walked along the path.

"Would you please tell me what's wrong? I don't know

what I did." And it was starting to tick her off, or make her sick to her stomach. She wasn't sure which at the moment.

"This isn't the time," he whispered.

He was right, of course. They'd walked through the jungle for almost an hour in silence. She needed to work on curbing her ego. Maybe, if she'd have calmed down enough to ask sooner, they'd be in a much better place now.

Slowly, they started to decline. The path became less crowded with bushes and flowers before it began to etch into the ground. The soil formed walls on either side of them until they hit a barrier of tightly woven vines.

Jason leaned closer to her. "Watch this."

Two of the natives moved to the front of the group and put their hands inside the brush. As they removed their hands, the verge shifted, revealing a tunnel beneath.

Mia gaped. There was no way she'd even dreamed there would have been a tunnel there before. Jason grabbed her arm again, coaxing her inside. She kept her focus in front of her so she didn't think about how tight the walls were, or how one earthquake or other natural disaster could bury them alive—not to mention the spiders who liked to live underground.

Had this been one of their tunnels at one time? Was it *still* one of their tunnels? She worked to control her breathing. At the academy they conditioned recruits to close quarters like this. However, back then she'd been prepared. She'd done yoga and relaxation exercises to keep herself from freaking out.

Those training drills had been far worse than this narrow tunnel. If she'd lived through basic ops, she would live through this, too.

Orange flowers lined the walls, glowing with some sort of natural light, maybe similar to fireflies on Earth, but with a consistent glow that gave just enough illumination for her to see. Eventually, the tunnel started to brighten again before they stepped into a deep valley.

Sharp cliffs of gray, shimmering rock surrounded them on all sides, and tall trees extended even higher above the rock. Rather than a bright blue sky, though, a faint blue-green glow shimmered in and out above, like the energy shields over the colony on Corillian Major.

"What is this place?" Mia asked.

Jason grabbed her chin and tilted it forward so she was looking in front of her, rather than up. "Careful. You're going to trip, and you're missing the best part."

He wasn't kidding.

A city of rock and trees rose before them. The buildings seemed to emerge from the cliffside, built up against them if not chiseled from the stone itself. Even more, smaller structures wove around and up the ashen-trunked trees, as if living symbiotically with the surroundings, rather than taming the world to their whims.

Streets paved from smooth rocks that glittered under sparkling lights in the simulated sky ceiling wound throughout the city. The natives in those streets moved closer to the buildings as they passed. She supposed she couldn't blame them, if they'd been living this close to the Perseverance colony and remained undetected for so long.

The male warrior behind them nudged Mia with the dull end of his spear. She nearly fell from the jab. Jason said a word, and it was firm enough that she hoped it meant he was defending her. The warrior replied and pointed toward a grand cavern in front of them.

"Ka'Raziel is in the city hall," Jason murmured. "We're to walk fast so we draw less attention to ourselves and don't scare the people."

Mia nodded. "Got it. They can ask a little nicer next time, though."

He glared over his shoulder. "Agreed. Come on."

He pulled her closer to him, keeping an arm around her waist. Not in a romantic way, but rather one of protection and guidance. Despite what had happened between them, she appreciated he still wanted to keep her safe in this new and foreign culture.

They moved through a long hallway with huge wooden doors that seemed carved directly into the rock. She wished one would open, so she could tell if they were actually doors, or some kind of alien decoration.

More of the illuminating flowers wove through the ceiling in an intricate pattern that reminded Mia of petals floating on the wind. Small pools of water reflected the flowers above, adding to the light around them.

Mia leaned over a pool to see the reflection, and a small mound of water rose, giving it the shape of a flowing pillar.

"It's a drinking fountain," Jason whispered.

"It's beautiful."

"Yeah, well, you've activated it, so you better take a drink before they get offended."

The procession had stopped. They all stared at her. One warrior folded her arms.

"They take the natural resources seriously here." Jason motioned to the fountain. "Please, drink."

She nodded and leaned toward the pillar. The water chilled her lips. There wasn't a hint of the metallic taste she'd grown accustomed to at the academy or at home. It actually tasted like nothing, and her body reveled in the simplicity, as if this was what it had been craving all its life.

Jason pulled her back.

She stumbled, wiping her mouth on her arm. "Wow."

"Exactly." He took a sip of his own before the pillar sank into a small pool in the floor.

They continued through the vast, underground space

until they reached a thick, intricately designed, wooden door. Two warriors on each side slowly pulled the massive frame open.

Swirled roots made up the door frame, spreading out and widening from the entrance before thickening into solid-looking benches that lined the room. They had the same soft color of the Great Eater tree, but that couldn't be right. The pits beneath the tree ate people, didn't they?

The ends of each bench swirled up and converged at the far center wall of the room and molded into an intricately braided throne. On it sat a woman with deep-toned skin that was wrinkled around her eyes, and silver streaks in her dark hair. Glowing flowers, like the ones in the ceiling, adorned her hair.

About ten feet from the throne, Jason bowed deeply. Mia followed suit.

"Ka'Raziel," he said, and then proceeded to speak in the woman's language. The only thing Mia recognized was the woman's name.

The chieftess turned to Mia. Unlike the warriors, her gaze didn't contain any aggression, merely curiosity. She began to speak, making sure to pause so Jason could translate.

"Ka'Raziel welcomes you to their city, Malashra," Jason translated. "We are allowed to stay for the remainder of the day since our conversation will probably last to dusk."

Mia nodded and smiled at the woman. "Thank you for your hospitality."

Jason translated, and the chieftess continued to speak, using her hands and entire body to illustrate.

"I've been told you come from a ship that has crashed from the heavens. Like our friend, Griggs, you are from another world hidden in the stars." Ka'Raziel clenched her hands into fists. "We have always lived at peace and seclusion with our home. We respect that fate has brought you here, but that does not mean we should interact."

Wow, that wasn't exactly the welcome Mia had hoped for. They needed dialog to make peace. That was textbook Psychology 101. She needed to find a way to build trust, or she was skunked.

Ka'Raziel pointed to Jason. "We accept Griggs as a guest because he is kind, but he isn't one of us. With you and your ship, we will accept you the same if you respect our desire to be left alone." She stood, holding up her arms. "Our city has remained hidden since the First Ones were formed from the Great Eaters' roots. We wish for it to stay this way, so we are not attacked by the Vincent."

The Vincent. Mia liked that translation. Mia turned to Jason. "Does she know that Vincent is interested in mining some kind of fuel source so he can get his own colony running more efficiently? And does she also know that he plans to conquer the land for his own? Is she prepared for that kind of a fight?"

Jason's skin seemed to pale, and he sighed, relaying Mia's questions to the chieftess.

Ka'Raziel's dark eyes narrowed and her lips pursed together before she took in a slow breath and began speaking again. Jason waited a few minutes for her to take a pause in her story before beginning to retell it.

"The fuel source you speak of is the Life Flower," Jason said quietly. "It is the heart of this city. The roots are all connected together throughout the planet. All come together in the ground beneath our home. It provides them with something similar to what we refer to as electricity. However, it lasts longer and is easy to harness without harming the planet. The Life Flower is fueled by the souls of those claimed by the Great Eaters, returning to the planet to be the light and guidance for all."

So they believed the energy source was sentient, and it sounded like they revered or worshiped it.

Mia didn't believe in the religious implications, but energy was nothing more than a type of power. It was perfectly possible that the excess energy of these Great Eater trees could be tapped and used to fuel everything from generators to ships. But draining that much could have horrible repercussions to the ecosystem. Anyone with basic environmental biology training would know that. The question would be whether or not they cared.

Mia took a small step forward. "Do you have a way to defend yourself from the Vincent?"

Ka'Raziel's hands fisted. She spoke in her choppy language.

"We will not need to fight. The planet will protect us," Jason said.

"Ma'am, I really—"

Jason cut Mia off with a stern shake of his head, then he mumbled something to Ka'Raziel that seemed like an apology. She gave him a gentle smile before speaking softly, much like a mother would. He gazed at Mia next. "She says we should settle in for some rest since we walked a long way."

Mia scowled. This woman shouldn't be dismissing them. The danger was real. They needed to listen.

Jason tugged her back a step. "Not now."

She glared at him, but she had to remember that he'd been dealing with these people for a long time, and he knew when they were at the edge of outstaying their welcome.

She lowered her head. "Thank you."

Ka'Raziel must have understood that word because she held her hands together and raised them. She didn't need to speak for Mia to know what she meant: You're welcome.

The doors opened, and the warriors escorted Mia and Jason out of the room. As soon as the throne room was shut off again, the warriors nodded their heads to Jason—ignoring her—and walked away.

"Does this mean they're not going to follow us around anymore?" Mia asked.

"Not closely," he said. "We'll always be watched. They have eyes everywhere. Either it's a scout, a hunter, a warrior, or through the Life Network that the flowers are connected through."

"The flowers can spy for the city?"

"The flowers can do a lot of things," Jason said. "It's part of what makes their civilization so strong."

That kind of a network would be important for Vincent to take over. After all, if the flowers could be used to watch the entire planet, that would give him an avenue for even more control. He'd have to figure out how it worked, first, of course.

She swallowed. "Do they have any defense? Any weapons?"

"Not beyond what you've seen."

"The spears," Mia said. "Which are great for defending against the wildlife, but not so much against Chrona and his men."

Jason gave her a sideward glance. "Assuming Vincent can find them here."

"It's only a matter of time before they figure it out."

"I don't know. You see that glow above us?" He pointed upward as they left the city hall and stepped into the dirt streets. "That's created by the Life Flower as well. It's a projection of sorts. From the outside, this looks like a huge lake, not a metropolis."

She shook her head, amazed and frightened all at once. "All of this power, and they can't protect it."

"They are by hiding," he pointed out.

"All they're doing is buying time."

"Maybe it's strange to you that there are people whose

first reaction to a problem is not violence, but most of us *want* peace," he snapped.

Mia laughed. "Right, you're Mr. Peaceful. Weren't you the one who caused a pirate freighter to crash into its command ship?"

"They were threatening a civilian ship. I only fight when there's no other choice."

"And if what you've told me is true, these people are soon not going to have another choice."

Jason grimaced and started walking again.

"Come on, Griggs, buy a clue. Once Chrona catches wind of how to get in here, every last one of them will have a gun pointed at their head. Fighting is a necessity of life. It's our core means of survival."

He shoved his hands into his pants pockets, refusing to look at her. "We don't all have the same drives."

Mia tossed up her hands and pressed onward, moving ahead of him. She'd come all this way, risked getting in trouble with her captain, and for what? To see this beautiful place and not to be able to protect it?

When he grabbed a hold of her arm, she balked, considering his touch, before raising her gaze to meet his.

He let her go. "I don't want to fight with you about this."

"It's not about you and me." She held up her hands to the city around them. "It's about protecting all of this from Perseverance."

The darker the artificial sky became, the more the glowing flowers strewn between the buildings glowed. There was a peace about this place, like a shrine, and it needed to be protected as such.

"This city is incredible. Do you want to see Chrona take it from them?" She turned to Jason. "What is he going to do to these people? I doubt he'll want to create some kind of an alliance. He certainly didn't want to do that with my ship and we're the same species."

"Which is a shame, I know. Chrona could be doing so many more wonderful things for his crew, things that don't involve practically enslaving the women and forcing Earth's way onto a planet that is nothing like home." He eased his hand into hers and drew her down a new path.

It was quiet here, almost serene. Every part of her wanted to relax and take it all in, but there was too much at stake. Almost anything could be going on outside these walls and no one would even know it.

Stars, when the captain found out she'd taken off without final clearance, he was going to spit jet fuel. She'd half-hoped that she would avoid an insubordination charge by returning with a treaty, or at least a plan. How was she supposed to tell them that the natives' plan was to hide?

He'd laugh at her, and she was pretty well done with people laughing at her. She'd proven herself. Excelled. She could figure out anything.

She just had no idea how to figure out this.

How could you teach common sense to people who were so sure that they were doing the right thing, but their decision would end up getting them all killed?

The trees hovered over them like walls before the path widened up to a pool of water similar to the one Mia had found in the cave, only the size of a large pond. Like the water fountain, pillars formed in different places within the pond waters. Children laughing and splashing each other swam through the small cylinders of water as they rose from the surface. It reminded her of a park where she used to play on Earth. Of course, that was man-made, while this was simply a product of this fantastical ecosystem.

"I do want to protect this place," Jason said. "It's why I refuse to join Chrona. Even if I'm the only one who fights, I need to stand against him. I won't leave this planet until I know these people are safe."

A splash fight broke out in the water, three girls against two boys.

Jason smiled before a more somber expression covered his face. "Vincent is going to do everything he can to stop your ship from leaving."

"I figured," she mumbled. "It's a good thing Bernard and the rest of the crew are working hard to get the Alpha Cent back in the air." The sooner the better, though. None of them had signed up for a war. They'd only wanted to save lives, and maybe brush elbows with greatness.

Jason grimaced. "There was a small cargo ship that crashed a while ago. There was only one survivor. I helped her repair her ship, and she was almost home free, until Chrona found her." He looked down. "All of the different parts of her ship suddenly stopped functioning. Eventually, she gave up and joined Perseverance."

"He sabotaged her?"

Jason nodded. "I can't prove anything, but it's all that makes sense. They used pulleys and makeshift cranes to drag her ship into the compound. I never saw her again."

Mia shivered. "Did you ask Chrona?"

Jason nodded. "He just made excuses while he hauled her ship into their compound." He pursed his lips. "I know she's okay. Physically, at least. Chrona would never intentionally hurt her when they have so few women."

The two boys tried to corral the girls between two fountains, before the girls joined forces and advanced on them.

Jason laughed as the boys screeched. He gave Mia a gentle tug toward the water. "Do you swim?"

"Yes," she said. "But no, I don't have a change of clothes."

"They'll dry." He pulled her toward the pool.

She squealed as he tugged extra hard on her and sent her

tumbling into the water. A pillar formed and caught her. A shriek left her lips as the wet warmth cushioned her fall. She startled, expecting it to be cold, like the drinking fountain. Maybe this was some kind of a hot spring.

She splashed at Jason, laughing. He dove in next to her. A pillar caught him as well and he backstroked across the pool, hovering in the air.

"It's warm!" He sounded just as surprised as she had.

"It's like magic." Mia laughed.

He smiled at her. "It's the Life Flower."

She let the warmth run through her hair. "It's unbelievable."

And it was. This place was like a fairytale fantasy. Now, more than ever, she wanted to see this preserved. So much could go wrong if this place fell into corrupt hands.

She splashed some of the warm water on her face. The sensation invigorated her, easing away some of the tension.

This wasn't right, though, for her to be safely tucked away underground when the ship above was still a target. Despite the beauty of this place, she still had a responsibility to the crew of the Alpha Cent. She needed to help get them home. Jason, too.

But her heart needed to make sure this native city remained safe.

She just wasn't sure she could do both.

"I guess this place *is* a sort of magic in its own way." He stood in the pool and lifted her to her feet.

The water formed a circle around them, curtaining them from the children and pressing Mia and Jason closer together.

"Stop that." She stumbled into Jason as the ring of water tightened.

"I'm not doing anything."

She spun toward him. The water trickled up her back. "It's going to drown us."

"No, it's not."

A cascade of colors exploded through the water. In the distance, beyond the sound of a waterfall in reverse, the children laughed.

Jason's face glowed in red, yellow, and green light. "The Life Flower would never hurt us, not unless we gave it a reason to."

"Has it hurt anyone before?"

He pulled her tighter as the waters closed in. "Not that I know of."

The laughter outside grew louder. The lights danced on all sides like being stuck inside a Christmas tree.

Jason traced his fingers down the side of her face. "Do you really want to help me to protect this?"

She looked up at the lights. The warmth, the closeness, the notorious Jason Griggs—it was like having everything she'd ever wanted in a relationship handed to her.

"Yes." And she meant it. There were many things in the universe that were meaningless. This was not one of them. This was as close to heaven as she'd ever been.

He eased her chin to face him. "Good."

He lowered his lips to hers. The lights winked out, and he pulled her closer. The laughter heightened. She folded in to him, letting the warmth and serenity of this place enclose them in this one perfect moment in time.

She could stay here forever if she let herself, but she'd just made a promise to this place, to these people, and she intended to keep it.

She lowered her gaze and pulled away from him. The cylinder of water surrounding them dropped with a splash, revealing the children standing in the water, smiling at them.

Mia looked back to Jason, but he just shrugged.

The kids started laughing again, all their attention still on Mia and Jason. A few blushed and turned away. The others pointed. The question was: had the kids played a trick on them or had the planet, the Life Flower, taken it upon itself to draw them together?

A jitter swirled in Mia's chest and heat rose in her cheeks. What was she doing?

She moved to the water's edge. "Is there somewhere we can get some sleep? I have a feeling tomorrow is going to be a long day."

Her stomach churned. Her wet clothes clung to her as she stepped toward the shore, back toward reality.

"It probably will be." He helped her onto dry ground, his voice a little different. Harsher. More businesslike. Maybe he'd come to the same conclusion she had. "There's going to be a lot for you to talk about with Captain Stevenson."

She gave him a grim nod.

Tomorrow's conversation might cost Mia her career, but the words needed to be said. The UGA could not turn its back on these people and leave this incredible culture to be decimated by the likes of Vincent Chrona.

Jason pointed down the dirt street. "I have a little house down there."

Mia shook out her hair. "You have a place of your own, here?"

"Yeah. It's not much, but Ka'Raziel wanted me to have a safe place to hide if I needed one."

"She seems to like you." Mia wrung the water out of her shirt.

"She does, and I want to make sure it stays that way." He walked toward a bush. "They've been good allies and friends."

The bush behind him started to shake. The leaves came

to life, and long vines leapt out, surrounding him. In less than a second, he was engulfed.

"Jason!" She lunged for the vine, searching for something, *anything* to set him free.

"Hold on," he called. "I'm fine."

She eased away, her heart rattling. "Wh-What?"

The vines abated. Jason stumbled, his clothes disheveled and his hair sticking up.

He laughed, smoothing back his hair. His *dry* hair.

He pointed a thumb at the bush. "Clothes dryer."

Mia gaped at him, then stared at the swirling leaves behind him.

"These bushes need an inordinate amount of water to survive. They sprout up around ponds and lakes." He held out his hand, caressing the leaves. "It's a pretty amazing way for the environment to adapt to the constant storms. These things drink up all the extra water when it rains for days. It keeps the ponds from overflowing."

Whoa. It was like everything on this planet was alive. Well, lots of things on Earth were alive, too, but this stuff was alive with a capital 'A.'

Jason held out his hand to her. "Do you want to try it?" The leaves reared up behind him, almost like it had heard his question.

"Does it hurt?"

His smile was maddening. "It just tickles a little."

She let him draw her to the bush. The vines started to swirl as she stepped closer. Her heart rattled. She wanted to run, but a thick, deep-purple creeper wrapped around her hip.

She cried out as the vine pulled her to the bush, where several thinner vines swept over her, tugging at her clothes and dragging through her hair like dozens of little fingers.

Mia stood still, frozen, her heart beating frantically, until the vines abated, returning to the bush.

She let out the breath she'd been holding and ran her hands over her dry clothes. They weren't even damp.

Jason snorted. "Pretty cool, huh?"

She gaped at him. "I can't believe it."

He nodded. "I can't even count how many times I said that in the first year." He pointed to the bush. "The first time I stumbled into one of those, I thought I was a goner."

"I guess that was a happy discovery."

"Most of them are. Once you figure out what will eat you and steer clear of those, the rest of the planet is pretty helpful."

He reached out his hand, and she slipped her fingers into his as they continued down a dark dirt path.

It seemed oddly right, strolling quietly in this spectacular place. She should be afraid, or at least wary, but she understood why the Bobonians would want to stay hidden here. She didn't ever want to leave, either.

Jason's house was a small, round blob at the end of the road that looked a lot like a giant, dark green tomato. He pressed on the front, and a door appeared out of nowhere.

Stepping inside, Mia couldn't help but smile. A small kitchen lay nestled in the rear lined with appliances she wasn't quite familiar with. She assumed they functioned similar to a stove and an oven, but they seemed chiseled from stone and were probably made to utilize the energy of the Life Flower.

Beside them a tiny pool of water bubbled up from the ground. She waved her hand over, and the fountain rose for her to take a drink. To the left was a small room she assumed was a bathroom, and in the very front of the house was a futon, already open.

To some, this would be a glamorized closet; to her, it felt like a home.

She sat down on the futon. "Why wouldn't you stay here all of the time? It's like they've adopted you."

"Kind of. I don't want to take advantage, though. We're neighbors and friends. I appreciate all they do, but if I'm being honest, I like my home in the trees more. I don't feel like I belong here." He sighed. "I'm not quite sure where I belong anymore."

Mia patted the spot next to her. "You'll find home again."

"I hope so."

"Sleep sounds good." She laid down.

His eyes lingered on her, and she flinched. She hadn't meant anything suggestive by lying on his bed, but now that she had, she wasn't sure what to do. She started to sit up.

Jason cleared his throat and ran his fingers though his hair. "I can sleep on the floor if you like."

Her chest tightened. That wasn't what she wanted at all. She mustered up a friendly smile and patted the mattress beside her. "I can share. No spooning, though."

He held up his hands, a playful grin on his face. "Wouldn't dream of it."

"Good. It's going to be a big day for both of us. We need our rest."

His lips thinned slightly before he nodded. He dropped his belt to the floor before he slipped into bed beside her, facing away.

Mia's stomach fluttered. Had he expected more? *Hoped* for more?

The kiss in the water had been a little more than they'd shared in the woods, but she'd thought it was just the atmosphere getting to them.

Then again, he'd admitted to not having much contact with women. Had he really been alone, without any sort of emotional connection, for thirty years? That was almost enough to make her roll over and spoon *him*.

She didn't want to start something that neither one of them had any business finishing, though. Jason wasn't just a pretty face on a poster. He wasn't just a hero to look up to. He was a flesh-and-blood man. He deserved more than that.

Mia curled up into a ball and hugged herself. Jason Griggs could have any woman he wanted. So many people looked up to him, including her. He needed the right person, someone who could make him happy. In another time, another place, maybe that could have been her. But today? Now?

She supposed that depended on tomorrow, and whether or not she had the guts to stand up for what was morally correct. Jason was right; he'd gotten lucky over and over again. Normal people didn't get away with insubordination, even for the right reasons.

If Stevenson didn't cave and chose to support Chrona, she'd be forced to choose between the career she'd aspired to her entire life and the possibility of saving this place.

Mia closed her eyes.

"You okay?" Jason asked.

"Yeah." But in truth, she wasn't okay at all.

Chapter 16

JASON

Jason startled awake and sat straight up in the bed. There was always a certain reverent silence here, but tonight the air tingled. The flowers in the walls dimmed, then flicked brighter. They'd never done that, not in all the years he'd stayed there.

A scream ripped through the night, followed by another. A deep roaring sound filled the air. The dry tang of smoke drifted in through the windows.

He jumped to his feet and shook Mia. "Get up."

"Huh?" she asked.

"Get up!" He ran to the window. Sure enough, a smoky haze filled the clearing. He grabbed his belt from the floor and made sure he still had his gun, along with all of his knives.

Mia popped out of bed like a hardened soldier and charged out of the door. She uttered a loud curse and grabbed hold of her gun.

"The fire is coming from the center of the city," she said.

Jason stepped farther outside and gazed toward the blaze. Smoke billowed overhead, going through the shield that was supposed to protect the city from outsiders. He couldn't see the outline of the lake above anymore. What he did see made his stomach churn: fire licking the window frames of all the houses along the left cliff side.

Guns fired off, and Jason's worst fears were confirmed.

"Chrona," he growled.

Mia cocked her gun. "Looks like he made his move sooner than we expected."

"How'd he find the city?" Jason put a hand to his forehead. "What if I led them here?"

"If you did, it happened a long time ago. This isn't the kind of attack you plan on a whim." She grabbed him by the shirt, pulling him toward her. "Snap out of it. We need to focus on helping the people."

On that they could agree. But which time had he had been careless? Of course, it was always a possibility that maybe one of the scouts had given away the location. There were an endless amount of opportunities day after day for anyone to make a mistake. He loaded his gun, glad he made the trade for extra ammunition only a few days before. It'd be a great pleasure to use Vincent's own resources against him.

Mia ran ahead. She aimed her gun high and shot. One of Vincent's goons fell out of a window. She fired off a few more shots, and two more fell.

Damn.

"Is there a way to get the water from the pool to put out the fire?" she asked, sighting another target.

"I'll try." He vaguely remembered having the water system explained to him. Somewhere was a failsafe for just such an unthinkable situation. He dashed to the pool they'd romped in only a handful of hours before and frowned. The water was eerily flat. He waved his hand over the surface, but there was no response.

The water should be tingling with the energy of the Life Flower, not only for children to play in, but also vibrating with the communications of the warriors. Vincent must have done something to cut off the living waters, disabling the communication system. Each lake had a manual trigger, though, and a way to sound an alarm. No one else must have made it to a pond yet.

He scrambled along the edge of the water. *Where is it? Where is it?*

"Where is it?" He slammed his fist into a tree trunk beside the water before he spotted the rich, red stone embedded into the border of the pool. There. That had to be it. He lifted his foot and smashed his heel into the stone.

A deafening horn blasted throughout the city. Any warriors who weren't already attempting to aid the citizens came streaming out of the unspoiled houses. Jason spotted another one of Vincent's crew raise a gun.

No way. Not on his watch. Jason fired before the guy could shoot his own gun and turned before the man hit the ground.

There were more humans in the upper windows, waiting to strike. Jason attempted to knock a few more out. His aim wasn't quite what it used to be and definitely nowhere near as good as Mia's, but the men in those houses dropped down. At least they weren't shooting at the Bobonians anymore.

Mia ducked behind a large root as a few bullets riddled the ground at her feet. Jason dove next to her.

"The two of us aren't going to be able to take them all out," she shouted over the noise.

"The warriors will help."

"Do they have guns?" Mia asked, her tone grave. He shook his head. "What about a long-ranged weapon of any kind?"

Another shake of his head, and he scowled. "They know what they're doing. They train full out and—"

"They thought hiding was the best way to avoid this," Mia pointed out. "We need help. Real help. I need to get Captain Stevenson and bring the crew over."

"*You* need to get him? *We* need to get him."

There was no way he'd let Mia out of his sight with Chrona and his goons prowling around. Who knew what other traps lay in store for them?

"What we need to do is get as many Bobonians out of here as we can," he said. "Then we can get Captain Stevenson and fight."

"Or both. We can do both." Mia peeked over the roots and shot her weapon. "Separating isn't a bad idea."

"The people first," Jason said.

He lifted his gun to shoot another Perseverance soldier running down a Bobonian girl. The guy fell, and bullets throttled the other side of the root they'd hidden behind. Their window for leaving would be small. Eventually, Vincent's men would figure out a way around their hiding spot. Jason grabbed Mia and pulled her between the trees.

Mia scooted under a branch. "I hope you know where you're going."

"Me, too."

They ducked and weaved their way between the buildings and the forest, taking down any of Vincent's men who got in the way. As they got closer to the main cavern where Ka'Raziel's throne sat, they got caught in a stream of citizens being ushered inside by the warriors.

Jason's stomach sank. Of course they'd run to her and hide, trapping themselves in the process. That was probably what Chrona was hoping for. They'd be sitting ducks in there.

Jason ran to the nearest warrior. "*Evacuate the city. Those men will kill you all.*"

"*Do not order me, other worldling,*" the warrior seethed in his own language. He gave Jason a hard shove into the cavern.

Somehow, Jason had to find the chieftess and talk her into fleeing. He searched throughout the cave, almost forgetting about Mia until she returned to his side.

She pointed toward the right. "There's an opening there."

Sure enough, everyone seemed to be going left, flowing into a secret passage he'd never seen. Whatever the strategy was, he had to trust they had a plan to stay safe. So while everyone went left, Jason went against the flow toward the right. He curved around the wall, hugging it close and avoiding the warriors—until he got to the door to the receiving hall.

The two warriors guarding the way pointed their spears directly at him.

"*Other worldling,*" one said in his own tongue. "*You keep moving before we worry you are like the others.*"

Jason squared his chest and glared. "*I demand to see the chieftess. Take all of my weapons if you insist, but she and I will have words. It's for the safety of the people.*"

The chieftess's daughter, Adaranla, moved out from behind the other warriors. His eyes softened, and he pleaded with her, "*You need to run. I know how these men think. It's the only way you will survive.*"

She stared at him for what seemed like an eternity. Somewhere behind him a child screamed, and her expression hardened. "*I will stand for him. Let him see my mother.*" Adaranla moved to the door. The other warrior hesitated. "*Now, Gamolfan.*"

Gamolfan didn't respond, only huffed and did as he was told. Adaranla ushered them inside before shutting the entrance.

"*We must be careful who sees Ka'Raziel. My mother is focusing all of her energy on the escape paths. Your conversation with her must be quick.*"

Jason nodded, then turned to Mia. "Talk fast. Got it?"

"Got it," Mia said.

Ka'Raziel sat on her throne, her hair extending toward the ceiling, floating as if the strands reached for the world above. The flowers interspersed in the flowing tresses glowed bright yellow, casting most of the light in the room on the closed-eyed woman as she gripped the armrests of the throne so tightly, her greenish-tan skin was several shades lighter.

Jason bowed quickly. *"I'm sorry to interrupt, chieftess, but it's important that we leave this city. Hiding won't save you this time."*

Ka'Raziel shifted her gaze to him and he saw only the whites of her eyes. *"We survived other invasions. We will survive this one. The Great Eaters will provide for us."*

He needed to make her understand. *"Humans are different. You've seen this. The Vincent will not just give up. He will keep on coming."*

She shook her head. *"When the Vincent thinks he has destroyed us, he will leave and find a new land to conquer."*

"But he does not want to just conquer. He wants the power of the Life Flower. He will take it if you let him."

Her vacant stare bored through him. *"The Life Flower cannot simply be taken. It is a living thing. It will fight him."*

Skies, he hoped so, but if they were wrong, their entire civilization was about to end. *"Don't you owe it to the Life Flower to fight for her, out of love and respect for all she has given you?"*

Screams sounded outside. The room shook.

Ka'Raziel blinked, and the whites of her eyes eased back, allowing her pupils to focus on him. The wild tendrils of hair settled on her shoulders.

She grimaced. *"Perhaps the Life Flower could use our assistance."*

Yes! He stood taller and placed his hand on his chest. *"We can help mobilize your warriors."*

She waved both of her hands—the Bobonian equivalent to shaking her head. *"First, they will get our people to their hiding place. Then they will defend the Life Flower, and our home."*

Her hair started to swirl again, and a thick ball formed in Jason's stomach. *"What about you? They need to lead you out, too."*

"My presence quells the Great Eaters, allowing my people to pass through their tunnels. I will see every life in my care safe before I attempt to protect myself."

Jason quickly translated everything for Mia.

She glared at him. "If she stays, she's going to die."

His stomach lurched again. "Probably."

Mia took a step forward. "Chieftess, unless you have a plan to take your city back, it's going to be gone for good. You have to come with us and seek out assistance from the Alpha Cent. They'll listen to you, respect you, and help you defend your home."

Jason translated as she spoke, and while he didn't know if Mia's words would make a difference, he appreciated the passion with which she spoke. She might be the only other person on this planet who wanted to protect this place as much as he did.

Ka'Raziel tilted her head before shaking her hands again. *"The best way for me to help is to stay here and ensure the safety of as many people as possible. My presence will not make your argument more convincing. Go and get your Alpha Cent."*

The room shook again. Shots fired just outside the door.

Ka'Raziel tightened her grip on the throne, and the flowers in her hair brightened. *"Do not let the Vincent harm the Life Flower. It is the source of all life."*

Jason cringed. "That's what I was afraid of."

"What did she say?" Mia asked.

"If Chrona gets the roots, everything dies."

Her face became a mask of determination. "Roots good. Vincent bad. Got it."

Jason turned to the chieftess. *"I will die before I let him kill our planet."*

Ka'Raziel bowed her head. *"That is why you are* The Griggs. *My warriors will follow you if needed."*

He bowed once more to Ka'Raziel before moving to leave the room. He quickly filled in the blanks of the conversation to Mia as the guards closed and sealed the door.

Mia's gaze carried over the chaos. "So what now?"

"We get to your ship and get backup."

Jason moved into the main cave. Vincent's men shot into the fleeing Bobonians like cowards. Every ounce of his being screamed at him to throw himself between the innocent and the bullets, but his death would mean nothing if this place still fell into Vincent's hands.

"Somehow, we've got to get out of here without them catching us."

The people of the city pushed and shoved through the holes in the intricate root system that made up the leftmost wall of the cave.

"She's sure that the Great Eater roots aren't going to make shish-kabobs of her people?" Mia aimed at one of the invaders on the far side of the room and fired. That dirt bag dropped to the ground.

Jason glanced at her, certain he would have missed that shot by yards. "That's what she said."

She started heading for the roots. "That means that those tunnels go to the surface. Let's go."

Jason hesitated before following. The trees had always been a mystery to him. By their bases was death and in its sap was life. The greatest of healing ointments could be tapped from its trunk. He still wasn't willing to believe, though, that whatever Ka'Raziel was doing in her throne room could stop those ancient trees from doing what they instinctually needed to survive.

People crowded everywhere, and when Vincent himself entered the cave and began firing into the air, panic rose to terror. A man ushered his children to the roots, and Mia got knocked into the crowd.

"Jason?" She reached out toward him.

He pushed his way against the flow of Bobonians. "I'm coming."

Vincent closed in on them, and Jason tried to ignore the look of pure delight on the man's face when he saw Mia. An arm slammed into Jason, pushing him to the ground. Feet trampled over him. He fought to an upright position, using the wall of the cave for support.

Nearby a child wailed, separated from its parents. Jason helped the Bob-ling up and handed him off to an adult native. The whole time, he searched desperately for a crown of short, blonde hair among the brown-haired Bobonians.

A lump formed in his throat as she screamed his name again. Three men dragged her toward Vincent.

"I see you've found a really nice one," Vincent called out, looking directly at Jason. "She's strong-spirited. Those will be good traits to pass down to our children."

Jason pushed through the crowd, only to get pulled back.

Vincent stroked Mia's cheek with the edge of his gun. "I wonder if you'll be hard to break or if you'll come to me willingly." Vincent was screaming, making sure Jason heard over the cacophony.

Jason was going to kill that scum-sucker with his bare hands.

Mia spat in Vincent's face. She twisted and kicked before the guy holding her dropped to the ground. Mia bolted two steps toward Jason when Vincent grabbed her arm and yanked her back.

He laughed, his dark gaze landing on Jason as his smirk widened, issuing a challenge: *Come and get her.*

Jason clenched his hands into fists. He didn't care if this was a trap. He was going to cut out Vincent's heart and shove it down his throat. He pushed through the crowd, only to be drawn farther back by the throng.

"Griggs?"

Jason startled, hearing his name next to him. Adaranla shoved him toward the roots. "Out Griggs, out." Adaranla pushed him.

He fought against her and the people around him. "No. I can't... Mia."

"Out," Adaranla repeated, maybe the only word of English the chieftess's daughter knew.

She and her people pressed him into the roots and out of the main chamber, far from Mia.

Adaranla pushed Jason and the others into a hollow room, butting Jason far closer to the base of a Great Eater trunk than he ever wanted to get without his sap-collecting gear. The natives gathered tight, holding him in, staring at the ceiling.

"I have to get back to Mia," Jason said.

"Out," Adaranla said again, looking up like the others.

Above, an oval hole opened in the ceiling, showing a blue sky beyond the canopy of trees.

My God, this is the belly of the beast.

The ground under his feet began to shift, and like an elevator, they all rose to the surface, only to be spat out onto the grass. Jason rolled three times before getting his bearings and crawling back to the hole, but the opening closed just before he got to the edge.

Adaranla touched his shoulder. "Out."

Jason rolled over and looked at the sky. He was out, but he'd left Mia there. Vincent would do who-knew-what kind of disgusting things to her as soon as he got her to Perseverance.

Jason gritted his teeth and stood. He wouldn't give Vincent that chance.

The natives all fled to a location deeper in the jungle. Jason glanced in the direction of the Alpha Cent. If he ran with everything he had, he could get there in twenty minutes —maybe.

There was no use thinking it over. That was his only chance.

He sprinted through the jungle, jumping over branches and through bushes. His lungs burned, his stomach cramped, but he kept pushing. This wasn't just about the planet anymore. Chrona had too many men, and Jason couldn't save Mia on his own.

His chest thickened. Never in his life had he worried about being alone. He'd always been able to conquer anything. But tonight, being pushed through the crowd and away from Mia, he'd never felt so small.

The Alpha Cent came into view just as the cramp in his stomach started to double-knot.

Gunshots sounded from the ship. The captain, Bernard, and Commander Cortenz stood at the base of the docking bay, firing rounds into the jungle. Vincent's men—dozens of them—cased the perimeter of the ship, just inside the trees. Chrona must have split up his men for a coordinated attack, taking on the Bobonians and the new ship all at once, the power-hungry worm.

Jason had to act fast. The numbers were not in the Alpha Cent's favor.

Jason snuck up behind the goons and placed hungry flower roots, looped, behind each one. He whistled twice, like a Keeka bird, and Dobby slid out of the trees above him.

"Were you there the whole time?"

Dobby's ears lifted as he growl-barked softly.

"It's okay, buddy. I wouldn't expect you to take them all

down on your own. Thanks for looking out for my new friends, though." Jason pointed to the vines. "Can you get your buddies to help me out?"

Dobby wagged his tail and made the same call he had earlier, calling the animals of the forest. Within seconds, a wall of Tank Beetles rammed the Perseverance soldiers, making them stumble. They each flew from view as the hungry flowers drew in their prey.

Holy cats! He half-expected that his little trick wouldn't work again. The squirrels dropped out of the trees and the rest of the soldiers spasmed, screaming, and they dropped into the brush.

Too bad he couldn't figure out a way to get these guys underground.

He found one of the talking trees and tapped the pattern for "danger come quick" into the coarse, padded leaves. Hopefully, one of the warriors was nearby to hear the message and come help. The threat against the ship might have been temporarily dealt with, but it was only a matter of time before they returned.

Ka'Raziel had said her people would follow him. With any luck, Jason would be able to convince the warriors to work with Captain Stevenson or they were all skunked.

He took a moment to catch his breath before shouting out, "Captain, it's me, Griggs."

"Griggs?" Bernard called. "If it's you, what are we supposed to be doing later?"

"Getting a drink. I've got a few stories to share."

The captain and Bernard spoke quietly amongst themselves as Jason stepped out into view with his hands raised. All three of them relaxed when they saw him. Captain Stevenson waved him into the docking bay.

Behind Jason, the native warriors charged forward. Captain Stevenson raised his gun again.

"Don't shoot." Jason put himself between the two groups. *"No attack,"* he shouted in Bobonian.

The warriors growled and held their spears at the ready. None of the Alpha Cent crew lowered their guns, either.

Jason tried again. *"These are my friends."* He said it again in English for the captain. *"And we need to work together to get rid of the Vincent once and for all."* He paused before adding. "They have Mia. We have to get her back before it's too late."

"Those men took more than just Mia," Bernard said. "Leslie is gone, Erin..." He sighed. "Ashley." There was a tenderness in his voice when he said her name. Maybe the kid had a thing for her.

Captain Stevenson stared at the warriors, his eyes wide. "We will work with these native men and women if they're willing to help. I have a feeling we'll need all the help we can get."

Jason relayed the information to the warriors. They formed a tight circle with their bodies and spoke amongst themselves for a lot longer than Jason liked. When they broke apart, a warrior gave Jason a salute.

"Yes," the warrior said. He tapped his chest. "Lowan."

"Griggs." Jason mimicked the same movement. *"Good meeting, Lowan."*

Lowan ignored him and marched his way to the docking bay. *"Show us how to destroy the Vincent."*

"What?" Commander Cortenz asked.

Smirking, Jason followed all of the warriors onto the Alpha Cent. "Vincent is about to get the fight of his life."

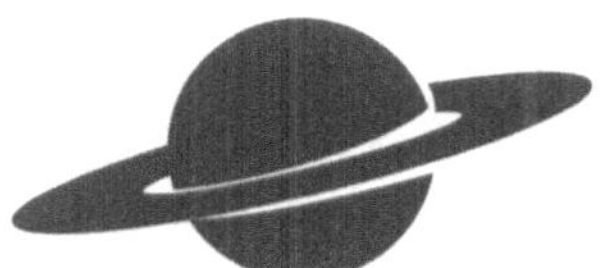

Chapter 17

MIA

Vincent pushed Mia toward another of his men. "Toss her in with the others who still need to be rehabilitated."

The guy grabbed hold of Mia, keeping her tightly restrained as he dragged her through the compound. She kicked and tugged at him, but there wasn't much she could do with her hands tied behind her back.

She shouted for help and kicked up a cloud of dust as they pulled her along, but the men's gazes only dropped over her as they passed, as if contemplating a prize to possibly bid on later.

Skies, she hoped that wasn't true.

Near the center of the compound, two women tilling a garden stood as the guards dragged Mia past. Their faces were covered with grime. One held a large, rounded belly.

They both grimaced. The second woman covered her mouth as tears gathered in her eyes. They must have known all too well the type of *rehabilitation* she was in store for.

Mia's captors pushed her toward a small building close to the main center complex. Heavy, misshapen bricks made up the exterior instead of wood. The inside was lined with metal doors, and she knew she was headed for some kind of a holding cell.

The man opened a chamber, removed her bindings, and shoved her into a dark room, slamming the door shut behind her. Mia waited a good ten seconds before she growled and punched the wall.

She'd been careless, letting herself get caught up in the confusion, and they'd grabbed her. Stars on high, she should have been ready for that. All of her training pointed to staying focused in mass confusion. That had been a textbook evacuation scenario, and she'd failed horribly. Now she was paying for it in the likes of a jail cell.

She ran her fingers through her hair. There was no point in beating herself up over foolish mistakes. She needed to pull herself together and focus on getting out.

Mia sighed and gazed up at the ceiling. Every cell had a weakness; that was one of the many lessons she'd learned at the academy. No building was perfect, so when taken captive on enemy ground, a soldier needed to take stock of what they were dealing with.

She grazed the cool metal with her fingers. The material seemed thin but strong. The seams were wide, and the bolts stuck out, like the structure had been made quickly. Was the entire compound like this, or was building a prison an afterthought, and they'd constructed these walls quickly once they'd had a need for them?

She heard a sniff and spun to the darkness. Someone moved. Maybe more than one someone.

"Hello?" She moved deeper into the room until the darkness shifted into several silhouettes.

Okay, good. She wasn't alone. Now she just needed to make friends so they could get the heck out of here. "My name is Mia. Have you been here long?"

No response. The figures simply shifted closer together.

"I'm from the Alpha Cent. We crash-landed here a few days ago."

Someone laughed without mirth…a woman's voice. Was crash-landing so common?

"Oh," someone moved on the ground. It looked like she held her head.

If these people were all shoved into the dark like this, they must be petrified. If this was the first phase of rehabilitation, Chrona needed to get a new handbook. Making them sit in the dark wasn't going to do much more than drive them all crazy.

She tried again. "Listen, if we work together, maybe we can get out of this."

A quiet chuckle made the rounds through the cell, but still no response.

Okay, so they didn't think escape was an option. Maybe they'd been here a long time or had even tried to get out themselves. If Vincent had beaten them down to nothing, then she might be on her own unless Jason made it to the ship to get help.

That is, *if* he'd gone to get help.

Jason was a hero, and heroes were born to save people, but there were a lot more Bobonians to save than there were Mias. The Captain Starlight from the comic books would have gone for the bigger win, sacrificing his friend, and maybe even himself, to save as many people as possible. She couldn't fault him for that. It was who he was, and it was the right thing to do.

Deep down, she hoped that he cared enough to put her first, but she couldn't sit here like a damsel in distress. She needed to start planning her own escape.

The figure on the ground sat up. "M-Mia?"

"Leslie?" Mia crawled across the floor to the other woman. "They got you too?"

Leslie nodded as Mia grabbed her hand. Her skin was smooth, and nowhere near as pocked and bloody as it'd been after her encounter with the hungry flower.

"I was finishing up a repair on the outside of the ship with Ashley and Bernard when the ship was attacked." Her grip on Mia's hand tightened. "We fought them off, but not well enough. Bernard barely got away. They captured Erin by the perimeter. She was looking for water."

"Alone?" Mia shook her head.

"Cortenz was with her. They'd found a small spring that tested positive for drinkability." Leslie shifted her weight. "We tried to fight off as many of them as we could, but there were just too many."

That sounded like a major offensive, maybe more than Captain Stevenson was ready for. "What happened after? Did they take out the rest of the crew?"

"I'm not sure," Leslie said.

So they might be alone after all. "Okay, noted." Mia stood. "Have you been able to get any information from anyone else here?"

Leslie shook her head. "No one wants to talk, and Ashley is in another area, probably because they knocked her unconscious. I hope they're taking care of her and didn't just throw her in a cell."

Mia took in a deep breath, gaining more resolve. "We have to get out of here."

"Yeah, but how?"

That was the question of the hour. "There are three of us in here, right?" She squinted in the dark. "Where is Erin?"

"They dragged us both into the compound, but then we got separated. She must be in another cell." Leslie eased up from the floor. "They probably divided us so we didn't band together and cause a riot. I guess they forgot about me being here when they brought you in."

"Or they didn't think it mattered anymore." Which was another reason to believe that help wasn't coming.

"Last I heard, there was a firefight not far from here," an older, rougher, female voice said.

Mia turned toward the voice. "A firefight? Then they're still going against the Alpha Cent."

The woman moved closer, coming into clearer view in the dim light. She was tall, with a muscular build that would put most men to shame. She didn't seem much older than Mia, but there was a degree of experience around her eyes that Mia lacked.

Maybe she was like Jason—landing here decades ago, but barely aging, or maybe aging backward.

"The Alpha Cent, is that your ship?" the woman asked.

Mia nodded. "And you are?"

"Abigail." The woman held her hand out for a quick shake. "I've been here for a while. Every time I convince them I'm ready to join the colony, I've tried to escape. They keep threatening me, but I know how badly they need us, so I keep trying." She looked around at the others. "There's a guy on the outside. Some of the girls think he'll help."

"Captain Starlight," another voice whispered.

Abigail shook her head. "I think they're all delirious, searching for comic book heroes, but there *is* someone out there who refuses to join the colony. He's super resourceful." She straightened. "We just need to get to him, and we need to do it fast."

A man's muffled voice shouted somewhere down the hall, like he was barking orders.

She turned to Mia. "I don't think it'll be long before things get ugly. None of them have resorted to violence or forcing themselves on us, but we've all heard rumblings of trophy wives."

Mia shivered. "I'm not sure I want to know what that means."

Another woman moved closer. "It's true. Vincent plans on granting mating privileges to whoever does his dirty work the best in a given month."

Mia stiffened. "He can't do that."

The girl shrugged. "A few of the women have already agreed. He lets them walk free in the compound." She held up her hands. "The rest of us are here *for our own protection,* so he tells us."

Mia gritted her teeth. There was no way she, or anyone from the Alpha Cent, was going to be anyone's reward for a good day's work.

She rubbed the woman's shoulder. "We're going to try to get you out." And to Abigail, she said, "How long have you been here?"

"Too long. My ship crashed ages ago. They dragged it here into the compound and are using its systems to help run the colony. At first, I thought I was an equal with Vincent Chrona and the others, but that didn't last long." She frowned. "There have been several crashes. More than they want you to know. Chrona has managed to recruit or overtake all of them."

Mia's stomach churned into knots. "Are you the only one who's still trying to fight him?"

"There are others. We aren't allowed to interact with each other much, so it's hard to band together. Most of the women are afraid for obvious reasons."

"We don't have time to band together with anyone," Mia said. "I've got to get out of here now so they don't take over my ship and strip it apart. We're still planning to get off this planet."

Leslie nodded in agreement. "The two of us working together should be able to get further than working on our own."

"Three of us," Abigail said. "They won't be prepared for it. Only two guards are on duty at any given point of time here. Most of the women here have lost the will to fight. That's why they've started accepting their fate and joining the mating agenda."

Mia shuddered that they had an almost socially acceptable name for what was really sexual slavery. This wasn't acceptable on any planet in the UGA. Vincent was insane to think he could get away with this.

Well, it stopped right here as far as Mia was concerned. "All right. We need to get the guards in here and then jump them. From there, we can unlock all the other cells. If we show unity, then the other women might join us."

"And then?" Leslie asked.

Mia lifted her chin. "We go after Chrona and end this."

Leslie and Abigail nodded.

Good. At least she had two people willing to take their destinies into their own hands.

Mia pressed against the hastily constructed walls. "So the compound is made up of Vincent's ship and other ships he's conquered over the years?"

Abigail nodded. "Yes, all of the security systems and other technology is supplied by our old power sources."

The less technology for them to fight against, the better. "We'll need to disable those power sources."

"First, we need to get out of here," Leslie said.

Mia gazed at the two other women. "You ready for this?"

"Yes," Abigail said. "I've been waiting for this for a long time."

"Time to create a diversion," Mia whispered to Leslie. "Did you, by any chance, have Takaki Mendura as a defense instructor?"

Leslie laughed. "One of my favorite classes."

Perfect. Mendura specialized in teaching women to kick men's asses. Step one was catching them off guard.

Mia leapt across the cell and pushed Leslie into the wall, shouting, "I can't believe you sold us out."

"Someone had to steer our ship in the right direction," Leslie countered, shoving Mia.

"I'll kill you!"

The cell doors opened and one of the guards came in. His partner stood in the doorframe, his massive bulk blocking the light.

"Hey!" The first tried to pull Mia and Leslie apart. "Stop fighting each other, or I'm going to have to sedate you both."

Behind him, Abigail swept out the legs of the guard in the door. He went down with a hard thud. She grabbed hold of his head and smacked his skull into the ground until he stopped fighting.

The guard on Mia and Leslie made the mistake of looking away. One swift kick to the back of his knees brought him down. The drop kick to the back of the head took him out.

Abigail and Mia dragged the unconscious men toward the rear of the cell before stripping the guards of their clothes and weapons.

A few of the women were crying. Mia wanted to tell them to steel themselves, but she remembered her sister on Earth. Her eyes had always been wide, and she'd covered her mouth when Mia had explained what she went through in basic training.

Some of these women might be medical personnel, botanists, or maybe even just family of officers traveling as part of a crew. Not everyone was a hardened soldier.

As she and Abigail changed into the men's uniforms, Leslie helped the other women up.

"Keep quiet, and follow us," she told them. "No stragglers. If you want out, you listen and stay close."

Mia strapped a gun belt around her waist.

Abigail put the strap of a larger gun over her shoulder. "I've been with these women for a long time. You need to know that it's just the three of us in this. The rest of them are broken.

Mia moved to the door. "Yeah, I figured."

A man's voice sounded down the hallway. "Parker? Smith? Where the hell are you?"

Mia glanced at Abigail and then Leslie. They each gave a quick nod, their features icing over. The women behind Leslie clung to each other.

"Parker?" The voice was closer.

A shadow fell over the open doorway.

"What the...?"

Abigail grabbed the end of her gun and swung, lunging through the door. Someone gasped before a *thunk* echoed through the hall and a body slammed to the floor.

Mia stepped out beside her. "That was effective."

Abigail nodded, grabbing the guard's gun and handing it to Leslie. "The less gunfire, the farther we can get before the rest of them figure out what's going on."

Mia pulled the man into their cell.

"I'm not very good with one of these." Leslie held up the weapon.

As the head of alien biology, she probably spent more of her time in a lab studying dead things under a microscope.

"You've got this. Abigail and I will go first. Once we carve a path out, I need you to find the rest of the women and get them out."

She balked. "Me?"

Mia raised a brow. "Would you rather be in the front?"

Abigail handed Leslie the guard's key band. "Just wave this in front of the door."

Leslie nodded, her expression hardening. "I got it. And I'm sorry. I'm with you."

Good. The last thing they needed was another handicap. They moved into the hallway, Abigail first, Mia behind, and Leslie prodding the others forward in a tight cluster.

More voices sounded around the corner.

Mia nodded at Abigail. This was it.

'Ready?' she mouthed.

Abigail nodded.

They turned the corner, Abigail charging like a kamikaze pilot. The men shouted before raising their guns. One fired.

"Stop!" one shouted. "It's the women."

Abigail shot first and Mia sprayed below the guard's knees with successive fire. Four of the men fell. The one who'd told the rest to stop raised his weapon and fired. Mia's arm seared in pain, but she raised her gun and fired again. The guy fell to one knee and shot.

Someone behind Mia screamed and a *thunk* echoed above the gunfire.

Dammit!

Ducking, Mia shot and the man fell, but more screams came from past their cell.

She took cover as bullets sprayed over her head from behind them. Two men entered the hallway from the rear as another shot from the front, leaning around the corner.

Crouching, Mia grabbed her shoulder and hissed as her hand came back red.

Abigail shot, and the man around the corner fell.

Another two blasts rang out and the hallway grew silent. In the rear of their group, Leslie stood, her gun shaking in her hand and two men lying on the floor, one in a growing pool of blood.

Mia made her way to her. "Hey, you did what you needed to do."

She nodded.

Mia gave her a shake. "I need you to go down these cells as quickly as possible and help get the women out." Mia leaned down and grabbed a key from another guard. "I'll take this side."

Leslie shook her head as if clearing her vision before she focused on Mia. "Yeah, I got it." She headed for the first door.

"Abigail touched Mia's shoulder. "You okay?"

A red bloom had spread around the slash in her purloined uniform. The sting burned deep, but she could still move it.

"I think I'm okay."

Several women filed out of one of the doors Leslie had opened down the hall.

Abigail's eyes narrowed. "You *think* you're okay, or you *are* okay?"

Mia shrugged and winced. "I've never been shot before, but I'm pretty sure it's just a scrape." A star-blasted nasty scrape, but she'd live. She got lucky.

"Good. Let's do what we need to do and get the hell out of here."

Abigail walked among the bodies on the floor as Mia headed for the other cells.

Moving to the first door, she swiped the key. The room was empty. She tried the next cell and found that one empty too.

"Mia?"

She spun to the voice. "Ashley?" Mia gave her a hug.

"Is everyone out of the other cells?"

"As far as I can tell, yes."

Perfect. Hopefully, their luck would hold out.

Down the hall, Leslie crouched over the body of a woman with a puddle of red surrounding her hair. Leslie covered her mouth, crying. Maybe they weren't as lucky as Mia had thought.

She couldn't dwell on that, though. She needed to get the rest of them out.

Mia turned to Ashley. The captain had called her a jack of all trades. She certainly seemed collected, despite being knocked out when they'd locked her in a cell. "Get as many of the prisoners as you can to the Alpha Cent."

Ashley looked back to her. "What about you?"

"We're going for the power source. We'll hit Vincent where it will hurt him the most."

Ashley pulled a small sidearm off one of the men on the floor and straightened. "I should go with you. I'm a strong fighter."

"Which is why I need you leading the others out."

Down the hall, Leslie held her temples and slipped to the floor. Most of the color had drained from her face as she stared at the bodies of the men she'd fired on.

Mia leaned closer to Ashley. "Leslie is doing great, but I think she just shot a man for the first time. I don't think she's taking it well."

Not that Mia had ever shot anyone before today, either, but she'd been trained to block that kind of emotion out. It would hit her later. For now, she'd keep pushing it out of her head.

She motioned to the women leaving the cells, most of them cowering and clinging to each other. "They need someone strong to lead them or they're going to freeze."

Ashley nodded. "All right. I'll get them out." She peered down the hall. "Do you think we'll find the Alpha Cent in one piece?"

"It has to be." Because the alternative meant they were trapped there.

"You're right. Let's do this." Ashley walked down the hall and took Leslie by the arm to lead her out.

Mia readied her new gun and gazed at Abigail. "That leaves you and me to sabotage Vincent's systems and end his madness once and for all."

"Sounds like a party." Abigail cocked her own gun.

They peeked out of the jail door. Overhead, another storm cloud blew in. If Jason was right, they might not have much time before the planet worked against them. "Which way to the compound energy reserves?"

Abigail pointed farther into the colony. "Almost all the power lines lead to the back of the compound. The power center must be by the rear fence. That's where the wall he erected is strongest."

Mia checked to make sure no one was coming before sprinting across to a stacked pile of metal crates that had probably once held food.

They made their way forward, moving from object to object, doorway to doorway, until they got to the rear fence.

Three guards stood in their way.

"Now what?" Abigail asked.

Mia held up her gun. Weapons were always a last resort, but they were well past the last resort phase.

Abigail looked to the front of the compound, where the other guards had started to gather. "They'll hear."

Probably, but unless these two guys were complete idiots...

Gunfire sounded from the front of the camp. Abigail and Mia ducked between two crates. They wouldn't try to kill Leslie and the others. After all, they needed them to breed.

Maybe Captain Stevenson was mounting an offensive? Mia could hope, but she couldn't bank on it. Right now they could only count on themselves. Everyone else had enough on their plates.

Mia took aim at one of the guards blocking their path, but his partner slapped his shoulder and motioned for him to follow. They both headed to the front of the camp.

Abigail wrinkled her brow. "Did that actually just happen?"

"Don't pass up the rations that the enemy leaves behind. Let's go."

They scooted around the side of the building.

The walls looked like exterior ship casings, maybe even the bolstering ramparts to an engine room.

"Jesus," Abigail said. "I think that's my ship."

"You probably could have gotten out of here if they didn't rip it apart."

She shook her head. "It was stupid of me to trust them."

Mia held her gun at the ready. "Don't beat yourself up. Let's just get even."

A few guards were at the entrance. Mia used the handle of her gun to knock them out. She and Abigail got lucky with whatever was going on at the main gates. They needed to keep attention away from them as long as possible.

They snuck through the halls of Abigail's ship. It seemed ancient in comparison to the Alpha Cent. And Vincent had been here even longer, and Jason longer than that. Had technology really come so far in only thirty years?

"The controls are connected to the bridge," Abigail said. "This way."

Mia followed her, trusting the woman to lead the way, and hopefully not lead Mia to her demise. The ship shook beneath them, and a grinding hum filled the corridor.

"What is that?" Mia asked.

Abigail shook her head, staring at the ground. "I'm not sure. It can't be what it sounds like."

Mia cocked her head. "What do you think it sounds like?"

"Nothing." She motioned for Mia to follow. "Let's go."

They slipped onto the empty bridge. So far, so good. As long as Vincent and his crew stayed distracted, they could make their move. If she could power down the compound, it'd make things significantly easier for Captain Stevenson to get in.

"Let's see what kind of chaos we can create," Abigail whispered, pulling herself beneath the control panel.

Mia leaned down beside her. The system was a little outdated, but the academy trained in all of the basic ship functions, and those hadn't changed over the years—only gotten more elaborate. The core remained. It just hadn't been used in the stars-knew-how-many years.

Mia slipped in beside her, wiggling beneath the narrow opening beneath the control panel. She pointed out the blue and red entwined wires running to the tertiary splicer plate. "This looks like perimeter power."

"Yeah, and I just cut the lights and the fences."

Mia snorted. "That one's bound to piss him off." She cut her red wire, being careful to leave the blue attached to keep the main power operational. If they had an infirmary here, she didn't want to hurt anyone who might need the machinery.

Abigail pulled out a few plain black wires and cut them. "If this is labeled correctly, those were wired to the jail building. Anyone we missed can now get out on their own."

"What's this?" Mia's fingers hovered over a red button.

Abigail swatted her hand away. "Self-destruct."

Mia balked. "Seriously? I thought those were a myth?"

Abigail's lips thinned. "Not for spy vessels."

Whoa. She glanced at Abigail. No wonder she'd kept fighting them. This chick was probably trained to take less crap than Mia was. Still, a self-destruct button might be a little excessive, no matter what kind of ship this had been.

Someone grabbed Mia's ankle and yanked her out from

beneath the console. The seams of her uniform caught on the tiles as she was dragged across the floor. Mia struggled, reaching for her gun, before Vincent kicked it out of her hand.

His eyes blazed as he stepped back. "You set the women free."

He was mad about the prisoners? He must have already been inside the ship before they'd started cutting power to his security systems outside.

"They weren't yours to keep." Mia scooted farther away as Abigail eased out of the console with her hands raised.

He pointed a gun at her, then Mia. "You will not destroy everything I've built. I *will* make you understand."

Chrona reached for Mia.

"Bite me." Abigail kicked him, and he stumbled.

Mia jumped to her feet. They'd already done everything they'd come to do. They just needed to get out. "Come on."

She bolted through the door and into the hall before crashing right into the arms of another of Chrona's goons. She kicked at the guy's ankles, but he slammed her against the wall. The room spun for a moment, and Mia closed her eyes.

Dammit! They'd been so close.

She took a step, but the walls closed in and spun. She grabbed a side rail to steady herself.

Vincent moved into the hall, holding Abigail by the hair with a saber pistol pointed at her temple. If he touched the trigger, let alone pulled it, Abigail's brain would be scattered across the walls of her former ship.

Chrona smiled. "Nice try. I *do* love your spunk." His grin turned malicious. "I'm definitely saving you for myself."

The room spun. The guard behind Mia pushed her down to the floor.

"That's it." Chrona dragged Abigail along with him.

"Women belong on their knees. You'll learn that soon enough."

Mia's eyes wouldn't focus. She blinked, trying to hide the impairment. "Screw you."

He snickered. "Certainly, as soon as I get you back to my rooms."

Mia squared her shoulders. "I'll never let you touch me."

"I'll tie you down if I have to. In fact, I think that would be fun."

"Don't count on it," Jason's voice called out.

Mia gasped as Jason pointed a gun at the man holding her. Captain Stevenson, Bernard, and three of Ka'Raziel's warriors stood behind them. More warriors came in from her left from the far side of the hall.

The guard who'd hit her raised his gun, and a spear flew past Mia's face, impaling the man's hand against the wall. He stared at his skewered palm for a moment before screaming. Another Perseverance guard fired at the same second Jason did. The guard's body jolted before slamming to the floor.

Mia tried to walk, but the hallway seemed to pulse. The Perseverance soldier must have hit her harder than she'd thought.

Vincent didn't lower his saber pistol. Instead, he shoved Abigail at Jason and wrapped an arm around Mia. She felt the cold steel of the military-grade weapon pressed into her stomach as Vincent pulled another gun out of his waistband and pointed it at Jason.

He let out a dramatic sigh that seemed to be for show more than anything else. "As always, Griggs, you're in my way."

Jason had taken a few steps closer. His gaze flashed to Mia, concern mixed with horror, before the blank visage of a hardened warrior returned.

"Let's trade, Vincent, our last one," Jason said. "You give

me Mia, round up your men, and prepare for the justice of the UGA, and in exchange I won't kill any more of your people."

Jason held his weapon out to his side. It was useless at this point, anyway. Even if he were to shoot Vincent in the head, the man's fingers would still slide onto the trigger, and Mia would have a hole the size of Kansas in her stomach. She took shallow breaths, trying her best not to move as her vision started to clear.

The warriors behind them shuffled their feet. They must have seen what a saber pistol could do before, or they would have already ambushed Vincent from behind.

Jason holstered his gun and put his hands out to his sides. "Come on, Vincent. The unnecessary bloodshed needs to end."

"It does," Vincent agreed. "But this is one trade I'm going to have to refuse."

Chapter 18

JASON

Jason knew Vincent wasn't going to accept his offer, not when he had so much to lose. All the same, Jason had to buy time because time was the only gift he could give Mia, when there was a star-blasted saber-pistol pointed at her...time for him to figure out how to disarm the lunatic without that sadistic weapon going off.

"We don't need to do this. Everything just got out of hand." Jason took a steady step forward. "We're just two guys who got stranded here. We've both been desperate in our own way, but these people can help us. Don't you want to go home?"

"This is my home." Vincent's grip on Mia tightened. "I had nothing going for me on Earth. I was never the captain of my ship. My role was a mechanic. When we crashed, the captain died and my commander was weak. Someone had to take control so we didn't die."

Jason nodded and inched closer. Behind him, the warriors set their footing. He held out a hand, warning them to stay back.

He focused on Vincent. "You did good. This is stuff you should be rewarded for."

"I should be, and I am, by creating this new life for us here. Our society functions just fine. Successfully, even." Chrona paused. "No one is being forced to do anything they don't want to do, though. We're survivors, not monsters."

Says the man who just threatened to tie up a girl in his rooms, and had that same girl in the kill-range of a military-grade sniper weapon. Jason resisted the urge to leap for the gun. A younger, less cautious Jason would have taken the chance. He wasn't that man anymore, though. Not with Mia's life on the line.

Still, Jason had him talking. That was a step in the right direction. He needed to keep up the façade that they were friends.

How had Mia worded it before? "I *respect* your drive to make the best of your situation."

Vincent raised his gun higher, pointing it at Jason's face. "See, I think you're blowing smoke up my ass, because I know you want her." He yanked on Mia's hair, and she grimaced. "Which makes me want her more." He smelled her hair, the crazy slime ball.

Jason gritted his teeth to keep himself from plodding forward and breaking his ever-loving nose.

"We need women, Griggs. Without women, we don't have a colony."

"But there's nothing for you here." Jason moved closer, maybe too close. If Vincent stopped concentrating on holding two guns, he might realize Jason could almost reach Mia. "We have a chance to leave. Let's take it."

Vincent growled. "Everything is here. We have an opportunity to create one of the greatest civilizations in the galaxy. All we need is to tap into the energy running underneath that native city." He shook Mia slightly. "They haven't even begun to explore the potential of this world. We can put this planet on the map."

Wow, he was definitely a nutcase. "At the price of the people who already live here? The natives have a thriving culture—a living, breathing community."

Jason could feel the Bobonians shifting behind him. One of them gripped their spear, just inside his peripheral vision. Jason glanced at the warrior and shook his head. If spears flew, Mia would die.

"They're only savages. Did you see how they ran? They're cowards who don't deserve what this planet has to offer."

That was about all Jason could take. He made a grab for Vincent's gun with his right hand while swiping the saber pistol with his left. The military weapon went off, searing a three-foot hole in the floor at Mia's feet. She kneed Vincent in the balls and grabbed the saber pistol.

"Careful with that," Jason said, pushing Vincent against the wall and struggling for the other gun. "There are too many of us." Jason swung, cracking Vincent in the jaw. "Just give up."

"I'm not giving up to an egotistical imp with no sense of vision." Vincent head-butted him and Jason stumbled, shaking his head.

"Freeze." Mia held up the saber pistol.

"Don't touch the trigger!" Jason and Vincent yelled at the same time.

Mia's eyes went wide, and she looked down at the gun.

He could see it in her expression. She had no idea how to hold a saber pistol without it going off.

Billy, or Captain Stevenson...or whatever the hell he was calling himself these days, and the commander appeared on either side of her and reached for the weapon...slowly. Hopefully, they knew how to disarm it.

A spear throttled across the room, impaling itself in the wall centimeters from Chrona's head.

"No." Jason held up his hand. "I got this."

Vincent snickered. "You're still as arrogant as the day we met." He started circling. "You're nothing without your little fighter plane. You're just a kid lost on a planet looking for some senior officers to come and bail you out."

Jason wiped his mouth with his sleeve. "Yeah, well, this kid is about to kick your ass."

A *boom* echoed through the room, and a five-foot hole appeared in the wall. Circuits fizzled and sparked around the burned edges of the orifice that had cut clear through to the next room. Mia sat against the opposite wall, gaping, the godforsaken sniper weapon lying at her side.

Jesus! Saber pistols should all be tracked down and destroyed.

Vincent lunged at Jason, slamming him against the far wall. The man probably had a good hundred pounds on Jason, and he'd learned how to use his girth to his advantage. He shoved his thick arm against Jason's neck, pinning him.

Billy and Cortenz eased the saber pistol into a metal box. Mia's co-pilot, whatever-his-name, helped her up off the floor. The three Bobonians in sight each held a Perseverance guard against the wall.

Vincent's fetid breath puffed in Jason's face. "You're never going to learn, are you? We're not on Earth, and you're not going to luck your way into saving the day again."

"Looks to me like you're already skunked," Jason rasped, clawing at Vincent's arm.

Vincent's nose flared. "Looks to me like you're already dead." He brought the gun up to Jason's forehead.

"No!" Mia jumped on him, grabbing the gun.

Vincent laughed. "Maybe I need to teach you a lesson through more extreme methods." He kicked Mia in the gut. She grabbed her stomach and wheezed.

The stupid, useless co-pilot jumped out of the way, leaving Mia clutching her stomach.

Jason growled. "Leave her out of this."

"Both of you seem to think you have a say in the matter."

Billy moved toward them as his commander backed away balancing the container holding the saber pistol.

"Be careful what you do next, Captain." Vincent glared at Billy, then cracked Jason over the head with the butt end of the gun.

Stars blasted across Jason's vision. He slipped to the floor as Vincent released him.

The room spun around a blurry figure raising a gun in the direction where Mia had been.

Billy held up his hands and stopped his advance. "No one else needs to get hurt."

"Then keep away and let me do what I've been called to do. This is my destiny."

Destiny? For real? Jason closed his eyes against the stars and hazy vision, and lunged at Vincent. He heard the weapon cock.

This was it. Last chance. He could either be the hero everyone thought him to be, or the only woman he'd ever opened his heart to would die.

Chapter 19

MIA

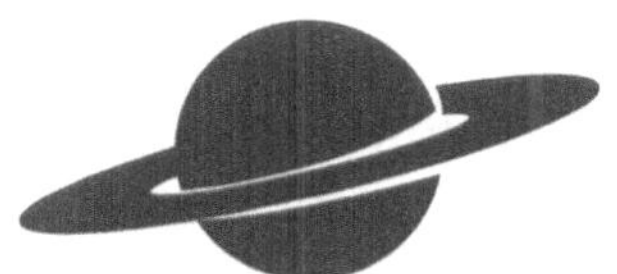

Mia's breath hitched as Jason jumped at Vincent and pulled the gun down. A loud boom echoed through the chamber, and Jason cried out, gritting his teeth and gasping for breath.

They continued to struggle for the weapon, blood smearing across the floor beneath Jason.

Mia snapped out of it and lunged for them, adding her hands atop Jason's in the struggle for the weapon.

"Give it up, Vincent," Captain Stevenson called out, his gun trained on them, but he knew as well as Mia that he didn't have a clear shot, and there was no way Jason was going to let go of the gun and give Vincent another chance to shoot someone.

Sweat broke out on Jason's brow, and Mia's gaze dropped to the growing smear of blood on the floor.

Jason paled.

"Hold on," she whispered to him through gritted teeth.

Jason blinked repeatedly. If he passed out, she'd be on her own holding Vincent back. Of course, she didn't have a hero complex. She could step away, giving Captain Stevenson a clear shot. But there would still be a chance that someone else would get hurt, and Jason was starting to swoon.

She kicked Vincent's leg twice. Jason's eyes rolled back, and in what were probably his last moments of consciousness, he threw all his weight on Vincent.

Mia pushed her own weight into the fall, and Vincent went down with them. She released the gun and sidled away, staying on her feet as the two men hit the floor.

She steadied herself, slipping on the blood, before kicking Vincent once in the head, and then spin-kicking the gun out of his hand. The weapon slid across the floor, stopping a few feet away from Bernard, who paled before a look of determination crossed his face. He picked up the gun, cocked it, and joined Captain Stevenson in advancing.

The captain yanked Vincent off Jason and pulled the man's hands behind his back.

Vincent laughed. "You haven't stopped anything. When I attacked the natives, I was doing them a favor, forcing them to evacuate before the city came tumbling down around them."

"What do you mean?" Jason groaned, blinking like he could barely see.

Mia knelt beside him, touching his forehead. He was far too cold. Blood pooled inside a bullet-sized hole on the top of his foot.

The walls shook around them again, just like they had when Mia had first boarded.

"What is that?" Mia pulled Jason's head to her, trying to give him some comfort before they could risk taking off that boot and seeing how bad the injury was.

"It's my ship's drills," Abigail said. "But why?"

Vincent snorted. "Your ship was the final piece of the puzzle we needed. It took us a while to break through your security and recalibrate the drills, but they are more than doing the job."

"The job of what?" Abigail asked.

Jason's skin grew paler. "Stay with me," she whispered. "Stay awake."

Vincent cackled. "Your drills have already tapped into the root structures flowing beneath Perseverance. By now, they've started to extract the oils running through the veins of all those massive trees."

The Life Flower. He was extracting the power source from the city, from the planet. "It can't be," Mia said. "We cut all the wires." Except the main line she'd thought might be feeding their infirmary. *Dammit!*

Abigail shook her head. "That wouldn't matter. We cut external power. Those drills are part of the ship."

Mia gripped Jason as her heart wrenched tighter. "But all those people..."

Vincent snarled. "You should all be thanking me for letting any of the natives live. They were only an annoyance."

Captain Stevenson looked at Abigail. "This is your ship? How do we stop the drills?"

"You can't." Vincent grinned. "They're on an automated cycle. You might as well let me go because this planet is already mine."

The walls around them shook again.

Mia and Abigail had cut the power. That should have at least slowed Chrona down, but this ship was far more than a power source. It was now the harbinger of death to this planet, and that wasn't something Mia could allow.

She kissed Jason on the forehead and eased him to the floor.

"Give up," Vincent told Captain Stevenson. "Join me, and I'll give you a cut of the profits. You'll make your children and your children's children rich beyond their wildest dreams."

Not in this lifetime. Mia took off down the hall.

Boots slammed on the flooring behind her, and Abigail entered the control room just as she did.

"Don't try to stop me," Mia said.

Abigail shook her head. "No way. I'm here to help. Just promise me you'll get me off this rock when this is all said and done."

"Deal."

Abigail moved into the room. "You need two people to hit the self-destruct."

"I thought it was just a button?"

Abigail opened a panel, and a red button appeared. "Both at the same time."

Failsafe. That made sense.

"How long will we have to get out?"

"Eight minutes."

Whoa. This was going to be close.

Mia's arm burned and the bleeding started anew as she pulled herself under the control panel and found the blue button. "Got it."

"Okay," Abigail called. "On three. One, two, three."

Mia slammed the heel of her palm onto the button.

The floor beneath her vibrated. The drills screeched but continued syphoning the life blood from the planet.

"Did you hit the button?" Abigail asked.

"Yes." Mia hit it again, and a flood of blue gas hit her in the face.

Abigail yanked her out by the ankles. "That's not the self-destruct." She grabbed a canister from inside a panel in the wall and sprayed it into Mia's face. "Breathe deeply."

Mia complied, and her stomach lurched. She rolled over and vomited across the tiles.

Abigail threw the canister. "This time press the red button."

The red button...stars, she knew that.

Wiping her mouth on her sleeve, Mia crawled back beneath the panel. The ship vibrated, the shake deepening.

"You're not color blind, right?" Abigail asked.

Mia gritted her teeth. She deserved that. "No. I have the red button."

"Good. Three, two, one."

Mia punched the button.

An alarm blared along with red, flashing lights. Classic signals that they had to get the heck out of there before the whole place blew. They sprinted down the hall.

Mia pulled Jason up, and Abigail took his other arm.

Searing pain burned through Mia's injured forearm as they dragged Jason toward the exit.

"What have you done?" Vincent screamed over his shoulder as Captain Stevenson shoved him down the hall.

"What I should have done the second I crashed," Abigail muttered.

"Come," Mia called to the warriors, who poked their prisoners with the spears, more worried about their duty than the impending doom that they probably couldn't even fathom.

Jason groaned. The lights flashed red on his face. "Is-Is that a self-destruct warning?"

"Yup." Mia continued to drag him.

"Stars!" He moaned again. "I take a nap and the whole world goes to hell."

"What can I say? I like to do things big." She shifted his weight on her shoulder. "My dad used to tell me bedtime stories about a hero called Captain Starlight who used to blow things up all the time."

He huffed out a pained laugh. "Yeah, but not when I was still inside them."

They moved out into the sunlight and followed the colonists and the others toward the main gate.

Mia looked at Abigail. "How far do you think the blast radius is?"

"It will only take out the immediate vicinity. The point of the self-destruct option was to keep sensitive information from getting into the wrong hands, not to hurt anyone."

They eased Jason to the ground just outside the main gates.

She felt his head. "How are you doing?"

He smiled. "Great. You want to go dancing?"

She laughed. His boot was still soaked with blood. He was probably delirious, but he wouldn't be dancing any time soon.

The ground rumbled, and the trees waved as the boom echoed through the area. Vincent cursed and kicked as Captain Stevenson continued to drag him away. What few lights were still on in the compound flittered out, their source of power—Abigail's ship—destroyed.

"It's over," Mia whispered.

Jason gave a weak nod, his skin devoid of color.

Mia glanced around, hoping to see someone with medical supplies. "You need a doctor."

He sighed. "I'm going to live. I promise."

"You think I'd let you die?" She managed a chuckle. "What kind of hero would I be if I did that?"

"A pretty bad one," he mumbled. "Which means I trained you all wrong."

Mia planted a kiss on his forehead. "Your reputation will be ruined. I refuse to allow that."

"You're a peach."

Abigail crouched beside them. "So, Captain Starlight ended up getting saved by a girl. Why am I loving this so much?"

Jason puffed out a laugh, then groaned in pain.

Mia smiled. "Take it easy."

Abigail chuckled as she pushed herself to her feet. "Keep the flyboy alive. I'll go find a medic."

Chapter 20

JASON

Hours later, Jason blinked as Doctor Kelex shined a light in his eyes. Again.

"My eyeballs are there, I swear," Jason told her.

"You've been through a lot, Captain. It's better to be safe than sorry."

Jason sighed. He just wanted to find a nice, soft bed to sleep in for a few days straight. "I feel fine. I'm just tired."

The doctor cocked a brow. "You feel fine because you're all jacked up on the best painkillers and nerve blockers the UGA has to offer. Don't mistake that for being fine."

Jason rubbed a deep ache in his spine, which was strange, if he was as jacked up as the doc seemed to think he was.

Across the room, a medic finished shining a light in Mia's eyes and spoke to her before tapping his fingers over a datapad and moving on to the next person.

Mia rubbed the top of her head and winced, smiling at him. They'd cut off the sleeve of her uniform and bandaged her arm.

Jason's stomach sank. He should have been there to make sure she didn't get hurt.

Life didn't work that way, though. He couldn't be everywhere, and with this little spitfire, he'd drive himself crazy if he tried.

He had to remember that she didn't need his protection. She'd proven that.

He'd keep that little tidbit to himself, though. Teasing her was far too much fun.

Jason tapped his palm on the gurney beside him. Mia walked over, her tread stiff, and without the *I'm-going-to-kick-your-ass* gait that he'd grown to adore.

It had been a risk to point Vincent's gun at himself, but it had been a risk worth taking since she was still here to look like death-warmed-over with him.

The mattress jumped as she plopped beside him. "Are you going to live?"

"Yeah. Sorry to disappoint you." He took a moment to enjoy her smile. "I got lucky. It was a clean wound. The bullet went straight through my foot."

"Only you would think that was lucky."

"Hey, I still have a foot. And it won't take that long to heal. I'm an optimist, what can I say?" Anytime you finished a mission alive was lucky. After she'd been out in space for a while, she'd realize that.

The doorway slid open and Billy—no, Captain Stevenson —approached them.

"I've got Chrona and his main followers locked up in the brig," he said. "As much as I wanted to confine them all, we don't have the space." He adjusted his stance.

Jason hoped that he still didn't make the kid uncomfortable. Jason laughed to himself. *Kid...* Billy looked older than Jason now. It was quite a bit to get his head around.

"A few of the others swore they only followed Vincent for the sake of survival," the captain said. "They don't have any interest in actually carrying out his mission."

"And you believe them?" Mia asked.

Billy—Dammit!—*Captain Stevenson* nodded. "Our ship psychologist does, too. The fact that they want to stay behind and help rebuild Malashra is a good sign as well."

He looked across the room at the other people being treated by his small medical team. A smile played across his lips. He was proud of his people, and with good reason. With that many casualties, their training was really shining through.

"The men in the brig are being very vocal about what they plan to do once they escape. Dr. Johnson is about to sedate them so we don't have to deal with any more problems." He returned his gaze to them. "Once we get back to UGA territory, we can hand them over for trial."

Jason gripped the edge of the bed. This wasn't a UGA world. All those men had coming to them was a slap on their hands and some community service time. "Galactic law states that Ka'Raziel and her people get first crack at them," Jason said.

Billy shifted his weight again. Jason wished he hadn't sounded so harsh, so commanding, but the Bobonians deserved justice.

"The laws have changed some since you've been active," the captain said. "But they will get a say in what justice should look like." He turned to Mia. "These men committed crimes against female members of the UGA as well, so they will probably be prosecuted for crimes against humanity first."

Jason pursed his lips. What he wanted to do was pull Vincent Chrona out of the brig and fight him one on one, sans guns. The idiot needed to be put in his place—in front of his men, if possible. The UGA would never allow that, though.

"We should be ready to take off within a week, as long as there aren't any more interruptions," the captain said.

Stars, it was hard dealing with him being a captain. This kid was barely able to keep his shit together when Jason had known him. Billy had done good for himself, though. He'd earned Jason's respect in ways that he probably never would have in the seat of a fighter plane.

Mia rubbed Jason's shoulder. It was a few seconds of bliss in all this craziness.

"It's going to be amazing to get you home," she said. "Everyone's going to be so excited."

There was a little glimmer in both her and Billy's eyes. He could see the media storm now.

When he was younger, he'd ignored his face in all the news feeds. He knew, though, that he'd always been great fodder for the reporters on Earth.

It was later, after saving that civilian cruiser from the space pirates, when he'd started enjoying the attention, the parties, the girls.

The media were probably the ones who'd given him the honorary rank of Captain, when he'd only been a lieutenant commander when he'd disappeared.

He smiled at each of them. These two, and maybe the rest of the Alpha Cent crew, were about to be immortalized in the history feeds. Too bad it wasn't going to be as soon as they thought.

Jason sighed and shook his head. "I have to stay here for a little while longer. If there's any hope of rebuilding, I need to make sure the process goes smoothly between the Bobonians and the people who are staying behind to help. I'm the only one who speaks both languages."

The hand on his shoulder stopped moving. Mia's touch turned to stone. He probably should have dropped that little bomb on her alone. She deserved that much. There just hadn't been time.

Mia lowered her hand to her lap and stared at her fingers.

She looked frail in that moment, and he hated himself for it. She was probably the biggest badass he knew, next to him. And oddly enough, he liked it.

She raised her gaze. "You're right. There's still a lot that needs to be done here." She turned to her captain. "With your permission, sir, I'd like to stay and help with the rebuild."

Whoa. Now *that* was unexpected. Every vibe he got from her was the headstrong hero type. She belonged in the stars, getting in trouble with her superiors and saving lives.

Heroes swooped in, saved the day, and left the cleanup to others. It was just the way they were made.

Which seemed a little odd, come to think of it, since there wasn't even a question in his mind that he should stay and be a liaison between the Bobonians and the humans.

He cocked his head at her. "You sure?"

"I'd hate to miss out on such a huge opportunity. We might be able to convince the people of this world to join the UGA."

Captain Stevenson frowned. "That's not really the job of a pilot."

"I know." Her hand slipped into Jason's. "But they know me now. The natives will hopefully trust me, and I can help keep things running smoothly."

Billy grimaced. "The only reason the Alpha Cent is in one piece is because you were flying her. I can't take the risk of fighting our way out of this planet's atmosphere, and then having the nebula pull us back down. Bernard is good, but he isn't you."

Jason cringed. The g-forces when his plane bad been crashing down...the way the nebula had come alive around him... It had taken months for the nightmares to abate. It had taken everything he had to keep his one-manned fighter from breaking apart.

Mia must be one hell of a pilot to bring the Alpha Cent down in one piece. The damage he'd seen appeared to be mostly from hitting trees during the last few minutes of the crash. All the other ships that had come down were in far worse shape.

"He might be right," Jason said.

Her eyes flashed at him. He had to look away.

He hated siding with Billy on this one. "They need a damn good pilot to get them out of this."

Her nosed flared. "Bernard is good."

Billy snorted. "Bernard is a good kid, but he probably peed himself on the way down. I need a pilot with balls, excuse my French."

Mia's chin lifted.

It had been a long time since Jason had disappeared, and things had obviously changed, but he had the feeling that she'd fought hard to get that kind of respect, and it looked like she relished it. Good for her. She deserved it.

"I need you, Walton," Billy said. "I'm sorry, but I can't approve you to stay."

She nodded, torn somewhere between duty and disappointment.

Billy cut through the tension by plowing on to the topic at hand, just like a good captain should. "We're timing the storm to choose our escape vector. It seems like the best chance is going to be in about five days." His gaze carried between them. "I suggest you two take care of whatever unfinished business you have in that time."

Jason's cheeks heated, and Mia flushed a damn cute red. It took everything he had not to pull her down onto that cot and give her a kiss to end all kisses...commanding officer watching or not.

She straightened. "Deep Space Supply Station Seventeen

will be in-line to bring the Alpha Cent in for a standard over-haul on the way to Earth."

Billy's eyes narrowed. "Yeah. So?"

Mia took a deep breath. "With your permission, I can get the Alpha Cent there and pick up a ship to return ASAP to assist Lieutenant Commander Griggs. Bernard is more than capable of flying the easy trip to Earth."

Billy folded his arms. "You actually think anyone is going to risk coming back here?"

She held her beautiful head high. "I landed this ship. I could certainly land a one-man craft with better maneuver-ability, especially now that I know what to expect."

Jason opened his mouth to say god-knew-what, but her gaze lanced him.

Instead, he closed his lips and pretended to adjust his bandage. Damn, she was beautiful when she wanted some-thing, and far be it for him to interrupt when he wanted the same thing.

Billy smiled. "You certainly are every bit the spitfire your instructors warned me about."

Mia's cheek ticked. "Is that a bad thing, sir?"

Billy shook his head. "Nope. Not at all."

She jumped off the cot. "Good. Because I'm also inter-ested in studying the time differential, if there is one." She turned to Jason. "I want you to count time starting at my departure. I'll run clocks as well, and we will match them up when I return. I'm guessing they won't be the same."

Jason raised a brow. "What if you get back and I'm an old man?"

"With my luck, you'd just get younger and more ornery."

He laughed. "Ornery. I like that one."

Billy shook Jason's hand. "It's a pleasure to have you back, Lieutenant Commander." Then, to Mia, "I need you ready to depart in five days. Will you be staying on the ship?" His gaze flashed to Jason.

"I think I'd like to show her more of the planet," Jason said. "Especially if she'll be coming back."

Billy smiled wryly. "Showing her the planet...riiiight." He saluted and headed out the door. "Five days," he called over his shoulder.

Mia looked down at Jason's bandaged foot. "Are you up for the walk to Malashra? It might be too soon for that much activity."

Malarsha... He'd have to get used to all the new names people would start calling things. All he really wanted to do was return to his little hut and decompress, but that was too small for both him and Mia.

He slipped off the gurney, testing his weight by taking a step. "It actually feels pretty good. As long as we take it slow..."

"Painkillers," Doctor Kelex called out from across the room. "Remember, without me, you'd be lying in that bed whimpering like a puppy lost outside in the rain."

Jason smiled. "Then can I have a doggy bag?"

The doctor nodded. "Give me a few minutes."

"Walking on it might hurt it worse," Mia pointed out.

"I know, but I'd rather recover with the tribe than here. I think that it's important that they see me. There's a shortcut we can take."

His mind returned to the elevator-like ride he'd taken to escape. It worked both ways, and it certainly explained a lot about how the warriors and hunters got around so quickly.

Mia put his arm over her shoulders so he could use her for support. "Fine, but you're not putting pressure on it. I'd carry you, but something tells me you'd fight too much about it."

"I don't think even the natives would let me live it down if you carried me into the city."

She snorted as the doctor gave him a bag.

"Directions are inside on the bottles," Doctor Kelex said. "Don't deviate. You'll regret it. Right now you're running on nerve blockers, but they'll start to wear off within six hours or so."

Yeah, he wasn't looking forward to that.

The doctor pointed to Jason's injury. "And keep that foot elevated as long as possible." She handed Jason a crutch before he turned to Mia. "Make sure he uses this, and don't let him walk too much."

Mia nodded.

Obviously, the doctor had no idea how far they were planning on walking or that they'd be navigating a jungle. Tonight would probably be painful, painkillers or not. Being wrapped in the arms of a beautiful, headstrong, capable woman, though, would make it all worthwhile.

Jason's crutch actually made a fairly decent walking stick as they made their way through the brush. Mia did her best to assist him while keeping back enough to help him save face with the natives who he was sure were watching them.

Something dropped out of the trees, and Mia grabbed for her sidearm.

Jason threw out his arm. "No. It's Dobby."

His Bobonian friend pushed up onto his hind legs, balanced somewhat by his long tail.

"Hey, buddy." Jason scratched him behind one of his long ears.

Dobby dropped down on all fours, sniffed his injured foot, and moaned.

"Yeah, bad man shot Griggs. I'll be fine, though, I promise."

Dobby returned to two feet again and put Jason's arm over his shoulder, like Mia.

"You guys." Jason laughed. "I'm not a complete invalid."

Dobby moaned and barked at Mia.

She smiled, maneuvering them forward. "Yes, he can be incredibly stubborn."

Jason frowned at her. "That's not what he said."

She shrugged. "That's what I heard."

A two-toned nut-stealer rat scampered up a tree beside them. Dobby hissed, dropped Jason, and bolted up the same tree. Jason grabbed Mia for support before he regained his footing.

"What was that?" Mia asked.

Jason looked up into the trees. There was no sign of either Dobby or the rat anymore. "Have you ever seen a dog freak out over a squirrel?"

"Of course."

"Same thing."

Mia held his arm to help him over a fallen tree. The sounds of Bob enveloped them: clean, pure, and everything an unadulterated planet should be. Hopefully, humanity wouldn't change this. Worlds like this really needed to be protected.

Mia gazed up at a cluster of seedling hungry flowers clinging to a tree as they passed. She smiled, and Jason warmed inside.

The normal human reaction would be to smash those little guys before they grew up into something big enough to swallow someone. They didn't need to be destroyed, though. The Bobonians had learned to live in harmony with the planet. Everything had its place, and all things were respected. Vincent had called the natives *savage cowards*. In truth, Perseverance could have learned a lot from them.

Mia expertly navigated around a patch of sticky webs. She'd picked up on how to hone in on her surroundings far faster than he'd done when he'd first crashed here.

He leaned on her, passing the last spider warren. "Heck of a few days, huh?"

Mia shoved away some of the brush. "That's an understatement."

Dammit, he hated small talk. He hated beating around the bush even more. He loved this planet, and he loved... The slight jungle haze cast a glow over Mia's skin, the strong lines in her face, the determined set of her jaw.

Screw it. He needed to know what was really going on. The pilot in him needed to know the mission, the stakes, and the intended outcome.

He stopped and turned to her. "Are you really coming back?"

She cocked her head to the right. "Yes, of course."

Part of him wanted her to say *no*, to confirm that she would be safe. "Reentry in a one-man fighter is going to be a bitch. I scored a 257 on my last pilot reflex scan, and I barely held on." He didn't mean to brag. That was the highest score anyone had ever seen on a response test. He just wanted her to realize the danger.

She smirked. "I scored a 260."

He balked. "You did not."

Her grin widened. "I was the first person ever to beat Captain Starlight—and a woman, no less." She laughed. "Boy, were the guys I tested with pissed."

Damn. This girl never ceased to impress him. Now he had a new goal: Get back into a pilot's seat and score a 261. She, of course, would then be gunning for a 262, but friendly competition that kept you sharp also kept you alive. He was good with that.

He needed to stop shoveling crap, though. If he was really fifty-four years old, he needed to put it all out there. He ran his hand down her cheek. "If you are coming back here to be with me, and you crash on reentry, I'll never be able to forgive myself."

Her gaze dropped to the ground. She stepped away. "I'm not just coming to be here with you. This is an amazing opportunity. How many times do you get to put a brand new planet on the map, let alone make sure it is protected?" He raised a brow, and she laughed again. "I mean, unless you're Captain Starlight. What is this, your fifth new planet?"

He smiled. "Sixth, but who's counting?"

She stepped closer. "You're really worried about me?"

Okay, thirty years ago the correct response would be to say *yes* and then talk about trying to protect her and keep her safe forevermore. Somehow, he was reasonably certain that response would earn him a crack across the mouth.

Truth was, though, that the damsel-in-distress type who'd always fawned all over him back home had never really interested him like Mia did. This girl could kick a guy's ass three ways from Sunday. It was a rush to be fighting alongside someone rather than constantly worried she might break a nail and cry.

How could he tell her that, though, and sound genuine? He took a deep breath, feeling like a dinosaur when in his own mind he was still a twenty-four-year-old in his prime.

He leaned on his crutch and met her gaze. "Yeah, I'm worried because the nebula isn't safe, but if anyone can get back, it's you. And..." *Okay, here it goes.* "I want you here. I enjoy your company. I like how you appreciate this world as much as I do." He gulped. "I think the warriors will respect you because I respect you."

Her brow furrowed. "Just respect?"

He shook his head, taking her chin between his fingers. "It's a hell of a lot more than respect, and I think you know that." He leaned down and brushed his lips over hers. She was warm and soft and everything a woman should be. If he'd met her before crashing on Bob, he'd probably have hightailed it into his plane and made a run for it.

Now, though, this connection—this sense of finding his equal—sent a tingling through his core. This could be *it* for him. He never really thought about what *it* was, but now that he'd found her, he wasn't willing to give her up without a fight. Too bad he had to crash and be stranded on an alien world for thirty years to finally realize what he wanted and have the balls to go for it.

They'd only be here for a few months while the city was rebuilt, and then Jason would see to it that all humanity, including him and Mia, left the planet, allowing the Bobonian culture to grow and thrive without human intervention. It was the right thing to do.

That would mean bringing Mia back to the real world, though. She wouldn't be tied to a planet with him. She'd be open to a universe of possibilities.

He turned and looked into the trees. He wasn't ready to think about that yet.

Right now, it seemed like he had her. Now he just needed to figure out how to keep her, no matter what planet they were on.

Chapter 21

MIA

Mia closed her eyes, feeling the imminent pull of planetary re-entry, wishing she had the controls. Today, though, she had more important things to attend to.

"Preparing to enter the atmosphere," Bernard announced over the intercom.

Mia squeezed Jason's hand. "Are you ready?"

"I don't think I have a choice." He turned to the window, where a quarter of the Earth, mostly covered with clouds, but as beautiful as ever, zoomed up and filled the window.

His grip on Mia tightened as he leaned back in his chair.

She held firm, here for him no matter what. The debriefing on Deep Space Supply Station Seventeen had been grueling for Jason. It had seemed like half of the staff had been sent there to try to prove it wasn't really him, while the other half was there to kiss his ass and make him feel welcome. She guessed she shouldn't have expected less. This was a lot for everyone to take in, maybe Jason most of all.

She'd tried her best to cut through the red tape and get information on Jason's parents, but she'd hit a black hole. The only communication that came back to her was that "the family had been notified." Not very helpful. However, that did allude to the fact that there would be *someone* waiting for him. They just had no idea who.

She'd been lucky enough to score a twenty-minute intergalactic call to her sister when she'd reached the supply station with the Alpha Cent five weeks ago. She'd asked June to get information about Jason's family, but most of the files had been secured at the request of the Griggs household not long after Jason had disappeared. Apparently, the pressure of being the family of Captain Starlight had been a little much for them, even after his presumed death.

Her sister had found a few men and women named Griggs in the military with locked personnel files. June thought that might be a good place to start, but beyond that, they weren't able to get any solid information on who Jason might be coming home to.

Jason frowned, closing his eyes.

The *not knowing* was killing him. He'd called for his father a few times in his sleep over the last few weeks and opened up to her a few days ago about how thoughts of his family haunted him day and night. She wished she could have given him some comfort, but the military would only allow essential information to travel through the communication pathways.

Mia grimaced at the bureaucracy. Jason Griggs was a hero, for goodness' sake. They couldn't spare a few megabytes of data to tell him if his parents were alive?

June had told tell her that the media was already abuzz. No one could believe Captain Starlight was coming home. His action figures were selling at astronomical bid prices on the web, just like they had when he'd first disappeared.

For Mia, only ten weeks had passed since the Alpha Cent had landed at Deep Space Supply Station Seventeen and they'd reported to the world that Jason Griggs had been found alive. After she'd spoken to her sister, she'd grabbed the first plane they'd been willing to "sacrifice" for her to return to the planet Jason had lovingly referred to as *Bob*.

She and Jason had spent about a month rebuilding the city, and then an additional month working on rebuilding and fostering diplomatic relations with the Bobonians, and then another five weeks on their journey home. However, due to Bob's time difference, nearly a year had passed since the reports of Jason's rescue had hit the news feeds.

Mia's sister had said the reporters were still camped out on her parents' lawn, hoping for word. Why the news thought her family would be a priority to anyone in the military, she didn't know.

June had started joking with her, referring to her as "her little sister, the hero." She didn't know about all that, but it was going to be nice to be home for a few weeks.

"Hold tight," Bernard called over the speakers.

Mia smiled at the sound of his voice, so much more sure of himself that when they'd last flown together. Over the past year, the Alpha Cent had been running maneuvers near the Centroid asteroid belt. Bernard had earned his wings in the school of hard knocks...or careening asteroids, as it might be. Mia was glad Captain Stevenson had lobbied for the honor of bringing her and Jason home.

The ship began to shake. Jason's breath hitched and she had to remind herself that it had been thirty years—longer than her lifetime—since he'd felt the gyrations of reentry.

Her gaze carried over the strong etch of his jaw and his nearly perfect skin. He barely looked older than her. The medical world was about to have a field day when they saw him. Hopefully, they would not have to fend off age-defying scientists as well as the alternate energy engineers to keep the newest planet in the universe safe.

The rattle evened out, and Bernard coasted them over the

North American Continent until they reached UGA head-quarters in Anchorage.

Jason rubbed his face after the engines throttled down, and the green lights came on in the cabin.

Mia stood, trying to act as natural as she could to ease his nerves. "Home sweet home."

His expression read blank when he turned to her, the perfect, unreadable visage of a well-trained academy veteran. His eyes told her a completely different story, though.

"You okay?" It was a dumb question. She knew he wasn't okay.

He drew her into his arms. "I never thought I'd see Earth again." He held her, his hands shaking slightly on her back. "I'm not sure I belong here anymore. So much has changed."

She gave him a kiss. His touch was tentative, lacking the passion they'd shared so many nights in the small, quaint Bobonian hut they'd called home.

"Do you still belong with me?" she asked.

He touched his forehead to hers, smiling. "You know it."

"Then you belong here because I'm here."

He shook his head. "That's not what I meant. You have a family to come back to. I have…"

She put her finger over his lips. "The UGA has been assholes, not sending you more information. I'm sorry about that. But no matter what, my family will be here, and you will always have a home on Earth with us."

He pulled her into his arms. She thought she heard him sniff, and she just held him, letting him work out whatever was going on in his head. For now, just being here was the most she could do for him—making sure he didn't feel alone. If she had her way, he'd never be alone again.

He laughed, drawing away and wiping his eyes. "Look at me, the big hero."

She ruffled his hair. "You're just tired, but you'll always be my hero, no matter what."

Bernard cleared his throat from the doorway. "Not to break up your mushy romantic talk, but there's a welcoming committee gathered on the landing pad. Time to turn on that legendary grin, Captain Starlight."

Jason stiffened. "Civilians? My family?"

Bernard glanced at Mia, then to Jason. "It doesn't look like it. I'd say it was a pretty official gathering, with some reporters, from what I could see."

Jason flinched. "Great."

"Shall we?" Bernard waved them through the door, and they followed.

As they neared the already-opened exit ramp, the sound of the crowd began to echo off the walls. Jason's jaw seemed clenched so hard, Mia could practically hear his teeth grind.

"It's okay." She squeezed his bicep. "I'm here."

He gave a curt nod. "It's just been a long time."

Captain Stevenson stood on one side of the exit, Commander Cortenz on the other. The captain beamed with a broad smile, and he began clapping as they drew near. Jason's breath hitched as they stepped out onto the gangplank, and the crowd rose into a roar.

They'd landed in a huge, pristine docking bay. Royal and presidential insignias, some familiar, some unknown, hung on the walls near the ceilings.

Stars, this was the massive receiving chamber set aside for...

Mia tensed. At the bottom of the platform, the Prime Minister stood and smiled, clapping her hands.

Dammit. If the Prime Minister was here, that meant this was an exclusive military event. Even if Jason's parents were alive, they wouldn't be able to attend due to security protocols.

Cameras flashed by the dozens, and people held up banners.

"Welcome Back, Captain Griggs."

"Starlight Returns to the Galaxy."

"Welcome Home, Mia."

"Mia Brings Back the Starlight."

Jason snorted. "Looks like I have a little competition for the hero award."

Mia closed her gaping jaw as a young officer in a very crisp, pristine UGA uniform walked up the gangway.

He saluted Mia, then Jason. "Lieutenant Commander Griggs, they've given me the honor of walking you out, sir."

Jason startled, probably not used to people knowing his actual rank. He remembered himself and returned the salute.

The younger man straightened his already stiff posture. "Sir, if I may, it is an incredible honor to be here to represent the UGA and our family." He lowered his hand from his forehead.

Jason visibly balked. "Did you say *our* family?"

Captain Stevenson stepped out and placed his hand on Jason's arm. "If I may, I'd like to introduce you to your nephew, Lieutenant Junior Grade, Jason Nathanial Griggs."

Chapter 22

JASON

Jason stared, forgetting to breathe, looking into eyes far too much like his own. After a moment, he was able to get his lips to move. "Are-Are you Jillian's son?" Stars, his sister had named her kid after him?

The officer smiled. "No, sir. Aunt Jillian has all girls. Nat Griggs is my father."

Jason took half a step back. It couldn't be. It wasn't possible. "Nat was sixteen when I left for my last mission."

Jason's nephew kept his posture stiff. "You've been gone a long time, sir."

Jason fought the tremble in his lip. This kid was little Natty's son?

Shit! He really *had* been gone thirty years.

He'd missed his baby brother growing up, getting married, and having kids. Stars of Mars, how much more had he missed?

He reached out to shake his nephew's hand. "I'd really like to spend some time talking as soon as all this is done." Hopefully, this kid would be able to fill in the blanks that the UGA couldn't.

Natty's boy saluted again. "I'd like that very much, sir." He spun, the perfect, stiff soldier. "Now, if you'll follow me, sir, ma'am?"

Cameras flashed as they walked down the gangway. Jason tried to remember the best angle to give them for a perfect picture, the best place to stop and pose, ensuring a portrait to light up the news feeds, but he couldn't do anything more than scan the crowd. Thirty years ago he would have eaten up this kind of attention, but now, he just wanted to pull this kid leading him to the podium into a quiet room and ask him questions.

A woman in a tailored black suit stood smiling beside the lectern. "Lieutenant Commander Griggs, welcome home." She reached out to him. Her tightly pulled-back blonde hair seemed to stretch her features.

He shook her hand. "Thanks."

She smirked before turning to Mia. "Air Pilot Walton, good work."

Mia shook her hand vigorously. "Prime Minister, it is an incredible honor."

Jason cringed as the leader of the North American Federation faced him. "Sorry, ma'am. I didn't realize..."

She smiled warmly. "No offense taken, Lieutenant Commander. You have thirty years to catch up on."

She leaned closer to the microphone and started speaking. A sea of faces looked up at Jason. In the past, he'd make eye contact with every single one of them for at least 1.5 seconds...longer if it were a pretty girl. Connections with fans were a must.

He sickened himself thinking about it. Yeah, he'd done every last crazy thing they said he'd done. He'd discovered worlds and saved lives...and he'd eaten up every second of the accolades. What an idiot he'd been.

In the end, it all meant nothing when he'd been stuck on an alien world, fighting for his life and struggling to make friends with the natives.

The Prime Minister continued, "And in agreement and support of the UGA, we'd like to officially grant Jason Griggs the title that the world has known him by since I was a child."

He turned to her, his brow furrowed.

She held up a pin with three stars encased in a blue oval. "Congratulations, *Captain* Griggs." The crowd erupted in cheers as she placed the pin on Jason's uniform.

Tears glistened on Mia's cheeks as she applauded.

Jason appreciated her sincerity, but she should be the one getting a promotion. She was the one who'd saved him, not the other way around.

The Prime Minister continued her banter as Mia reached out and took Jason's hand.

"Well deserved," she whispered.

Jason shook his head. "If you say so. All I did was hole up on a jungle planet for thirty years."

"And find another planet, represent and support the ideals of the UGA, and fight off an illegal occupational force. Didn't you listen to a word the Prime Minister said?"

He shrugged. "No, not really. I've never listen to their speeches when they…"

"Get out of my way!" A woman pushed through the crowd. "I *said* get out of my way."

Two security officers moved toward her from opposite sides of the crowd.

Natty's boy left Jason's side and pushed into the crowd ahead of them. "Stand down," he told the guard, although Jason doubted a junior ranking officer had the authority to tell anyone to do anything, let alone stand down.

The woman pushed ahead until she saw Jason. She froze, staring, her lips parted.

Jason's gaze carried over her long, curly, gray hair, her

lined face, and eyes that matched the junior officer at her side...eyes that also matched his own.

He gulped the painful ball building in his throat. "Mom?"

She reached up and touched her lips before she reached out to him. "Jason?"

He leapt off the platform, slamming onto the ground. She met him halfway, Natty's boy running interference, until she was in Jason's arms.

"It's you. It's really you." She grabbed his face and covered him with kisses. "Your father always knew you were alive. He always said you would come home."

Jason held in his tears, ignoring the maelstrom of camera flashes as he tried to scan the crowd. "Dad?"

Little Nat grabbed Jason's shoulder. "Grandpa died six years ago."

No. It couldn't be.

Jason ground his teeth together, pulling his mother to him. "Oh, Mom, I'm so sorry. Stars, I should have been here. I- I should have..."

What was left of his heart broke into a sob. He buried his face in her hair as the sound of cameras and people scrambling for a better shot erupted through the room.

"Let's get them to a more secure location." Mia's voice came from somewhere close, but Jason couldn't move, couldn't look up, couldn't care for anything other than holding his mother close, needing her like a child, and making up for thirty years of leaving her alone and wondering.

"But the ceremony!" The Prime Minister's voice rose above the clatter, probably closer to the microphone than she'd intended, and someone pushed Jason and his mother through the crowd.

The noise abated as they moved through a stark, white hallway, and they were ushered through another door.

Several people were inside, and rose to their feet when Jason entered.

Shit. Jason just wanted to spend time with his mother. The last thing he needed was another sit-down with higher-ups who he'd never even heard of.

Anytime he'd been pushed into a side room was always a pain in his ass. This was the part where he usually got yelled at, even though he'd just saved the universe.

"Jay?"

He stiffened, hearing his sister's voice.

Jason jerked up, still clutching his mother. Jillian's hands were over her mouth. A slight hint of gray held at her temples, and she'd gained about twenty pounds, but she'd never looked so beautiful.

"Jill?" He released his mother and hugged his sister. "I never thought I'd see you guys again."

She sniffed and pulled away. "David, my husband, is coming. His ship lands tomorrow, but these are my kids." She motioned to three women, probably in their late twenties or early thirties. "Mary, Simpka, and Allison."

The pain in his throat returned. They all looked his age or older. How could that be? The last family event he'd attended was Allison's christening, and here she was, now, a full-grown woman.

Allison pulled a little girl, about eight years old, toward her. "This is my little girl, Uncle Jay. This is Emily."

Stars... How? He crouched. "Hi, Emily."

She smiled and waved. There they were again—his eyes on a pint-sized person. And this wasn't even his sister's kid. This was his sister's kid's kid.

He looked up at his mom. "You're a..."

His mother beamed. "Great-grandmother." She held up her hands. "Funny how that happens, huh?"

And he'd missed it. He should be fifty-four years old by now. He should be giving her grandchildren himself.

"Hey, spitfire."

Jason turned. His breath caught, gazing into the eyes of his father. His world spun. He stumbled back.

The guy gaped. He held up his hands. "Jay, it's me, Nat."

Jason released his breath. Hell, he looked exactly like he remembered his dad looking the last time Jason had seen him.

"Natty?" Jason hugged him. "Stars, man, I can't believe it."

Nat tapped his back. "I knew you were too much of a badass to let a little nebula get you." He pulled away. "I see you've already met my son, Jay."

The Lieutenant Junior Grade nodded.

"Jay was happy to take up the family tradition where you left off. He's taking the UGA by storm."

"Not you?" Jason asked.

Nat shook his head. "Nope, I'm an accountant." He held out a hand to a pretty woman with short, brown hair. "This is my wife, Carmen."

Jason shook her hand. "A pleasure, ma'am." Skies, that sounded stupid, calling her *ma'am*, but how was he supposed to act when his baby brother, and his baby brother's wife, were decades older than he was?

He had some introducing to do too, though. Out of this whole fiasco, there was one bright shining star. He looked over his shoulder. "Where's Mia?"

Chapter 23

MIA

Mia tried to change the viewscreen on the wall in her private receiving room. She appreciated the quiet and the spread of food displayed on a table against the wall, but she wanted to know where they'd taken Jason and his mother.

Her sister, June, tied her blonde hair up in a messy ponytail before she plucked a deviled egg from a silver tray. "So, why didn't they give you a promotion? You're the one who saved the ship from crashing."

"I'm barely out of the academy." Mia turned away from the view screen, showing the reporters still out in the main hall.

"Who cares? Girl power and all that. You're the chick who saved Captain Starlight. You deserve all the props for that."

She obviously didn't understand how the UGA worked, which was fine. Jason, on the other hand, had thirty years of living up to the UGA standard. *Captain* was too tame a title.

Mia rubbed the back of her neck. They probably would leave him *captain* for a while, wait for him to do something amazing again, and then give him another promotion. Heck, if he managed not to piss too many people off, he'd probably have been a general by now. Although, through Jason's own admission, the chances of him not pissing off every commanding officer in the fleet were fairly slim.

June pulled Mia down beside her on the couch. "So, fess up. Please tell me the rumors are true."

Mia raised a brow. "Which rumors?"

"That you really stayed on that jungle planet because you were boinking Captain Starlight."

"Did you actually just use the word *boinking*?"

That earned her a playful punch in the shoulder. "Come on. Please tell me you know how good he is in bed. This is like every fangirl's dream come true."

Mia supposed it was. "I hated him at first, to be honest." She smiled. "But I guess he's an acquired taste."

June's eyes widened. "So you *did* boink him." She fist pumped in the air. "You go, girl. Now you have to tell me every last dirty detail."

Yeah, like that was ever going to happen.

The door opened and the Prime Minister walked in. Mia jumped to her feet and saluted.

June eased up beside her. "Is that who I think it is?"

The Prime Minister shook Mia's hand. "Pilot, things got cut a little short out there, but I wanted you to know that we are grateful for all of your hard work. Without your initiative, not only would your crew have been lost upon landing, but our new peace alliance with the people of Marshala would not have come to fruition."

Marshala—the planet Jason had referred to as *Bob* for so long. Marshala meant *Great Place* in the native language. It was already the name of the city they'd helped rebuild, and Mia couldn't think of a more appropriate name for their world to be registered under in the official UGA guidebook.

Mia gave the Prime Minister another salute. "Ma'am, I

was merely serving my planet and my people. I did what was needed for us to stay alive."

"Your insistence on preserving culture stands out the most." The Prime Minister returned the salute. "I lobbied for a promotion for you as well."

"Damn straight," June mumbled behind her.

"But the UGA apparently has levels of achievement to obtain. You are well on your way, though."

Being honored fresh out of the academy was almost unheard of. Except, maybe, for an upstart pilot who'd discovered a rogue, populated world while taking an unsanctioned joyride that should have gotten him court-martialed. But not everyone could be Captain Starlight and get away with it.

The Prime Minister continued. "What I *was* able to get them to agree to is assigning you to the ship of your choice. Now, we'd rather not unseat a pilot in good standing, so if you could provide us a list of possibilities and your interests, we'll have you well on your way to that promotion."

Wow. That was unheard of in itself. "Thank you, ma'am."

She nodded. "Frankly, we need more people like you out there who are interested in working with new worlds as opposed to altering them."

That meant Mia could be placed on another deep-space ship. Maybe an explorer rather than a search and rescue. She could be in the thick of it, searching for new worlds.

A smile crept onto her lips. She tried to not let it grow too wide. It'd be immature of her to go into a fit of giggles, but she was about to explode with excitement. Wait until she told Jason.

"Thank you, ma'am. I won't let you down." Mia took the Prime Minister's outstretched hand and shook. "If I may ask, how are the proceedings going for Vincent Chrona's trial?"

The Prime Minister grimaced as if a foul smell had wafted into the room. "The lawyers have finished submitting all of their evidence. Your testimonies will be needed as well, though I've been assured you won't need to be in court to give them. They can be delivered through a video conference."

She glanced at a screen over Mia's shoulder, showing Mia and Jason stepping out of the Alpha Cent for the first time.

"Mr. Chrona is expected to plead guilty to the charges to avoid a harsher sentence. We expect his defense council to argue for insanity."

"He's definitely insane." Mia tried to not let her bitterness show.

In truth, she didn't know what might have happened to her if she'd been trapped on that planet for as long as Jason had. She wasn't sure she would have fared as well. She might have joined the colony, just to be around other people, even if she didn't agree with their politics.

Then she'd probably try to dismantle it from within, of course. Needing company wouldn't change her need to do the right thing.

"The rest of the crew is getting off a bit lighter," the Prime Minister continued. "Some of them claim they did what they could to protect the women from the other men. Their stories are quite remarkable."

Mia hoped they spoke to the other women to corroborate which were decent, and which were on board with Vincent's impending reign of terror. "Whatever you need me to do to make this process as efficient as possible, I'll do it."

"We appreciate that, pilot." She glanced at June. "Please take a few more minutes with your family, and then we'll need a last debriefing with the UGA before you'll be released for a one month required R and R."

Required? "But—"

She held up her hand. "No buts. Enjoy your time on Earth, pilot."

What was she supposed to do on Earth for a month? "If I

may, ma'am, is the UGA enforcing an R and R protocol for Captain Griggs as well?"

A sweet smile crossed the Prime Minister's lips. "Of course."

Mia fluffed her hair as she and Jason walked up to his mother's house.

"You look fine," he told her.

But she needed to look more than fine. She pulled down the hem of her black cocktail dress. "I'm meeting your family for the first time. I need to make a good impression."

He laughed, pulling her in for a kiss. "You're the woman who bought me home. You've already made a good impression."

But that wasn't enough. Why did men always oversimplify things like this? Jason was the oldest son. His mom would have preconceived notions of the type of woman she wanted for him. She needed to make the grade, or things would be awkward.

Jason kissed her on the nose. "You are perfect, you look amazing, and they are going to love you as much as I do."

Mia smoothed her skirt. Hopefully, he was right.

Jason rang the bell and a little girl answered.

"Hello, Emily," Jason said.

Her gaze scanned to Mia, and her lips formed an 'O'. She ran back into the house. "Mom, Grandma! She's here. Mia's here!"

A middle-aged woman with kind eyes came to the door. "Hello, little brother." She gave Jason a kiss on the cheek then held her hand out to Mia. "Hi, I'm Jillian."

Mia shook her hand. "It's a pleasure. I'm Mia."

Jillian laughed. "Oh, we know. The president of your fanclub just answered the door."

Another woman with long, curly, gray hair came from the back of the house. "There they are." She gave Jason a hug and a kiss on the cheek, then turned to Mia. "Ah, Mia, you are even more beautiful in person than on television. I'm sorry for not introducing myself at the UGA, but I was a little over-whelmed at the time."

Mia smiled. "Understandable, ma'am."

She waved her hand in front of her face. "Now, none of that military hogwash here. You'll call me *Mom*." She spun and headed into the kitchen.

"Come on," Jillian said. "We're about to sit down to eat. You guys just made it."

They settled at the table, and Jason introduced the rest of his family. The warmth of the meal was only matched by the joy of a family gathering simply to be together.

The last time Mia could remember her family sitting down to a meal was when her grandmother had died. She needed to do something to change that, maybe even during the last two weeks of their required R and R. She'd love to just sit down and talk to her parents and sister, just like they used to do growing up.

They sat through the meal talking about whatever came to mind and laughing about nothing. This was everything a family should be, and she warmed to be a part of it.

Jason's mom placed a large dish of some kind of pudding on Mia's plate, and another on Jason's. "It's very exciting, you know, what you've done, Mia."

Mia looked up at her, not sure what she meant.

"You're a hero." Little Emily beamed from across the table.

Allison smiled. "It kind of sucks, despite all the leaps and bounds we've made over the last three hundred years, that all people lauded as the real-life heroes were still men. Well, not anymore." She raised a glass of wine to Mia. "Let's hear it for the UGA's newest, and best, hero."

Mia's cheeks heated. "I only did what anyone else would do."

Jillian nearly spit her drink. "I would have run and hidden in a bush."

Jason placed his glass down. "On planet Bob, the bushes might eat you. That would have been a bad idea."

He watched as Mia took another scoop of her pudding and then set her utensil down. She wiped her mouth with her napkin.

Jason stared at her for a moment. "You're not going to finish that?"

"I'm kind of full."

"You have to eat it!" Emily screeched from across the table.

Allison put her hand over her daughter's mouth.

Jason laughed, leaning closer. "Family tradition. You need to eat the dessert or my mother will think you didn't like it."

Great. Couldn't they have a tradition that didn't revolve around a thousand extra calories?

His mom looked up from her own dessert. "Is there something wrong with the pudding?"

"No, it's fantastic." Jason picked up his spoon. "Is that fresh vanilla?"

"Of course. Nothing but the best for my long-lost boy."

Mia scooped another mouthful between her lips and frowned, feeling something hard on her tongue.

Jason smiled. "Everything okay?"

She wasn't sure what to do. Everyone was staring at her. Emily bounced on her chair, looking like she might blast off like a rocket.

Mia grabbed her napkin and held it in front of her, spitting whatever it was out and placing it on her lap. The room went silent.

Jason laughed, holding his forehead. "What did you just do?"

She nudged him. "Nothing. I'm trying to be polite," she whispered. "There was something in my dessert."

"She didn't even look at it," Emily wailed.

The entire table burst into laughter. Heat rose in Mia's cheeks. She'd messed things up, and she wasn't even sure why.

Jason grabbed her face and kissed her. "You're lucky I love you, you know that?"

This had to be the strangest family ever. "What are you talking about?"

He grabbed the napkin off her lap and rubbed the cloth around. "Let's try this again." He handed the wadded fabric back to her. "How about you open that up?"

Definitely an odd family.

She unfolded the napkin and found a beautiful, yet slightly pudding-covered, ring inside.

Her stomach sank as the diamond caught the light.

Oh, crap!

She gasped, turning to Jason. "I-I—"

He smiled. "You love me more than all the stars in the universe? Yeah, I know. I'm pretty irresistible."

She held up the ring. "This is beautiful."

He nodded. "My grandmother's ring."

His grandmother's ring?

Sweet stars in heaven. "I-I don't know what to say."

Jason smoothed his hand over her cheek. "Far be it for me to ever tell a woman what to do, but I think it would be pretty darned exciting if you said *yes*."

Emily finally blasted out of her seat. "He wants you to marry him, Mia!"

Yeah, she got that. The room fell into a hush again, with the exception of the squeak in Emily's chair every time she bounced up and down. The ring was gorgeous, despite the pudding caked around the edges of the stone. This family—maybe her new family—stared at her.

"Well?" Jason said. "You better answer, or Emily might pop."

Mia smiled. "Well, we wouldn't want that, would we?"

He shook his head. "Definitely not."

The sparkle in his eyes rivaled any star, and Mia knew he'd fly out and grab any celestial body she wanted and bring it home, if she only asked. He'd been her hero growing up, a pain in the ass on planet Bob, and in the end, everything she'd ever wanted, all rolled into one amazing person.

She leaned up close to his ear and gave him the only answer she possibly could. "You want me to marry you?"

She felt his smile against her cheek. "Yeah."

Mia pushed away. "Then catch me."

She jumped up from the table and flew out the front door as his family exploded in laughter. The door slammed at her rear and she bolted down the road.

"Walton!" Jason's boots pounded on the asphalt behind her.

He'd catch her.

She knew he would.

Heck, she even wanted him to.

But that didn't mean she wouldn't make him work for it.

DOBBY SAYS, "THANKS FOR READING!"

Thanks for reading! If you enjoyed the book I really hope you will be the best star pilot in the galaxy and leave a review. People who leave reviews are the first to get rescued when they crash land. (Or so I hear).

**And flip a few pages for a sneak peek at
Whisper s of Sorcery!**

ACKNOWLEDGMENTS

This may be getting old, but I have to thank my husband. I am domestically challenged, and wouldn't eat if it weren't for you. You are a great support for all this insanity, and I appreciate all you do! And Grandma, thanks for folding laundry or all my teenage boys would be living out of their laundry baskets wrinkles and all. (Ummm... maybe their mom would be, too.)

A lot went into bringing this book to life. I had an idea about a new pilot crash landing on a planet, and accidentally saving her hero. I had the basics, but I knew it needed more. Special thanks to Frankie Blooding for thinking it over, and coming up with the band of rogue brigands on the planet. The addition was fun, and breathed some extra life into the story. (Not to mention the little boost in page count that tipped this over the edge from being a novella to a full novel.)

Thanks to Two Betas Editing for looking this over and giving me a poke to strengthen some of the characters and the descriptions.

Scarlet West, you can't stop doing what you do, because I really look forward to your thrashing insightful comments. You help me make my worlds better. Keep at it, girl!

Amy McNulty, thanks for fitting me in for a line edit. Someday I will get better at this scheduling thing. (Yeah, I know I said that last time.)

Tandy Boese, you rock. What else can I say? I cannot catch typos if my life depended on it, and you managed to see things that three other editors missed.

Nicole!!!! Nicole Conway, you captured Mia and Jason beautifully in the cover art, and Dobby couldn't be cuter. Thanks so much!

And last but nowhere near least...

Thanks again to my readers. I hope you enjoyed this little adventure. Anything 'outer space' will always have a special place in my heart. I really hope you liked this one.

Hugs all around! Everyone rocks.

Yup... that means YOU, and don't let anyone tell you anything different.

ABOUT THE AUTHOR

Jennifer M. Eaton hails from the eastern shore of the North American Continent on planet Earth. Yes, regrettably, she is human, but please don't hold that against her.

While not traipsing through the galaxy looking for specimens for her space moth collection, she lives with her wonderfully supportive husband, three energetic offspring, and a duo of poodles who run the spaceport when she's not around.

During infrequent excursions to her home planet of Earth, Jennifer enjoys long hikes in the woods, bicycling, swimming, snorkeling, and snuggling up by the fire with a great book; but great adventures are always a short shuttle ride away.

Read more at www.jennifereaton.com

WHISPERS OF SORCERY

Chapter I

The dry, black-spotted leaves crumpled in Damon's fingers. A slight breeze wafted the particles from his palm and scattered them across acres of similarly blackened foliage. Just last summer, this land had provided half the *cara* fruits in the kingdom. Now...this.

A boy strode across the field toward Damon. One of his guards advanced, but Damon held up a hand and crouched to the child's height.

"Did the sorcerer send you?" the boy asked.

Damon nodded. "He did."

"Can he fix our farm?"

Pursing his lips, Damon scanned the ravaged fields. Sending fertilizer and farm hands was one thing, but how could they combat utter desecration?

A man approached more slowly, gripping a worn brown hat between weathered hands. "Sorry. He don't mean no disrespect. We're hungry, that's all." He shooed the child away.

Damon stood. "It's not a problem. Is this your field?"

"Aye. Thank you for coming. We're at a loss."

Unfortunately, so was Damon. He'd heard stories, but this was so much worse than he'd expected. All he could do was report back to Binal, and hope his father would send someone who actually knew something about plants.

Damon took in the farmer's sunken cheeks. "When was the last time you ate something?"

The man looked away. "I had a bit this morning. My wife and I agree, it's more important that the children eat."

Stars, had it really come to this, in the mightiest kingdom in the land? He grimaced. *Not while I still have strength to do something about it.*

Damon turned, walked back to his horse, opened his saddlebag, and pulled out the ration packs.

"What are you doing?" the guard holding the horses asked.

He held up the food. "What do you think I'm doing?"

"What are we supposed to eat on the trip back?"

Was he serious? "We'll manage."

"That's not enough to help. You can't feed all the people yourself."

Damon pushed past him. "Maybe not, but I can feed a few." He handed the pack to the farmer. "Bring this back to your family. I'll report what I've found, and see if I can send a botanist to help you."

The man clutched the pack to his chest. His eyes filled with tears. "Thank you, my lord."

Damon grasped the man's shoulder. "Save your thanks until we get you a bountiful crop."

The man smiled, lifting his chin. "Long live Esparon."

Damon's chest clenched as his gaze trailed across the dying fields, again.

He whispered, "Yes, long live Esparon."

The timid voice of the child and the tears in the farmer's

eyes traveled with Damon along the road back to the castle, blocking out the complaints of the two guards forced to ride without rations.

Blast them both. He doubted either of them had been hungry a day in their lives. Not that Damon had, either. Binal would never let him starve, but at least Damon knew enough not to complain in the face of others' suffering.

That child was young—too young to know such hardship. Damon needed to make sure Binal understood how serious the blight had become.

When they reached the stables, Damon handed off the reins and turned to the page. "I need to speak to see Lord Binal immediately."

The page lowered his head. "I will pass on that you have returned."

In other words, find something to do and wait until you are called. Typical.

Damon sighed and waved him away. It certainly wasn't the page's fault that his father was occupied. There was no reason to make the man's thankless job worse by arguing.

His two guards gave a slight bow, then walked away, shaking their heads. Let them be annoyed. They will have full bellies within an hour—more food than that farmer's family would probably see in a week.

"Hey there, Doxion." Guardsman Rayhan patted Damon's horse's nose. "I see you managed to bring his highness back in one piece." He turned to Damon, and his smile melted into a frown. His eyes widened. "Was it really that bad?"

Damon nodded, pulling off his gloves. "If this keeps up, we're all going to starve."

Rayhan moved closer. "Word has it that the battle mages are scoping potentials." He looked over his shoulder. "Maybe we're finally going to do something about those blasted witches cursing our country."

Damon blinked. "I don't know that there is any truth to that." He certainly hadn't heard about any attack on their eastern neighbors.

His friend shrugged. "You wouldn't be able to tell me even if you did know, but I'm okay with that." He smiled. "I threw my name out there, just in case."

"You what?"

"If we're going after the witches, I want to be right there in front. Someone needs to make them pay for what they've done to our land."

Damon squeezed his gloves until his hands ached. Nefarum's witches had been a bane to Esparon since before his grandfather's rule. They needed to be stopped, that was for certain, however... "War isn't always the best answer for a kingdom or her people."

"Sir?" A young boy in servants' livery hovered by the side of the stable.

Damon turned toward him. "Yes?"

"Lord Binal has requested your presence in the war room, sir." The boy wrung his hands. Damon's stance softened. His father intimidated the mightiest of soldiers. This child was lucky not to have soiled his pants in the presence of the high sorcerer.

"I'll be there shortly."

The boy bowed and disappeared around the front of the building.

Rayhan held out his hands. "The war room. You see? Rumors are not to be taken lightly."

"It's the day after quarter moon," Damon pointed out. "My father always holds council on the quarter."

"Yes." Rayhan pointed a finger. "But for the first time in seventeen years, he's invited you."

Damon's stomach fluttered and he grabbed the side of the stall. His friend was right. He'd always been sent on errands at the quarter moon, traveling Esparon and engaging the people, like today. Normally, his father would discuss his decisions and tactics with Damon in private, but actually being called into the room with the war chiefs?

"Congratulations." Rayhan punched his shoulder. "It's about bloody time."

Bloody. An interesting choice of words. He nodded and headed toward the castle.

Rayhan's voice came from behind him. "Put in a good word for me. I'd make you a great general!"

Damon gulped, and shivered despite the heat of the late day sun. His friend was too eager to see combat, but Damon was afraid that day may come sooner than anyone had hoped.

Anya sidled to the edge of the cliff. A thick ball roiled in her throat, and she forced it down. This was the same precipice her mother had fallen from. Resisting the urge to look down and see the place her body had been found, Anya closed her eyes and steadied herself as a gust of wind tossed her long, dark hair in her eyes. The airstreams could change at any time, and she needed to be prepared. The village could not lose another priestess.

Anya drank in the cool air and took in the clouds billowing across the crisp blue sky. Green, growing glory greeted her right up to the edge of her warding spell. On the outside, the grass darkened, turning browner in the distance. *That* was why she stood atop this mountain—to keep the death and gloom of Esparon on the outside where it belonged.

She closed her eyes and stretched her hands outward. Her fingers traced sigils in the air. An *antecedum* for power, the *triglenterum* for fortitude, the *carcelemnum* for joy, and the *veridas* for goodness. Her mother had taught these spells to her from the time she could walk. Anya just never thought she'd have to take her mother's place so young.

Closing off the ward with a swirling *kavas* string, her family's own signature spell, she stepped back and watched her ward bolster, grow, and connect to the neighboring wards in the distance. The shield was a tapestry of sorts, each village priestess weaving her own blocks in the quilt. In the east, the red swirling bands of Naomi, in the west, the mottled, blocky patterns of Armana's sigils filled the sky. Here, Anya's weave was neither colorful nor uniform. 'Sturdy is better than pretty,' her mother had always taught.

Anya wasn't sure that her ward was sturdy, and it definitely wasn't pretty, but none of the sorcerer's spells had broken through from the outside, so she must be doing something right.

With a flick of her wrist she conjured up a spider sigil in the air—a sinister little bug of her mother's design that crept along the ward, checking the weave for holes. Her mother probably wasn't the first person to say that *luck favors the steadfast*, but this, too, was an adage ingrained in Anya's very being: always recheck your work.

Mistress Lixiss would inspect Anya's ward again in about an hour. It wasn't that she or the high priestesses didn't trust Anya, but everyone knew the consequences of failure.

Anya looked out on the dry, dusty plains beyond the trees on the outside of the ward and shivered. She understood their caution. With so much at stake, it would have been better to pull in a priestess from a neighboring village than elevate Anya before she'd had time to prove herself. There just wasn't anyone else, though. So here Anya stood, sole protector of her stretch of the ward, like her mother before her.

Anya let her hands drop to her sides, her fingers curling into her white linen dress. Dirt clung to the hem, as usual. It wouldn't be a Warding Day without Lixiss reminding her about the importance of appearances. She released the dress, allowing the fabric to scrape the ground, again. What did it matter, when she'd get even dirtier on her way down the mountain?

She whispered the words to a locater spell, searching for the one soul who'd be happy to see her, no matter what she looked like. The incantation cascaded through the air, swirling and peaking until it burst over the grassy fields outside her village.

She padded down the path that led back to the valley, avoiding sharp rocks that would slice her bare feet. The countless journeys up and down this hill since her childhood made the otherwise perilous trip easy, which may have been one of the reasons they'd elevated Anya so soon—no one else was willing to climb these peaks.

Anya smiled, kicking a stone and watching it bounce down the decline. They had no idea what they were missing.

Circumventing the mountain path, Anya stopped as the sky opened over her province. No matter how many times she walked this path, the sight never failed to steal her breath.

Below, a team of winged horses in brown, black, and mottled gray tones grazed in the vivid green pasture. She grinned and bounded down the rest of the steep path at breakneck speed, the special bundle in her pocket bouncing against her thigh until her feet hit the soft grass. The cold, damp blades made her sigh, close her eyes, and raise her face to the sun. This is where she truly belonged. *This* was home.

Several horses moved toward her, their wings a riot of colors and textures. They were all beautiful, but only one held her heart. She scampered towards the tall, white stallion that all the other horses gave a wide birth to. The magnificent creature stared her down as she skidded to a halt in front of him. Anya bent in a theatrical, formal bow and then straightened.

Entor nuzzled her black hair, which seemed even darker up against his milky wings and pale coat. Anya giggled when the huge winged horse snuffled in her ear.

"Stop, that tickles." She tucked back her hair. "I have something for you." She pulled an apple from her dress pocket. "Just don't tell Finn." She checked the guard tower but saw no sign of the old man, who was probably snoozing again.

She couldn't really blame him. Guarding the horses had to be a boring job. Nothing had attacked these beautiful creatures in her lifetime, and thanks to the priestesses and the wards, that would never change.

Entor sank his teeth into the apple with a crunch. Another pony snorted behind her. She turned to find several horses inching closer, and one foal ventured near enough to reach his nose into Anya's pocket.

She jumped back. "Oh! I'm so sorry. I couldn't bring enough for everyone." She turned out her pocket to show them. "Perhaps if I enchanted my cloak to hold more?" A palomino mare tossed her head in annoyance while a feisty brown neighed and sniffed at her pocket, as if not completely believing it was empty.

Anya held back her grin. "I'll bring more next time, I swear!" The horses would hold her to that promise. She'd need to find a way to smuggle more fruit from the kitchens.

Anya leaned against Entor and laughed as a playful colt nipped her sleeve before she and the remainder of the horses dispersed, finally convinced Anya had no more treats to enjoy.

Entor remained at her side, his all-knowing eyes surveying her, as always. Most felt belittled beneath that gaze, but Anya met his stare. Entor didn't judge her age or lack of ability. To an extent, he was the only one that didn't look down on her and expect her to fail. At least that's what she told herself.

She kissed him on the nose and turned toward the simple dirt trail that led past the guard tower and through the trees. Reality lay within, and she needed to face it sooner or later. She tapped his flank. "I guess I'll see you on the other side."

Anya trudged along the path, across the field, and pushed through the gates leading into the village. The dark red roofs absorbed the sun's light, making them look like tarnished coins. The smooth stones of the worn-down road cooled her feet, soothing away some of the anxiety over making a public appearance.

Her mother had liked the socializing part of her station and had been a great conversationalist. Anya never inherited that gift. She felt all wrong and couldn't find the right thing to say when the townspeople approached.

"Good morning, Priestess," Mrs. Todd, the butcher's wife, had a basket beneath one arm. She smiled at Anya with a strange glint in her eyes. The people she protected looked up to her, maybe even marveled at what she could do, but none realized what a heavy burden magic could be.

"Good morning," Anya said with a small nod.

Her mother would ask Mrs. Todd how she was and about her three children, calling each by name. Instead, Anya quickened her pace, avoiding the issue.

Kiera and Cillian, the village newlyweds, and former schoolmates of Anya's, approached with their hands linked and their faces alight with smiles.

"Priestess," Keira said, giving a curtsy.

Anya cringed. In a time not long ago, they would have said "Hey Anya!" and asked her to roll down the hill with them to see who could get to the bottom the fastest without vomiting.

Those days, it seemed, were long gone.

"Can I trouble you for a blessing?" Keira smiled at Cillian. "We're trying for our first child."

Anya's eyes widened. Their first child? Grace of the moon, they were barely out of school! Then again, so was Anya.

She forced a smile. "Of course." She raised her hand over Keira and whispered a few words she remembered her mother speaking when the Parson's pigs hadn't been breeding. The magic unfurled within her, small threads inching their way through her arm and out her fingertips. The sensation prickled like hitting her elbow on something.

Keira jumped and stepped back, Cillian steadying her.

"Well met," Anya said. "I wish you a house filled with happy, laughing children."

The couple hugged. "Thank you, Priestess."

Anya nodded. Hopefully, their child wouldn't come out squealing with a pink, curly tail.

An older man and a middle-aged woman had stopped to watch the blessing, but now scampered away, wide-eyed.

Her stomach hardened. As a priestess of the order Anya would never truly belong among the villagers, again. She looked back to the happy couple walking hand in hand. She could have had that, in another life, one where her mother hadn't been taken from her so soon.

She wiped the burn from her eyes and headed out along the path towards the temple, rubbing her sore shoulders. She didn't remember her mother seeming so tired after reinforcing the ward. Maybe it was the extra effort of blessing Keira. Her mother had made spell casting look so easy. She'd made everything look easy. Maybe in time, Anya would get the hang of her new station.

She glanced up a familiar hill, and warmed, remembering

the small cottage and white fence she knew sat on the other side. Too bad she couldn't return to her old family home after tracing her spells each Warding Day. A nice nap would have been helpful before returning to the temple.

Another family lived there now, though, and her brother's family had moved to Hecit Valley on the other side of Nefarum. There truly wasn't anything left in this village for her but her duty.

Entor swooped down to land in front of Anya, his wings creating a gust of air that stung her eyes. A cloud of dust puffed around them and she coughed into her hand.

The tinkling of delighted laughter behind the trees made her grin. The children of the village were not supposed to approach the winged horses. They were especially not supposed to be outside the town border, but they loved Entor. She remembered her own glee, the first time her mother's horse, Zaman, had flown into the valley to claim her mother as his spirit match.

Of course, Entor hadn't claimed anyone, and probably never would. He was 'the bold white,' 'the wild winged stallion.' He was the horse that made the others scatter, and people point and watch, wondering what he might do.

His free spirit must have called to the children, just as it called to Anya, though. She, like this amazing horse, and those children hiding where they should not be, had no intention of conforming to what others considered civilized boundaries, much to Mistress Lixiss's and probably to those children's parents' chagrin.

As Anya strode alongside Entor's clopping hooves, the ornate shimmering blue roof of the temple peeked out over the treetops. The arching gables towered over every other building in Nefarum, and with good reason. The temple was the heart of their small oasis, the seat of the high priestess. Everyone in Nefarum understood the order's purpose. The protection of magic meant the protection of the world, and nothing was more important.

She wove her fingers into Entor's mane, soaking in the power that radiated from his presence. It seemed unfathomable that there were those in the world who would hunt him down and destroy him, just because of what he symbolized and the power he bore. But this was one of the many reasons she climbed the mountain each Warding Day: to keep the sorcerer and his cursed taint, out.

Chapter 2

Damon paused on the war room's threshold. Voices rumbled from within.

As a boy, he'd pressed his ear against the thick oak door trying to glean what the kingdom's most powerful voices were plotting.

Who was he kidding? He'd done this only a few weeks ago, but now his day had finally come. The famed high sorcerer had finally decided to allow him to stand at his side.

Damon inhaled and pushed the door open.

His father leaned over the edge of a long, warped wooden table. Binal had rough, strong features and dark eyes centered on what may have been a map. His long hair was the same dark shade of brown as Damon's, held back by a circlet inset with a stone imbued with power. Binal straightened to his full six and a half spans of height—an intimidating warrior in addition to a master sorcerer... Damon's polar opposite in so many ways.

The seven war chiefs from Esparon's territories looked up when he entered, and silence flooded the room. Damon shuddered, and resisted the urge to step back out. He'd waited too long for this. He was the prince. His voice deserved to be heard.

"Ah, Damon." His father offered a rare smile.

Damon gave a slight bow. "I've just returned from the north farms as you requested, sire." He took a few steps inside. "I fear it's worse than we suspected."

Binal gestured to the empty chair at his immediate right —a place of honor reserved for whichever chief held Binal's favor that month. Around the room, men shifted their weight. A few twisted their lips, some lancing him with a glare before looking away.

"Sit," Binal ordered.

Damon wiped the sweat from his brow as he took the offered chair. The eyes of the most influential men in Esparon were on him. Many of these men had sat in on his training. A daring few *educated* him one on one, taking far too much pleasure in beating down the son of their sovereign in the name of *toughening him up*. His knuckles whitened on the arms of his chair. He wouldn't give them the satisfaction of balking at their presence. He was no longer a child. Still, his mouth turned to chalk.

"As I was saying," Binal said. "We must expand our borders if we're to survive the winter."

Damon blinked. "Expand our borders? Respectfully, father, we need to see to our people before we drag them into another war. The crops..."

"Are failing," his father continued. "Krut is too far from Nefarum to feel the witches' wrath. Scouts tell me their crops are bountiful. I've decided they should share their good fortune."

Padraig of the Southern Hills cleared his throat. "With respect, my Lord, the boy has a point. Do we have the resources to mount an attack?"

Jeers and derisive laughs filled the war room, and Padraig's face reddened.

"With our army and my magic, we cannot lose," Binal said. "Unless you doubt Esparon's might, Padraig?"

The color ran from Padraig's face. The Southern Hills were a recent addition to his father's empire. For him, the sting of the sorcerer's might was all too fresh.

Padraig shook his head. "No, my lord. You're correct, of course."

Damon would have pitied the man if he hadn't personally toured the Southern Hills last month. Padraig's farmers were heavily tithed and suffered beneath his rule. After Damon had reported his findings to the court, he'd hoped his father would put an end to his people's unwarranted distress, but more pressing matters always seemed to get in the way.

"Liam, you will commit your land's warhorses for our soldiers." Binal addressed the oily man with crooked teeth that ruled the coastal region.

Liam bowed his head, his long nose almost touching the table. "Of course, Lord Binal. We would be honored."

Damon held back a snort. Liam had been kissing Binal's posterior for years, dangling his daughters in front of his father, hoping for a union. Most recently, those same daughters had been dangled in front of Damon. His father certainly had to see through such power plays and groveling.

Binal turned to Damon, his eyes narrowed.

Had his father sensed his misgivings? He sat beside the greatest sorcerer their land had ever known. He should have spent more time learning to create a wall around his thoughts.

"What say you about my plans, son?"

Damon licked his lips, glancing down at the map of Esparon and the few surrounding kingdoms his father had yet to conquer. What Esparon truly needed, was a swift end to any campaign, and a return to focusing on their people.

He met his father's gaze. "Have you considered sending an

emissary, telling them of our struggle and asking for their help?"

The chiefs watched Binal, waiting for his reaction.

"That would be an excellent plan," Binal said, and the chiefs began nodding in approval. "If I wanted to risk people on a fool's errand."

Damon's face warmed.

Perhaps his father purposely brought him here to make a fool out of him? He'd tasked him time and time again to go out and interact with the people, always making promises that his father never followed through on. How could he think Damon wouldn't put the people first?

His ideas were sound, though. He just needed to approach them from a new angle. Maybe one his father could understand.

"They could kidnap the king." Damon stood and pointed to Krut's castle on the map. "And ransom him for land rights."

Binal leaned his head back and laughed. The war chiefs joined in, the sound raising in a cacophonous symphony.

"You still have much to learn, my son." Binal's smile faded. "Always trying to avoid bloodshed. You must realize that carnage is inevitable in war. You must cut some throats to make the rivers of victory run red."

Damon held his grimace back and gave a stiff nod as he eased back into his chair. "Yes, Father."

He sat in silence as the chiefs and his father plotted the demise of the western country. He didn't understand why avoiding needless waste and violence was so repellant to these men. The old ways of war and death had not served them well—their people were suffering. A different approach might mean their survival, if they would only consider other options.

The meeting ended and the war chiefs filed out. Damon

began to stand, but Binal clapped a heavy hand on his shoulder.

"Stay, Damon. We must discuss something of importance." Binal took a deep draught of his ale.

Damon sat back down. "Yes, Father?"

"In truth, our attack on the western kingdom is nothing more than a stopgap. As you have confirmed, magic is swiftly draining from our land. We must take more drastic action to ensure Esparon's survival." Binal leaned towards Damon, his dark eyes pinning his son in place.

Damon had seen men die under that stare—grown men reduced to sniveling children, hardened warriors stripped to lifeless husks, twitching on the ground gasping for their last breath.

Refusing to flinch, Damon met his gaze. "W-What sort of action?"

"First, I must gain your vow that you will do whatever it takes to bring our country back to its former glory."

A muscle in Damon's jaw twitched. "Of course, you have my vow." How could he think any less of him? Esparon was his legacy, the people his own. He'd die for them, and his father knew this. At least, he'd thought he'd known. Damon shifted in his seat as his father's eyes continued to bore into his very soul.

Let them—let his father search his mind. The only thing he'd find was undying loyalty to his people. No, Damon had no taste for bloodshed if it could be avoided, but that didn't make him a coward. He would fight and die for Esparon if he needed to.

"Excellent. I should have generals as devoted as you, but I do not. I can trust only you with this task." Binal leaned back. "You're always spouting about a peaceful end to conflict. Well, I give you one. Do this one task, and I will spare Krut."

Really? Damon straightened, lifting his chin. "Anything."

Krut wasn't his responsibility, but war meant casualties on both sides. Sparing Krut meant sparing not only the soldiers, but the innocents living along the borders.

"I'm sending you into the heart of Nefarum."

Damon's eyebrows shot up. He grasped the arms of his chair, fairly certain his heart had stopped beating for a moment. "Nefarum? With how many men?"

"Alone."

Now his heart *did* stop. His hands tightened on the chair.

"You will smuggle a winged horse through the witches shield and bring it back to me."

"A-a horse?" Bringing back one creature wouldn't be difficult. He'd been riding since before he could walk, and winged or not, a horse was a horse.

Binal nodded. "Do this, and our lands will be fertile once more. Our crops will be abundant and life will flow back into our country."

Damon looked down, digesting his father's words. "How could one horse..."

"Leave that part of it to me."

Damon nodded. His throat parched as he swallowed. All Esparon needed was for magic to flow through the land once again. He could save the people, and stop another war. It seemed like such a huge gain, for such a small...

"You only need one horse?" Damon asked.

Binal's booming laugh filled the room. "I appreciate your confidence, but don't be foolish. These horses are not normal animals. They wield a great power. The witches will protect their source of magic to their deaths." He ran his fingers over the edge of his goblet. "One is all I need."

So be it. "What if I run into a witch?"

Binal slammed a hooked dagger onto the table between them. "Kill her."

Damon shuddered. Perhaps he could ask for a horse?

Surely if they had so many, they would be willing to give up just one.

"Da-mon." His father drew out his name. His eyes turned to lances again.

"I-I won't let you down, Father." He grabbed the dagger, shoving the blade into his belt.

"I know, Damon. I have complete faith in you."

Damon gulped, taking in the slight indent in the table where his father had slammed down the knife.

Certainly his mage tutors had reported back Damon's countless failures. Unless they were toying with him and never tried to teach him at all. What Damon had mastered were mainly parlor tricks and simple spells—nothing of the caliber of his father's war mages, and definitely nothing like the power the sorcerer himself wielded as easily as walking.

"You're underestimating yourself again."

Damon cringed. Of course his father knew his every thought. "I'm sorry, Father. I'm just not sure why..."

"Faelar tells me you unwove his battle shield last week." Binal smiled. "He's quite impressed. He's not sure how you did it."

Damon pursed his lips. "It's a deconstruction spell. It's useless in battle. It takes far too long. I..."

"What is around Nefarum?"

Was this another trick question, meant to take him off guard? "The witches' shield."

His father's smile changed, it seemed almost...proud?

Damon's breath hitched. "It's a shield. A giant battle shield!"

Binal nodded. "They are ready for an army, not a small, temporary hole. You will cut through their shield, and let it reclose behind you. The hags won't even know you're there."

Damon gaped. He was right! Damon could do this!

Binal got to his feet. "Make your preparations. You leave

at first light." The sorcerer swept from the room, leaving Damon alone at the table.

A slow drip echoed through the chamber, and a breeze whistled across the cracks in the foundation.

Damon swallowed at the lump in his throat. He would do anything to keep his father's favor and save his people from their fate. His hands curled into fists on the table. He could do this. All he needed was one horse, and he would be lauded for all time as the prince who saved Esparon.

Did you enjoy this preview?
Find buy links for this and more great books
From Jennifer M. Eaton on Goodreads
Or visit www.jennifereaton.com